# KATARINA AND THE BIRD

## THE SHIFTERS SERIES BOOK THREE

## ELIZABETH KELLY

EK PUBLISHING INC.

# KATARINA AND THE BIRD

(The Shifters Series Book Three)

**What happens when a cat and a bird fall in love?**

Jaguar shifter, Katarina Frost, isn't looking for love. And she certainly isn't looking for love with a tattooed bird shifter with a smart mouth and the ability to make her cat purr with just a single, scorching look. Cat shifters do not take bird shifters to their bed. Especially when the bird shifter is their employee. Too bad her cat didn't get the memo.

Ronin Smith doesn't care that Kat's his employer. He wants the sexy cat shifter, and he's determined to have her. His offer to help Kat during her heat cycle is a temptation she can't deny, and neither of them is prepared for the smoking hot, undeniable chemistry between them.

Kat knows she needs to keep Ronin at a distance. There's no future for a cat and a bird. But as her feelings for Ronin grow and a threat from his past tries to take him from her, Kat will risk everything to protect him.

# CHAPTER 1

The man shifted in his chair before leaning back and rubbing wearily at his temples. The glow of the computer screen illuminated the deep lines around his mouth and eyes, and he sat silently for a few moments.

The headache pulsed through him and, without opening his eyes, he reached into the top drawer of his desk and pulled out the bottle of pills. He took four, chewing them rapidly and ignoring the bitter taste they left in his mouth, before returning the bottle to the drawer.

He sat forward and clicked the computer mouse. A new screen popped up, and he stared intently at the creature pacing restlessly back and forth in the massive steel cage. He sighed. She had torn up the bed again, stuffing and fabric littered the floor of the cage, and he made a mental note to order another one. It would be the fourth one this month, but he needed her to be comfortable.

He reached out and traced the creature's face on the screen as she lifted her head and stared at the camera. Saliva dripped from her oversized fangs as she stood on her hind feet and snarled.

"Je t'aime, ma chérie," he whispered.

There was a knock on the door, and he minimized the video feed before giving a curt, "come in".

The door opened, and the dark-haired man wearing a grey suit with a dark green tie entered the room. "Good evening, Wyatt."

"Hello, Clay." He motioned for the man to sit down.

Clay sat in the chair and studied him silently for a moment.

"What is it?" Wyatt asked.

"You look unwell."

"I'm fine."

"Are you? Did you sleep last night?" Clay said.

"What is it that you want?"

"Perhaps I'm here just to inquire on the health of my friend."

Wyatt gave him a dry look. "It has been many months since you considered me a friend, Clay."

"Just because I disagree with how you're handling the situation doesn't mean I'm not your friend, Wyatt. I will always be your friend."

"Your solution is not the way," Wyatt snapped.

"Yours isn't either," Clay said gently.

"It is! I know it is! If you found the bird, I would make it work."

"You had him, remember? An entire month and you couldn't make it work."

"I needed more time."

"A month, Wyatt," Clay reminded him. "He volunteered to help, and when his tears didn't cure her, you took him prisoner and injected him with the virus repeatedly. It didn't work."

"I need more time," Wyatt repeated. "I need to study the

2

way his body works. I'll take more samples of his blood, perhaps his internal organs or -"

"You mean dissect him."

"I will do whatever it takes to save her, Clay."

"I know. But if you kill the bird to save her, how is that any different from what I want to do?"

"I'm not going to kill him! I *can't* kill him, remember?" Wyatt said.

"I remember. But torturing him, locking him in a cage, and injecting him repeatedly with the virus while you take his blood and samples of his flesh, isn't the answer, Wyatt. You would keep him a prisoner, make his life a living hell, to save her?"

"I would. I will discover the cure."

"And then what? You release the bird with a 'sorry about that' and hope like hell he doesn't go to the press?" Clay asked.

"He'll be well compensated for his time."

"What happens if he isn't the key, Wyatt? Will you torture him, keep him prisoner, forever?"

"He is the key!" Wyatt slammed his fists on the desk and growled. Dark fur sprouted on his face, but Clay showed no fear.

"You can't contain it, Wyatt. The virus is spreading," Clay said.

"What are you talking about? You killed Millie, remember?" There was a note of bitterness in his voice.

"It was necessary. She had already killed three of my men and bitten five others."

"Yes, and you showed all five of your men no mercy. Did you feel any remorse when you put bullets in their brain, Clay?"

"No," Clay said.

3

"Of course, you didn't. I had no idea there existed such darkness in you."

"You knew," Clay said. "It's why you brought me here. You need someone more than ever to clean up your mess, to do your dirty work for you, Wyatt. You need me."

"I need you to find Ronin!" Wyatt snarled.

"We think he's in the city. It's going to take time to find him."

"Then maybe you should leave and do the job I'm paying you to do," Wyatt said.

"There was an incident at a coffee shop in the city last week," Clay said.

Wyatt gripped the edge of his desk and stared at him. "What do you mean?"

"A coyote shifter went insane and shifted into a monster. At least, that's what they're saying on the news."

"Fuck!" Wyatt slammed his fist on the desk again as Clay scrolled through his cell phone.

"There were numerous witnesses, human and shifter."

"Was anyone killed?"

Clay shook his head. "No, there was a bear shifter and a jaguar shifter in the coffee shop. They held him off until an off-duty cop shot him in the head."

"Thank God. Were they bitten?"

"I don't know."

"Fucking find out, Clay! You know what will happen if they were!"

"Yes, Wyatt, I do," Clay said icily. "Five of my men, remember?"

"Do we know for sure that he was infected with the virus?"

"Yes. Saul went down to the morgue and examined the body. There's no doubt he was infected."

4

"But how?" Wyatt said.

"Obviously, Millie came in contact with more people than we thought before we contained her."

Wyatt leaned back in his chair. "Find out if the jaguar and the bear were bitten. If they were, bring them to me. Do you hear me, Clay? Don't kill them."

"I hear you, Wyatt." Clay stood and walked toward the door.

"And bring me Ronin!" Wyatt shouted as Clay shut the door behind him.

He clicked on the video feed and stared at the creature as she paced relentlessly in her cage.

"Soon, ma chérie. We will be together again, soon," he said.

---

"WILLOW? I NEED MORE PACKING PAPER IN THE KITCHEN."

There was no reply, and Kat stuck her head into the hallway. "Willow? Are you here?"

The apartment door opened and Willow, balancing a tray of coffees and a bag of donuts, slammed the door shut with her foot.

"What's this?" Kat asked.

"I thought we deserved a break," Willow puffed. She joined Kat in the kitchen and collapsed on one of the chairs with a soft sigh. "Moving sucks."

"It does," Kat agreed as she chose a donut from the bag. "But think about how much worse it would have been if Mal wasn't organizing it."

"God, you're so right." Willow rubbed at her lower back. "Do you know he created a spreadsheet for the move? It's colour-coded and everything. I have matching coloured

stickers to put on each box for each room. It's crazy, and I
_"

She stopped, her eyes widening. "Oh crap! I didn't tell
you what colour the kitchen was!"

Kat laughed and took a sip of coffee. "Mal emailed me
with detailed instructions, don't worry."

"Thank God," Willow said before biting into a donut.
"Thanks again, Kat. I appreciate you giving up your weekend
to help me pack. Ava was here last night, but she's got a shift
at the hospital today and tomorrow. Plus, she isn't feeling all
that great. She was even paler than normal last night."

"You're welcome." Kat sat in one of the kitchen chairs
and studied the half-empty cupboards. "Are you excited about
moving in with Mal?"

Willow nodded. "I am. I spend most of my time at his
place anyway, and when I'm not there, I wish I was, so it
makes sense."

"Are you going to marry him, Will?"

"Yes. I love him to death and can't imagine being with
anyone else. Even if he does drive me crazy with his orga-
nized pantry. The other night I moved all the cans in the
pantry around, and by the time I got up in the morning, he
had reorganized them. Who does that, Kat?"

Kat laughed. "Mal, I guess."

"I guess. I just never imagined that I would fall in love
with someone who was so strait-laced. I always assumed I'd
fall for a hippie with questionable hygiene habits."

Kat laughed so hard that coffee spurted out from her
cup to land on the table. Willow wiped it up with a paper
towel before grinning at her. "It's true. But it's Mal I love,
so I guess I'll have to live with the fact that he showers
every day. Now I just have to get him to ask me to marry
him."

"Um, I think he already has." Kat pointed to the bite mark on the back of Willow's shoulder.

Willow shrugged. "True, but I want the actual proposal, you know? The 'down on one knee, baby will you marry me' deal."

As Willow stood and began to wrap glasses in paper before shoving them into a box, Kat grinned at her.

"Speaking of love, how are things with you and Ronin?"

Kat sighed. It had been nearly two months since the night Ava was kidnapped by a dragon, and Ronin had barely spoken two words to her. "It's not love, Willow. Outside of work-related stuff, Ronin doesn't even speak to me now."

Willow gave her a sympathetic look. "I'm sorry."

"Why? One night of sex doesn't mean that I want to marry the guy. Besides, I only slept with him because it was my heat cycle, remember?"

"I remember."

Kat stood and started loading a cardboard box with plastic containers. "It was a mistake to sleep with him, and I would never have done it if I hadn't been in the middle of my heat cycle. It drives me crazy that I can't control it anymore."

"Could you control it before?" Willow asked. "According to my research, it's extremely difficult to control."

"Your research?" Kat paused in her packing.

Willow shrugged. "I'm naturally curious about shifters. What can I say?"

Kat smiled a little. "Well, when I was younger, I did have better control of it, I think. Now, not so much. Last month was a nightmare. I almost picked up a random cheetah shifter at the bar."

"Why didn't you?" Willow asked. "I mean, what's the big deal?"

*Because it's Ronin you want.*

7

Kat ignored her inner voice. "I don't know. I guess I feel cheap when I do something like that, you know? Or weak, maybe."

She closed the box, and Willow taped it shut before placing a bright red sticker on the top of it. "Is your friend Mark still unavailable?"

She nodded. "Yeah. My next heat cycle is in a couple of weeks, and I'm, uh, meeting with a few shifters tonight over at Bud's. They all have potential."

At Willow's curious look, she flushed slightly. "There's a website that can line female cat shifters up with other shifters who are willing to help them out once a month. I've never used it before, but, frankly, I'm getting a little desperate."

"You should ask Ronin to help you," Willow said. "We both know he'd be more than willing to have crazy hot sex with you once a month, no strings attached."

"I told you, Will, that's not a good idea. One – he's an employee, and two – he's a bird."

"Didn't you and Fenton used to date?" Willow asked.

Kat nodded. "Yes, but it was before he started working for our company."

"Ah. Back to the bird thing – who cares?" Willow said.

"Cats and birds do not mate, Willow."

"I feel like we've had this conversation before," Willow said teasingly.

"I just can't, okay?" Kat said.

"Okay. So, tell me about the guys you're meeting tonight. Are they all cat shifters?"

Kat nodded. "There's a tiger, a jaguar, and a cheetah."

"Which one has the most potential?"

"The tiger, I think. He's done this before and can provide references."

Willow laughed. "It's like he's applying for a job."

"He kind of is."

"Yeah, but don't you want passion, Kat? Excitement?"

"What I want is not to feel like I'm losing my damn mind once a month," Kat said. "I'm not looking for a relationship right now. I have a lot on my plate with trying to grow our client base, and succeeding at my career is very important to me."

"You have succeeded," Willow said. "The company would be lost without you. And if you were in a relationship, your mom would stop trying to set you up with random shifters."

Kat grinned. "True, but then she'd be harassing me non-stop for grandkittens."

"I would think she would be harassing your sister," Willow said. "She's the one who just got married."

She stared curiously at Kat when the jaguar shifter grimaced. "What?"

"My sister and her husband separated."

Willow's jaw dropped. "You're kidding me. They've been married less than six months – they're still newlyweds."

"Yeah, but when you come home to find your husband in bed with the maid, it kind of puts a damper on the newlywed bliss."

"Holy shitballs!" Willow said. "What an asshole."

"You're telling me," Kat said. "She kicked the asshole out, and apparently, he's already shacked up with the maid."

"Is that why you flew out to your sister's last month for a few days?"

Kat nodded. "I helped her burn all of his stuff and file the divorce papers."

"You burned his stuff?" Willow said.

"Yep. Jaguars can be mean when we want to, Will," Kat said with a grin.

"Yikes, remind me never to piss off a jaguar," Willow said.

"I tried to convince Emerson to move back to the city, but she's decided to stay where she is for now. She likes her job and has a pretty solid network of friends. But now that her marriage is over, my mother is positive that I'm her only hope for grandkittens. Emerson isn't going to be in a relationship anytime soon, and Mom's given up completely on my brother."

She picked up another box, and Willow helped her load the paper-wrapped glasses into it before grinning at her. "Maybe I should come with you tonight and help you pick out your new boy toy."

Kat laughed. "Not a chance, Willow."

"C'mon, Kat," Willow wheedled. "I'll be super helpful. You know I will."

"Nope," Kat said. "It's not happening."

---

WILLOW NEEDED A DIFFERENT TACTIC IF SHE WAS GOING TO convince Kat to let her help. Before she could think of one, the door to the apartment opened, and she heard the low rumble of Bishop's voice. "I don't know, Mal. She's been throwing up every day for the past two weeks but won't go to the doctor. She said she talked to one of the doctors at work, and he said there's a bug going around, but I'm worried about her."

Willow stuck her head into the hallway. "Hey, guys. How did that go?"

"Good. We dropped off your bed and the other furniture at the Goodwill and took the boxes to my place," Mal said before pressing a kiss on her forehead. "How's the packing going?"

"Good. Kat's almost finished the kitchen – she's been an absolute dream."

She smiled at Fenton and Bishop, who stood behind Mal. "There are donuts in the kitchen. Come have some."

"Hey, guys," Kat said as they joined her in the kitchen. She smiled at Fenton when he placed an affectionate kiss on her cheek.

Willow glanced at her watch. "Damn, I need to run over to Ginger's and pick her up. She said she would help do some packing tonight."

"Ginger's coming over?" Fenton said casually.

Willow nodded. "Yes. But I need to pick her up. Her car's completely wrecked."

"What?" Fenton said. "She wrecked her car?"

"Not exactly," Willow said. "It's a long story, but I need to go, or I'll be late. I told her I'd pick her up by three."

"Why doesn't her idiot boyfriend do something useful for once and drop her off?" Fenton asked

"Didn't I tell you?" Willow said. "She and Robbie broke up."

"What? When?" Fenton asked.

"Last week," Willow said before glancing again at her watch. "Gosh, I wanted to get the bathroom packed up before I picked up Ginger, but I've run out of time. Unless there's someone who could pick her up for me?"

She smiled sweetly at Fenton as Mal rolled his eyes and grabbed water from the fridge.

A dull flush covering his cheeks, Fenton said, "Uh, I could run over to Ginger's house and pick her up if that's, um, helpful."

"It would be so helpful, Fenton. Thank you!" Willow

said. "You're such a sweetheart. I'll text her and tell her you're on your way."

She kissed his cheek and winked at Mal as Fenton left the room. As soon as the front door closed, Mal said, "So now you're trying to set up Fenton and Ginger?"

"I don't have to try to do anything," Willow said. "Those two are so hot for each other, smoke is practically coming out of their ears."

Kat laughed. "They'll make a cute couple, and Fenton's a good guy. He deserves to be happy."

"Bishop, have a donut," Willow urged as he checked his cell phone.

"I'm not hungry," he mumbled.

Willow gave Mal an alarmed look. "You're not hungry?" She reached up and pressed her hand against Bishop's forehead. "Maybe you're getting the flu as well?"

He shook his head. "Nah, just worried about Ava. Mal, I know I said I would help with this last load, but do you mind if I head out? Ava will be home now, and I want to check on her."

"Of course," Mal said. "Now that he knows Ginger will be here, Fenton will stay to help. Go home to Ava."

"Thanks." Bishop left the apartment, and Mal glanced at Willow.

"Do you think Ava's okay?"

Willow looked away. "Yes, I'm sure it's just the flu."

"Willow?" Mal said as Kat gathered her coat and purse.

"She's fine, honey." Willow wouldn't look him in the eye, and she quickly hugged Kat. "Thanks again, Kat. Good luck tonight."

"Good luck with what?" Mal asked.

"Nothing," Kat said. "Call me tomorrow if you need some more help, okay, Will?"

"I will. Thanks again, honey."

"What's going on with Kat?" Mal asked once Kat left.

"Nothing," Willow said innocently.

"Why do I get the feeling you're lying?" Mal grinned at her as he wrapped his arms around her waist.

Willow gave him another innocent look. "I don't know what you mean, honey."

"Sure, you don't," Mal said before kissing her on the mouth. "Willow, are you sure you want to move in with me?"

Surprise washed over her. "Of course, I do. Why? Are *you* having second thoughts?"

"No. Although after the canned goods debacle last night, I'm considering putting a lock on the pantry door."

Willow laughed before squeezing him tightly. "I was just testing your observation skills."

Mal tugged lightly on her ponytail. "I love you, Willow."

"I love you too, Mal."

# CHAPTER 2

Ava took a deep breath before glancing at the bathroom counter.

"One more minute, Ava. One more minute."

Her stomach churned nervously, making her wonder if she was about to throw up. So far, the vomiting had been limited to the morning, and there was a small part of her that hoped she would vomit. That would at least give her some hope that she had the flu.

*You're pregnant, girl. You didn't need to pee on a stick to confirm it. You missed your period, and you're vomiting in the morning. Exactly how many signs do you need?*

She rubbed at her forehead. She might not be. Sure, the condom had broken when she and Bishop were having angry sex in his kitchen, but they'd been super careful since then, and what were the odds of her getting pregnant from one bout of unprotected sex? Extremely small. Minuscule, in fact.

*Not that minuscule.*

"Fuck it," she muttered before lunging forward and grabbing the stick from the counter. She scanned it, her hands beginning to shake. "Well, shit."

"Ava? What are you doing?"

She shrieked and whirled around, hiding the pregnancy test behind her back as she stared wide-eyed at Bishop. Her stomach groaned in protest, and she willed herself not to throw up on Bishop's shoes as he ducked into the bathroom.

"What's wrong?"

"Nothing," she said quickly. "What – what are you doing home so early?"

"I was worried about you." Bishop leaned down and kissed her gently. "How did your shift go? Are you feeling better?"

"Um, yeah, I am. I managed to eat some toast at lunch without throwing up, so…" She smiled nervously at Bishop.

"Ava?"

"Yes, Bishop?"

"What are you holding behind your back?"

"Nothing?"

He raised his eyebrows at her, and she sighed. "Okay, it's something."

"Are you going to tell me what that something is?"

She stared anxiously at him. "Honey, there's something I need to tell you, but before I do, I want to say that being with you has been the happiest time of my life. And I'm not expecting anything from you, okay? I'll completely understand if you don't want to be involved or if you don't want -"

"What's going on?" Bishop said in alarm. "Are you breaking up with me?"

"What? Of course not."

"This sounds like a break-up conversation." Bishop was growing more agitated by the minute. She followed him out of the bathroom as he paced back and forth in his bedroom. He was starting to swell, and his dark beard had thickened.

"Listen, I know I'm not the easiest guy to live with. I

16

spend a lot of money on food, I'm messy, and I sleep a lot, but I can work on that. And I know I don't talk about how I feel about you enough, but I'm trying, Ava. Just give me another chance, okay? I'm not used to this relationship thing, but, hell, it's a big adjustment, and grizzlies aren't all that great with change. But I love you, Ava. I love you and I -"

"Bishop, I'm pregnant," Ava blurted.

He stopped pacing and stared silently at her. After a moment, she said, "Bishop? Say something, please."

He remained silent, and she blinked back the tears. "I'm so sorry. I didn't mean for this to happen, and I know that there have been a lot of changes for you lately, and I swear, I'm not going to ask you for anything or expect you to be a dad if you don't want to be. I'll move my things out tonight if that's what you want, and I won't -"

He strode across the room, the pictures on the wall shaking, and wrapped his massive arms around her hips. She made a sharp squeal of surprise, her stomach heaving unpleasantly when he lifted her in the air and pressed his face against her belly.

"Bishop?"

"You're carrying my cub."

His voice was muffled against her stomach, and she touched his dark hair tentatively. "Yes, I think so. The pregnancy test I just took was positive, but I'll have to go to my doctor and get it confirmed."

He lifted his head, and relief flooded through her when he grinned like a fool at her. "You carry my cub in your belly!"

"Uh, yes. That's what being pregnant is," she said. Her voice was shaky with relief, and she uttered a moan, clapping her hand over her mouth when he spun her in a circle. "Bishop! I'm going to barf if you do that again!"

"I'm sorry, baby." He carried her to the bed and set her

17

down gently, urging her to lie down, before resting his large head on her hip and sliding his hand under her shirt. He rubbed her belly with his warm hand before lifting her shirt and kissing her bare skin.

"Are you happy about this?" she asked hesitantly.

He nodded. "Very. Are you?"

"Yes. And nervous."

He smiled at her. "You're going to be a great mom, Ava."

"You're going to be a great dad."

"I hope so," he said quietly.

GINGER STUDIED HERSELF IN THE HALL MIRROR. SHE thought she looked okay. She had used make-up to try to hide the black eye and the bruising on her jaw. Kind of ridiculous considering the black sutures and the swelling were impossible to hide.

She sighed and rubbed at her ribs gingerly. She didn't know why she was even trying to look good for Fenton. Sure, they had kind of – *almost* - shared a moment in the hospital when he was healing from being shot, but she hadn't spoken a word to him since that night.

Still, his silence hadn't been enough to stop her pulse from racing when she'd received Willow's text.

*He's just helping Willow out*, she told herself fiercely, as the buzzer to her apartment rang. She pushed the intercom button. "Hello?"

"Hi, it's Fenton. I'm here to pick you up."

"Hi, I'll be right down."

There was no way she was inviting him up to her apartment. She'd probably try to jump his hot cheetah bones if she did. A little shiver went through her, and she winced as her ribs throbbed dully. Thanks to that loser Robbie, she was in no condition to jump anyone's bones. She locked her door and walked to the elevator, keeping one hand pressed against her ribs. She was thankful to be alive. If she'd known that Robbie had been drinking when he picked her up from her shift at the hospital, she would never have gotten in the damn car with him.

As the elevator moved steadily downward, she sighed. It could have been much worse. Thankfully, no one else was hurt when Robbie drove off the road and into the ditch. Of course, he had walked away without a scratch while she had massive bruising from the seatbelt, a cracked rib, and a face that looked like a meat grinder had attacked it.

*Drama queen.*

Yeah, okay, maybe a little. It was only ten sutures, and Dr. Paulson was the best plastic surgeon in the hospital. He had sewn the cut himself, assuring her she would have minimal scarring, and she reminded herself again that it could have been much worse.

The elevator doors opened, and she studied Fenton's ass as he stood by the front door of the lobby. Jesus, he really did have an amazing ass. The thick blond hair, broad shoulders, and narrow waist weren't bad either.

She walked across the lobby and tapped him on the back. She wasn't tall but standing next to him made her feel even shorter. He swung around, the smile on his face fading as he studied her face.

"Um, hi," she said.

She loved his eyes and their odd combination of gold and green, but she took a nervous step back when the pupils turned to slits, and his fangs descended with a soft pop.

"Fenton?" she squeaked when he cupped the side of her

face that didn't have a Frankenstein-like slash across it and bent down.

"Where is he, Ginger?" His breath was warm on her lips, and she stared at his sharp, white fangs as he hissed under his breath.

"W-who?"

"Robbie."

"Oh, uh, I'm not seeing him anymore," she whispered.

"I know. Tell me where he's living now."

"Why?" she asked.

"Because I'm going to beat the shit out of him for doing this to you." His finger, rough but feather-light, traced the sutures that ran across her jawline.

She shivered all over. "He – he didn't do this to me."

"Where is he?" he repeated quietly. "He needs to learn what happens to men who hit women."

"He didn't," she said. "He didn't lay a hand on me, Fenton. I swear it."

"Was this from the car accident?" He touched the swelling on her jaw, his eyes glittering at her soft hiss of pain.

"Yes."

His eyes narrowed, he clearly didn't believe her, and she unzipped her jacket hurriedly before unbuttoning the first four buttons on her shirt. "I swear. Look, I have bruising from the seat belt."

She realized an instant too late that she was practically baring her breasts to the cheetah shifter before his fingers traced the line of bruising from her shoulder to the hollow of her breasts. She moaned softly and watched as the anger in his eyes turned to lust.

*Thank God I wore my push-up bra*, she thought stupidly as his fingers stroked across the curve of one small breast. He bent his head, and his mouth touched hers in a light brush that had her instantly craving more.

"Fenton," she whispered.

"Ginger," he muttered.

She made a sharp squeal of pain when his arm wrapped around her waist, and he pulled her against his hard body. He let go of her instantly, the light in his eyes fading and his fangs retracting, as she pressed her hand against her ribs and blinked back the tears.

"I'm sorry, love." He stared at her in shame, and she shook her head, trying not to gasp from the pain.

"No, it's fine. I just – I have a cracked rib."

"Fuck! I'm a fucking idiot," he snarled.

"No, you're not! You didn't know," she said.

"Why did you break up with Robbie?" he asked abruptly.

"He picked me up from work. I didn't know he'd been drinking. We got into the car accident, and I decided enough was enough. I was a moron for dating him in the first place."

They both turned when her neighbour, Mr. Sorren, walked into the lobby. Ginger blushed when his gaze dropped to her half-open shirt, but before she could tug her shirt together, Fenton's warm fingers quickly buttoned it.

"Everything okay, Ginger?" Mr. Sorren asked.

"Yes, thanks, Mr. Sorren."

Mr. Sorren switched his bag of groceries to the other hand. "I caught Robbie skulking around outside last night when Davey and I came back from the movies."

Fenton tensed, his body moving closer to her, as she blinked at her neighbour. "What? Are you sure?"

"Yeah. He was trying to get someone to let him into the building, said he had forgotten his key."

Ginger sighed as Mr. Sorren said, "You're not back together with him, are you?"

"No, I'm not," she said.

"Doesn't seem like he knows that," Mr. Sorren said.

"He will," Fenton growled under his breath.

A small smile crossed Mr. Sorren's face. "I'm Carl Sorren."

"Fenton Allard."

"Nice to meet you," Mr. Sorren said as he shook his hand. "Have a good day, Ginger."

"You too." She cleared her throat as Mr. Sorren disappeared into the elevator. "So, uh, are you ready to go?"

"Where does Robbie live?" Fenton asked.

"It's fine, Fenton. I'll text him tomorrow and tell him not to come around. He'll get the message," she said.

"And if he doesn't?"

"He will," she said.

---

"WILL," GINGER GAVE WILLOW AN AFFECTIONATE LOOK tinged with exasperation, "why, exactly, did you ask me over here to help you pack if you weren't going to let me help you pack?"

Willow kissed her forehead before plopping down next to her on the couch. "I thought it would be good for you to get out of your apartment."

"It is nice."

"When do you go back to work?"

"Not until next week." Ginger rubbed at her ribs. "A cracked rib really, really sucks, Will."

"Sorry, sweetie," Willow said. "Do you need to go home? I'm sure Fenton will drive you home."

Ginger gave her a suspicious look. "Are you trying to set me up with Fenton now that I've kicked Robbie to the curb?"

"What? Of course not," Willow said with a *butter wouldn't melt in her mouth* smile. "I would never do that. But, you know, he is single and a sweet guy. He's my favourite out of all of the employees."

"Honey, you're sweet, really, but Fenton does not want to date someone like me," Ginger said.

*Then why did he kiss you?*

*It was hardly a kiss!*

Willow touched her leg. "You've got that look on your face, Ginger."

"What look?"

"The 'I'm hiding something juicy' look. Spill it."

"It's nothing."

"Spill it, or I'll tickle you."

"You wouldn't!" Ginger said in horror. "I've got a cracked rib!"

"I know," Willow said. "And I'll still do it. You know I will."

"What kind of friend are you?"

"An awesome one?" Willow grinned at her. "What? Are you and Fenton already doing it?"

"No! This is the first time I've spoken to him since the night he was shot."

"He's been pretty busy at work," Willow said. "Plus, you were dating Robbie. Hey, have I mentioned how glad I am you dumped that loser? We all kind of hated him."

"Yeah, I know. Why didn't you say something sooner?" Ginger said.

"We were trying to be supportive."

"God, I have terrible taste in men."

"You really do, sweetie," Willow said cheerfully. "That's why you need to date Fenton. He's hot for you, and he's a good guy."

"He's not hot for me."

"Bullshit," Willow said. "He can't keep his eyes off of you."

"Ugh, I wish he would," Ginger said before touching the sutures on her face. "I look like roadkill."

"Oh, please." Willow rolled her eyes. "Now stop stalling and tell me what you're hiding."

"When Fenton came to pick me up, he kind of, sort of, kissed me."

"Really?" Willow's eyes lit up, and she leaned forward. "How was it?"

"Brief," Ginger said.

"Brief? So, no tongue?"

Ginger blushed. "Oh my God, no. There was no tongue involved, Willow."

"Shame. Why did he kiss you?"

"He thought that Robbie had, like, beat me up or something, and he was angry. He threatened to teach Robbie a lesson and didn't believe me when I said it was a car accident. I had to unbutton my shirt and show him the bruising from the seatbelt."

"Ooh, you took off your shirt? Now we're getting somewhere. Go on," Willow said.

"It wasn't like that, Willow."

"Let's see, you took off your shirt, and he kissed you. You're practically dating already."

"Willow…"

The front door slammed shut, and Mal and Fenton walked into the living room.

"Last load has been delivered to the house," Mal said as he sat on the floor at Willow's feet.

She kissed the top of his head. "Good job, honey."

"How are you feeling, Ginger?" Fenton asked.

"Oh, I'm fine, I was just -"

"Actually, she's a little sore. Do you think you could give her a lift home, Fenton?" Willow said.

"Willow." Ginger scowled at her as Fenton nodded.

"Sure, no problem. It's close to my place, anyway."

"It is?" Ginger said.

"Yes."

"Perfect! Thanks, Fenton, you're a doll," Willow said.

He flushed but jumped to his feet when Ginger, wincing and biting at her lip, tried to struggle up from the couch.

"Here, let me help you." Holding her firmly around the hips, his fingers practically touching her ass, he tugged her gently into a standing position. He continued to hold her as Ginger stared up at him.

Willow nudged Mal and gave him a quick thumbs-up before standing. "Thanks again, Fenton."

"What?" He dragged his gaze from Ginger's face but didn't release his grip on her as Willow studied his narrow pupils with interest.

"I said thank you for taking Ginger home, Fenton."

"Oh, right. No problem." He finally seemed to realize he was still holding her and dropped his hands. "Uh, ready to go?"

"Yes," Ginger said hoarsely.

Willow and Mal followed them to the front door, Willow's grin widening when Fenton bent and helped Ginger into her shoes.

"Thank you."

He nodded before helping her into her jacket. He zipped it up and Willow, grinning like a maniac and not caring one bit that Ginger and Fenton could see it, kissed Ginger's cheek. "Bye, sweetie. Thanks for your help."

"I didn't do anything," she said.

"You kept me company," Willow said. "Bye, guys. Fenton, get my girl home safe, okay?"

"I will."

The door slammed behind them, and Willow fanned herself. "Good gravy, you could practically see the attraction between them. It's adorable."

"Not so adorable when you can smell Fenton's lust for her," Mal said dryly. "More like excruciatingly uncomfortable."

"Aw, the pussy cat has it bad for my sweet Ginger," Willow said. "I guarantee you they'll be knocking boots as soon as Ginger's rib heals."

"That's romantic, Willow."

Willow laughed and threw her arms around him. "C'mon, big bad wolf, let's go back to your house."

"Our house," he corrected her.

She smiled and kissed him. "Our house."

CHAPTER 3

"Katarina?"

Kat slid out from the booth and smiled at the tall and lean tiger shifter standing in front of her. He was good looking in a conservative way with short brown hair and a clean-shaven jaw. His smile was large and warm as he leaned forward and pressed a polite kiss against her cheek. No dimple, but what did that matter?

*I bet he doesn't have a single tattoo either*, her cat pouted.

"Hi, you must be Jace."

"I am." He waited until she had returned to her seat before sitting down across from her. "It's nice to meet you in person finally."

"It's nice to meet you too," she said.

The waitress bounced to a stop at their booth. "Hi, hon, I'm Tori. What can I get you tonight?"

She leaned against the table and bent forward slightly. To his credit, even though the rabbit shifter's small breasts were nearly resting in his face, Jace kept his eyes firmly on her face. "Gin and tonic, please."

"Coming right up, handsome." Tori winked at him, and

before she could bounce back to the bar, Kat cleared her throat.

"I'll have another glass of wine, Tori."

"Oh, of course, you bet, Kat," Tori chirped.

*Score one for Jace*, Kat thought. Jace was the final – well, applicant for lack of a better word - she was meeting tonight, and neither the cheetah nor the jaguar shifter before him had been able to keep their eyes off of Tori's tits.

Not that it mattered, she told herself hastily. She was looking for someone to scratch her itch once a month, not have a relationship with. If they wanted to look elsewhere the rest of the month for a fun fling, it was none of her business.

"So, you're single, is that right, Jace?" Kat said. She might be hiring them as her own personal - *whore*, her mind whispered, and she cringed a little – itch-scratcher, but it would only work if the person wasn't in a serious relationship. She wasn't a goddamn homewrecker.

"I am," Jace said cheerfully. "Much to my mother's dismay."

Kat laughed, and the scent of Jace's sudden desire drifted to her. Well, he wanted her - that was a good sign. "My mother isn't exactly purring with joy that I'm single either."

Tori returned and placed their drinks on the table. Kat reached for her wallet, and Jace shook his head. "Let me."

"Thank you."

Another point to the tiger. She had paid for both previous applicants' drinks.

He paid Tori, giving her a generous tip, and she bit her bottom lip before stroking one broad shoulder.

"Well, thank you, handsome."

Kat rolled her eyes. She liked Tori. The rabbit shifter was a charming single mother with three adorable kits, but she had trouble containing her libido like most rabbit shifters.

28

Jace smiled politely at her before his gaze drifted back to Kat. Tori moved to the booth behind them and giggled softly. "You need another beer, handsome?"

Jace raised his glass. "To disappointing mothers."

Kat smiled and clinked her glass against his before taking a sip of wine. It relieved her parched throat, and she licked a drop of moisture from her bottom lip as Jace studied her closely. His desire was thickening, and she glanced at his hazel-coloured eyes. They would turn the colour of jade when he was aroused, and she felt a moment of panic when the thought of him aroused did nothing for her.

*Relax, Kat. You can't force an attraction all at once. Besides, when you're in your heat cycle, it won't matter. Any man with a goddamn pulse arouses you, remember?*

Yeah, she remembered. Although that hadn't been the case with her last heat cycle. She had gone to the bar, determined to break her streak with her vibrator, and had even flirted with a cheetah shifter. Unfortunately, for the first time since her monthly heat cycles had begun, her cat was consumed with need for one shifter and one shifter only.

*Yeah, and it's a damn bird, you tramp. A bird!*

*A bird with dimples and tattoos and a really great dick,* her cat purred.

Moisture pooled between her legs as the memory of riding Ronin in her office blossomed. God, but it had felt good when they fucked. The feel of his mouth on her nipples, even the way he sounded when he called her Kitten, did crazy things to her insides. She hated the nickname, but for some odd and incredibly embarrassing reason, Ronin calling her Kitten while they fucked made her want to come all over that thick cock of his.

"Katarina?"

She realized that she'd been sitting there blankly for

29

nearly a minute, and she gave Jace an apologetic smile. "Sorry, I was, uh, just lost in thought."

"No problem."

The tiger shifter inhaled deeply, a small pleased smile crossing his face, and she groaned inwardly. He could smell her need and thought it was because of him.

*That's a good thing*, she told herself. She tucked away the memory of Ronin and his hot, wet mouth and smiled again at Jace. "So, you run your own business?"

"I do," he said. "I'm in real estate. My company is small, but it's pretty successful considering the housing market right now."

"You must be very good at what you do," she said.

He shrugged modestly. "Mostly luck and a great team of employees, I think."

He paused before leaning forward and lowering his voice. "It does, however, allow me to be available whenever you need me."

She appreciated his discretion. The bar was packed and noisy, it was a Saturday night after all, but most shifters had excellent hearing.

"Are your cycles fairly regular?" he asked.

She nodded. "Most of the time. Sometimes it's off by a day or two, but it always happens within the same week each month."

He settled back against the cushioned seat before taking a sip of his drink. "That's good. It makes it a bit easier. Although, as I said, I have a fairly flexible schedule, so if it happens earlier, don't be shy in letting me know."

"Right," she said before taking a large gulp of wine.

"Katarina?" Jace reached across and took her hand.

"I prefer Kat," she said as his thumb stroked the pulse at her wrist. "Only my mother calls me Katarina."

"Kat, then." He circled her pulse again. "Have you done this before?"

She shook her head. "No."

"I can tell," he said. "Plenty of cat shifters do this. You know that, right?"

"Yes. Are you, um, servicing any other women at the moment?"

A grin crept across his face. "Servicing? That's a boring and technical term for it, Kat."

She flushed. "Sorry."

He rubbed his thumb across her wrist again. "It's fine. You can call it whatever you're most comfortable with. And in answer to your question – no, I'm not servicing any other women at the moment. I prefer to *service* one woman at a time."

The tiger shifter was racking up the points. Both the cheetah and the jaguar were servicing other cat shifters. The jaguar had been hesitant to bring it up and didn't provide details, but the cheetah had been ridiculously proud of his service record. He'd spent twenty minutes going over in intimate detail the three other cat shifters he fucked regularly and what exactly he did for them.

"Why are you free at the moment?" she asked.

"Natasha – she's a lovely lion shifter who works as a nanny – found her mate a few months ago," he said. "I haven't had any hits on my profile since then, and I don't actively go out searching for a female to," he paused and gave her a flirty little grin, "service."

She blushed and didn't object when he linked their fingers together. "At the risk of sounding arrogant, I'm very good at what I do, Kat. I've done this for a few years now, and I know both the importance of being available when you need me and the importance of," he paused, "stamina."

He squeezed her hand lightly. "Whatever you need, I can provide. Sweet and gentle or rough and forceful – I'll be whatever you want. I'm very adaptable."

She licked her lips. "I've been told that I'm, uh, a bit more demanding than most during my heat cycle. Sometimes I'm even a little aggressive."

He smiled. "I like demanding, and I can handle aggression. I do ask that you keep scratches and bite marks to places I can hide with clothing. Nothing on my face, neck, or hands. I have human clients, and it can be difficult to explain any marks that haven't fully healed."

"Of course," she said. "I try to keep that to a minimum, anyway."

He shrugged. "It doesn't bother me if you don't. Just as long as they're, like I said, easily hidden by clothing."

The tiger shifter was turning out to be perfection. He was exactly what she was looking for, and he was handsome with an easy-going personality that didn't drive her crazy. So why wasn't she happy?

She realized Jace was speaking to her, and she smiled apologetically. "I'm sorry?"

"I was asking if you wanted me there the entire two days of your cycle or if you just want an 'on-call' type of thing."

"Oh, uh, I hadn't thought about that," she said.

"You should," he said. "In my experience, most cats want you around the entire time. I've had a few in the past who were content to let me go back to work or home in between, but I'm not sure that's the best idea. The need seems to be less intense if you have access to me whenever you want."

"That makes sense," she murmured. "I think having you stay with me the entire time would be best."

"If you change your mind, you can just let me know, and

I'll go and come back whenever you call," he said. "Again, I'm pretty adaptable."

He squeezed her hand a final time. "Any other questions, Kat?"

She shook her head, and he released her hand before reaching into the inside pocket of his jacket. He passed several pieces of paper to her, and she scanned them as he said, "Those are my references and my medical records."

"Oh right." She dug into her purse and handed him a folded-up piece of paper. "These are, uh, my medical records. As well, I'm on the pill. I can provide you with a photocopy of the prescription if you want."

"No need," he said as he looked over her records. "If you prefer to use condoms anyway, we can. I just find this to be," he paused and gave her another flirty grin, "easier."

She smiled faintly, and he placed her records on the table. "If you need more references or have any other questions, just let me know, okay?"

"Okay."

He finished his drink and stood, and she mentally scored him another point. He seemed to sense that she needed some time to think about what he said, and she slid out of the booth and gave him a more natural smile. "Thank you, Jace. It was great to meet you, and I'll get back to you in a few days."

"It was lovely to meet you," he said. This time when he leaned down, he pressed his mouth against hers and kissed her in a sweet and gentle way that didn't raise her pulse even a little.

He straightened and smiled at her. "Talk to you soon, Kat."

"You bet." She watched him leave before sitting in the booth again and resting her head in her hands.

The tiger shifter was seriously perfect and was what she

was looking for. Did it matter that she didn't feel a lick of desire for him?

No, she decided, it didn't. Despite the way her last heat cycle had gone, she was confident that once Jace was in her bedroom, naked and willing, she'd feel something for him. God, she had to. She couldn't go another heat cycle with nothing but her vibrator. Besides, if worse came to worse, she could just close her eyes and pretend he was a smart-mouthed bird with a stupid dimple and tattoos that –

"Well, I think he had the most potential, Kitten."

Her eyes flew open, and she stared in shock as Ronin plopped down across from her. He had a bottle of beer in one hand, and he took a long swallow from it before setting it down on the table. She watched in stunned silence as he picked up her medical records and read them with interest.

"Clean as a whistle, I see," he said.

"Give those to me!" She snatched them back and shoved them into her purse. "Those are private."

He grinned at her, and she scowled. "What the hell are you doing here? Are you following me?"

He laughed. "Hardly, Kitten. This is a public bar and, I hear, a very popular place for the shifters to go. I figured I would check it out."

She stared blankly at him as her mind raced. Had he heard something? Had he –

"As I was saying, I think out of the three of them, this Jace fellow was the best. Don't you?" He winked at her, and a surge of shame and anger went through her.

"Were you eavesdropping on our conversation?"

He shook his head. "Nope. But is it my fault that you chose to sit in the booth behind me?"

"You could have moved," she snapped.

"I was there first," he said. "Besides, I think you knew I

34

was there. You can't tell me you didn't smell me – not with your kitten super sense of smell."

"I didn't," she muttered. It was true. She hadn't caught ever a whiff of his scent, but she had been somewhat involved in trying to find a living, breathing sex toy.

She drank the rest of her wine in three gulps and waved Tori down. The waitress came over immediately, and Kat had to swallow her hiss of jealousy when Tori put her arm around Ronin's shoulders and squeezed.

"You moved booths, handsome. Do you know our kitty cat?"

"Tori," Kat muttered. "Don't call me that."

"Sorry, sweetie." Tori gave her an apologetic look, and Kat forced herself to smile at her.

"As a matter of fact, I do know the lovely Ms. Frost. She's my boss," Ronin said.

"Oh, you're working for the security firm? You must be, like, pretty brave and strong," Tori said before twitching her nose at him.

He just grinned, and Kat was only slightly mollified to realize that he hadn't dropped his gaze to Tori's breasts even once.

"Tori," she prompted, "I need another glass of wine, please."

"Of course. What about you…." Tori raised her eyebrows at Ronin.

"Ronin."

"What a sexy name," Tori giggled. "I'm Tori, with an 'i'."

"Nice to meet you, Tori, with an i," Ronin said.

"I love your tattoos. Do you, like, have them all over?" she asked.

"Mostly," he said, and Kat rolled her eyes when she made a little squeak of delight.

35

"I'd love to see all of them sometime. Tattoos are so, like, sexy."

When Ronin didn't reply, she stroked his shoulder. "Can I get you something else?"

Kat could feel her fangs lengthening, and she retracted them with a grimace. It was evident that Tori was offering more than just another drink, and she clenched her hand around her empty wine glass as Ronin winked at the rabbit shifter.

"Another beer would be great, Tori with an i."

"Coming right up." She let her hand trail down his bicep before leaving.

Her nostrils flaring, Kat glared at Ronin. Unlike Jace, who'd dressed in a conservative dark suit, Ronin wore a stupidly tight t-shirt that hugged his broad chest and accentuated his bulging biceps.

"Where were we?" Ronin leaned forward, and she automatically leaned back.

"Out of your three applicants, I think Jace was the best one. God, the way that cheetah shifter went on and on about the other cat shifters he," he paused, and she blushed furiously when he said, "*services*, was even a bit too much for me."

"Keep your voice down!" She hissed as she glanced nervously around the bar. "Do you have any idea how rude it was for you to listen in on my private conversations?"

"Can I help it if I have excellent hearing?" he asked.

"You shouldn't have listened," she said.

"You're right, I shouldn't have, and I apologize. It was rude of me."

"Why are you even talking to me?" she asked. "You haven't spoken a damn word to me since – since…."

"Since you rejected my offer to wash your back *and* rock your world?"

She looked away as Tori placed their drinks on the table. Before she could pay, Ronin pulled out his wallet and handed some bills to Tori.

"Thanks, handsome," she squeaked again before reluctantly moving on.

Kat downed the glass in four large gulps as Ronin watched her with interest. "Wow, you like your wine, huh?"

"Why are you talking to me? You hate me," she said.

"I don't hate you, Ms. Frost. I figured you needed a bit of a break from my charming personality."

"Your personality is not charming," she said. "More like irritating and annoying."

"Ooh, my little pussy-cat is as sharp-tongued as ever."

"Let's get one thing straight - I am not your little pussy-cat. I'm your boss."

"Even outside the office?" he said with a grin.

"Yes." She glanced at her watch. "If you'll excuse me, it's late, and I -"

"Hold on," he said and wrapped his long fingers around her wrist.

Her heart rate jumped crazily, and her blood pulsed in her veins as he smiled at her and stroked the inside of her wrist with his thumb.

*Fuck, I am in so much trouble.*

"I did want to talk to you about something."

"What?" She hated the way she sounded so breathless and needy.

"I wanted to throw my hat into the ring, so to speak," he said cheerfully.

"Excuse me?" She gave him a blank look.

"I'd like to apply for the position of *servicing* you during your cycle, Ms. Frost."

Her jaw dropped, and she stared in mute surprise at him for a moment. "I – it's not a job position, Ronin."

"No? Then why did you just meet three shifters in what were clearly job interviews?" he said teasingly.

"Do you have any references?" she blurted out as her cat purred with delight.

*Goddammit, Kat!*

He smiled at her. "Do I need references, Ms. Frost? You do, after all, have first-hand knowledge of what it's like to ride my dick."

She shut down her cat's excited purring with a harsh snarl. "Sorry, but the experience was over too quickly for me to make an accurate judgement."

"There's that mean little pussy-cat again," he said with a grin. "But I'll give you that one since it wasn't my best performance. Not my fault, though – you took me by surprise."

Fuck, she was in trouble if that wasn't his best performance.

"But if you choose me, I'll be much better prepared. I'll get plenty of sleep beforehand, eat my veggies and do some power walking."

She almost laughed but bit it back fiercely. "Sorry, not interested."

"Are you sure?" he asked.

"Yes. You're my employee, Ronin. It's not appropriate."

"Sure, it is," he said. "I can keep my work life and my personal life separate, can't you?"

"If Mal and Bishop found out, I'd be mortified," she said.

"Why would they find out? I promise to be discreet."

She hesitated. Her cat was positively begging her to take

Ronin up on his offer, and it was hard to think past its meowing, howling insistence.

He leaned in and rubbed his thumb over her pulse. *His* touch sent her lust into overdrive, and she licked her lips nervously as he gave her a dark look of desire.

"What do you say, Kitten? Do you want me between those gloriously firm thighs every month or not?"

*Sweet baby Jesus, yes!*

She yanked her wrist out of his grip. "No, thank you."

Disappointment surged through her when he shrugged. "Okay."

For some reason, his easy acceptance of her rejection made her temper flare, and she glared at him. "You're such a jackass, Ronin."

"Am I?" he said innocently as he picked up his beer and slid out of the booth. "Have a great night, Ms. Frost. Good luck with the tiger shifter."

He walked across the bar and sat down at one of the taller tables. Tori appeared almost instantly, and she ignored the jealousy that surged through her when the rabbit shifter pressed her chest against his arm and shoulder, and Ronin didn't move away.

"Asshole," she muttered and grabbed her purse.

She wasn't about to stay and watch the rabbit shifter seduce Ronin. No way, no how. She stomped toward the door before suddenly turning and heading to the bar. She sat on an empty barstool as Porter stopped in front of her.

"Hey, Kat. I wondered if you were going to stop by and say hello."

"Whiskey, neat," she snapped.

He blinked at her in surprise, and she sighed before rubbing her forehead. "Sorry, Porter."

"No problem," he said. "One whiskey, coming up."

He placed a glass in front of her and poured some whiskey into the bottom. She drank it all in one large gulp, gasping as the fiery liquid burned down her throat before setting the glass down in front of her.

"Another."

Porter gave her an assessing look, and she hissed lightly at him. "Another, I said, Porter."

"Yes, ma'am," he replied and poured her another.

# CHAPTER 4

"Thank you for the ride home, Fenton," Ginger said as he parked in front of her apartment building.

He studied the two police cars parked on the street. "Why are there police in front of your building?"

"I'm not sure." She unclicked her seatbelt as Fenton shut off the car and opened his door.

"I'll walk you to your door."

"Oh, that's okay. You don't have to do that."

He took her hand and helped her out of the car. "I don't mind."

As they walked up the steps of her apartment building, she wondered if she should let go of the cheetah shifter's hand. He was still holding it firmly, and she decided it was too nice to feel his warm hand gripping hers to let go.

As they entered the elevator, he glanced at her. "What floor?"

"Seventh."

He pushed the button, his left hand still linked with hers, and she smiled tentatively at him. "Thanks again for the ride home. It was really nice of you."

"You're welcome."

"So, you live close to here, huh?"

"Yes. Only about fifteen minutes away."

"That's nice. It's, um, a nice neighbourhood."

The elevator doors opened, and they walked down the hallway. They turned the corner, and she stopped abruptly. "What the hell?"

The door to her apartment was open, the door frame cracked, and the doorknob hung uselessly. Two police officers stood in the hallway talking to Mr. Sorren, and Fenton tightened his grip on her hand as they turned toward her.

"Mr. Sorren? What's going on?"

"Ms. Billings?" One of the officers walked toward them.

"Yes? What – what's happening?"

"Your apartment's been broken into," the police officer said.

"Are you kidding me?" Ginger groaned as Mr. Sorren hurried forward.

"I'm sorry, Ginger. I didn't hear anything. Davey and I were leaving, and we saw that your door was open and called the police when we saw the, uh, mess inside. I'm so sorry."

"It's not your fault, Mr. Sorren," she said. Fenton dropped her hand, and she was just mourning its loss when he put his arm around her shoulders and drew her into him. She leaned against his hard warmth.

"What did they take?" Fenton asked.

The police officer hesitated, glancing at Fenton, before saying, "We don't think they took anything."

"What?" Ginger frowned at him.

"Ms. Billings, is there anyone who might have a personal grudge against you?"

She stiffened, and Fenton rubbed her shoulder soothingly.

"Yeah, my ex-boyfriend," Ginger said.

"Ginger? Are you okay?" Fenton gave her a worried look as they stood in her bedroom.

The room, like every other room in her small apartment, had been completely trashed. Her clothes and her bedding had been slashed with a knife, pictures lay smashed on the floor, and her dresser and nightstand tables were knocked over.

She didn't reply as one of the police officers walked into the room. "We're almost done, Ms. Billings. They've dusted for prints, and we're sending a unit over to speak to your boyfriend."

"Ex-boyfriend," Fenton grunted.

"Unfortunately, because your neighbours didn't see or hear anything, unless we get a hit off of prints, we can't arrest him," the officer said.

"It was him," Fenton growled. "Who else would it be? I can't believe no one heard anything."

"My apartment is an end apartment," Ginger said, "the walls are thick, and both Carl and Davey are older and don't have the best hearing."

She picked up a shirt and stared at the ripped fabric. "Maybe it wasn't Robbie. Maybe it was just a random break-in."

"It's a possibility," the officer said cautiously, "and we won't rule that out, but it seems odd that a thief would destroy your TV and your electronics rather than take them."

Ginger swiped at the hot tears that were starting to run down her cheeks and didn't object when Fenton put his arm around her again. She rested her head on his chest, and he stroked her dark hair as the officer said, "Do you have somewhere else you can stay tonight, Ms. Billings? Family or friends?"

"I have a brother," she said dully, "but he doesn't live here."

"You really can't stay here tonight," the officer said. "The door is completely busted, and if it was your boyfriend and he decides to come back…."

Ginger gave him a frightened look. "Why would he? He's made his point."

The officer didn't reply, and Fenton stroked her hair again. He hated how tired and defeated she looked. "She's staying with me tonight."

Ginger blinked at him in surprise. "No, Fenton. I can't do that. I'll just call Willow or Ava and -"

"Willow's in the middle of moving, and Ava's got the flu," he said. "You're staying with me, Ginger."

"I… okay," she said.

"Good," the officer said. "Now, we just have a few more questions, and then we're done."

———

"You have a nice place," Ginger said.

"Thanks. It's a bit on the small side," Fenton said as he took her coat and hung it on the hook on the wall.

It was a bachelor pad, and Fenton was right that it was small, but it was remarkably tidy for a guy who lived by himself, Ginger decided. She studied the bed, heat rising in her cheeks when Fenton said, "I'll take the couch."

"No, I will," she protested. "I'm not going to kick you out of your bed."

"I don't mind."

"Fenton, no," she said. "You'll never fit your giant body on that couch, and you won't get any sleep."

"You've got a cracked rib and bruising all over. You're sleeping in my bed tonight, Ginger," he said.

A sweet little shiver went down her spine, and she smiled at him. "Thank you, Fenton."

"You're welcome. Are you hungry?"

She shook her head. "No, just tired. Could I get a glass of water? I'm supposed to take some medication for my ribs."

He poured her a glass of water and then rummaged through the dresser beside the bed while she took her medication. He handed her a t-shirt. "You can use this to sleep in."

She took it from him with a smile of thanks. Robbie had been thorough in destroying her stuff. She didn't have a single item of clothing that hadn't been ripped or shredded, and she blinked back the tears as Fenton showed her to the small bathroom.

"There's no tub," he said, "but if you want to have a shower, you're more than welcome to."

"I just want to lie down, if that's okay? I'm exhausted."

She was less tired and more scared and depressed, but she didn't want to look like a weak little girl in front of Fenton. She closed the bathroom door and pressed her face into his shirt, and inhaled deeply. Disappointingly, it smelled like laundry detergent rather than Fenton, and she made a face at herself in the mirror as she carefully stripped down to her bra and underwear. She hesitated before unhooking her bra and sliding it down her shoulders. It would be super uncomfortable to sleep in her bra, and it wasn't like she had a whole lot in the boob department anyway. Fenton wouldn't even notice she was braless.

FENTON SEARCHED THE DRESSER DRAWERS FOR SOMETHING HE could wear as pajamas. He usually slept naked, but he didn't think that would go over very well with Ginger. He might occasionally smell the sweet scent of her lust when she stared at him, but she was injured and frightened, and he didn't want her to think he had brought her back to his place for sex.

He found a pair of shorts, and he stripped quickly before pulling them over his hips. Ginger was acting brave, but he could smell her fear. It covered her in a thick blanket, and a surge of anger went through him. He would find her dickhead ex-boyfriend and make sure that he never went near her again.

The door to the bathroom opened, and he turned around, his mouth going dry. His cheetah made a rumbling purr of approval, and he had to stop himself from crossing the small space and rubbing up against Ginger like a randy tomcat. Holy shit, but did it turn him on to see her wearing his shirt.

*Jesus, she's not wearing a bra*, he thought as his eyes dropped to her chest. It wasn't cold in the room, but he could see the outline of her nipples against the fabric, and his cat yowled happily.

He blushed furiously when Ginger crossed her arms over her chest. "Fenton? Are you, uh, okay?"

He nodded. Seeing her in nothing but his shirt had made his fangs pop out, and he turned away so she wouldn't see the evidence of his arousal. "Fine. Crawl into bed."

She didn't answer, but he could hear the sound of her slender body sliding between the sheets. He clenched his hands into fists as his groin stirred. Fuck, he needed to get control of himself.

"Goodnight, Fenton."

"Goodnight," he said gruffly before striding to the couch

and lying down. Ginger shut off the lamp next to the bed, and darkness enveloped them.

He stared up at the ceiling. He had excellent night vision, and he counted the tiles as Ginger moved restlessly in the bed. After only a few minutes, he heard the slide of tears down her cheeks, and the scent of her sadness filled the room.

He got up from the couch and crossed to the bed without thinking about it. "Don't cry, Ginger."

She made a startled little sob. "How did you know?"

He patted her hip gingerly through the blanket. "I'm a cat. We have excellent hearing, remember?"

"Right," she whispered. "I'm sorry to be such a baby."

"You're not," he said. "Don't say that."

"Will you lie in bed with me, Fenton?"

He hesitated, and she blushed. "I'm sorry, that was dumb. I shouldn't have -"

"I will," he said abruptly. He crawled into the bed beside her and pulled her carefully into his embrace.

"I'm sorry," she whispered again as she rested her head on his chest.

"You don't need to be sorry," he said. "Or scared. I'll keep you safe."

She lifted her head and stared at him. "You will, won't you?"

"Yes."

She rested her head against his chest again, her small hand rubbing almost absently through the hair. It felt perfect to have her touch him, and he closed his eyes and stroked her back, ignoring the way his dick stirred.

"Fenton?"

"Yeah?"

"You're purring." There was soft wonderment in her voice.

To his shame, he *was* purring - purring loudly - and he shut his cat down with an inward growl before clearing his throat. "I'm sorry."

"Why? It's a nice sound," she said before raising her head again to look at him. "Why would you be sorry?"

"I don't know," he said.

"Do cat shifters purr for the same reason that house cats purr?" she asked.

Christ, her hand had dipped to his flat stomach and was still rubbing. It was taking every bit of his willpower not to rub up against her soft body. If she didn't stop soon, he'd have to leave the bed before he embarrassed himself.

"Mostly," he said. There was no way he was telling her that he was purring because he was turned on.

"So, you're purring because I'm petting you?" She giggled as the scent of her sadness lessened.

"Uh, yeah, sure," he mumbled. He was purring again, the deep rasp rising out of his chest, and he was as hard as a rock. Panicking, he pushed down the blankets. "I should go back to the couch."

Ginger inhaled sharply, and he muttered a curse. She stared at his crotch, and his purring came to an abrupt stop as he yanked the covers up to his chin. "Fuck, I'm sorry. Uh, it's not what it looks like."

"Really?" Ginger asked. The scent of her fear had disappeared completely, and he took shallow breaths, trying to block out the new and intoxicating aroma of her need.

He groaned when she gently snuggled into him again and placed her hand on his stomach. "You know, I might not have the night vision of a cat, but I'm not blind, Fenton."

"I'm so sorry," Fenton said hoarsely. "I – I didn't bring you back here for this, I swear. I'm not some perverted feline who preys on women in distress."

She laughed, and his entire body stiffened when she slipped her hand into his shorts and wrapped her fingers around his cock. He purred again, the sound was loud and ragged in the dark, and she stroked him softly before grinning at him.

"That gets your motor running, huh?"

"Jesus, Ginger," he said hoarsely. "That feels so fucking good."

"I like you, Fenton," she whispered.

"I like you too." He cupped her face and pressed his mouth against hers. When she sighed and parted her lips, he slid his tongue into her mouth and stroked hers with a light pressure that made her moan.

"I've dreamed about kissing you, about touching your soft, sweet body," he murmured against her mouth.

"Me too," she said breathily. "I mean - touching you, not touching myself."

"Love, if you want to touch yourself, you go right ahead." He grinned at her soft blush before nuzzling her neck. He was purring so loudly it was embarrassing, but Ginger's soft little hand was still stroking his cock, and he was about two minutes away from pushing her on her back and burying himself deep inside of her.

He reined in his need for her and cupped her small breast through her shirt before rubbing his head against her shoulder. She giggled softly and used her other hand to pet his thick, blond hair.

"You really do like to be petted."

He grinned at her as he circled her nipple with his thumb. "I can't help it, love. It's the cat in me."

"I don't mind." She made a breathless little moan when he tweaked her nipple. "Would it sound trampish if I said I wanted to have sex with you?"

He shook his head. "God, no. I like a woman who isn't shy."

She squeezed his cock, and he groaned before wrapping his hand around her waist and pulling her toward him. He needed to get her naked – naked and under him while he –

He froze when she made a harsh cry of pain and clutched at her side.

"Shit! I'm sorry." He stroked her upper arm and gave her an anxious look. "I forgot about your ribs. Do you need to go to the hospital?"

"No, I'm fine," she gasped. "Don't stop. We'll just have sex slowly."

He studied her in the dark. Her face was pale, and her mouth was trembling, and he could smell the pain rolling off of her in heavy waves.

"Not tonight, Ginger," he said before tugging her hand out of his shorts.

She gave him a ridiculously adorable pout. "It'll be fine, Fenton. I want to have sex with you."

"I want to have sex with you too, and we will when your ribs heal," he said.

"This sucks," she muttered.

He nuzzled her neck again before helping her turn onto her side. "Get some sleep, love."

"I'm not tired. I'm horny," she pointed out.

He rumbled laughter before kissing the back of her neck. "Sleep, love. The more you rest, the sooner we can have sex."

"Fine." She took his hand and pressed it against her breast. He cupped it gently before leaning over her and kissing her.

"Good night, Ginger."

"Good night, Fenton."

## CHAPTER 5

K at swallowed the last of her whiskey, grimacing at the taste, before tapping the bar with one pointed fingernail.

Porter ambled over with the bottle of whiskey. "You sure you should have another, Kat?"

She squinted at him. "You're not my mother, Porter."

He laughed. "No, I'm not. But you're not driving home, Kat. Hand over your keys."

She scowled at him. "I don't need to give you my keys, Porter. I'm not stupid – I'll call an Uber."

"Okay," he said and poured her another.

She made herself sip at this one rather than downing it and ignored the sounds of Tori and her best friend Lori giggling. Lori had shown up at the bar twenty minutes ago and immediately glommed onto Ronin like he was a piece of lettuce.

Christ, the entire bar was filled with rabbit shifters, and all of them were horny for the damn bird.

*Not just the bunnies,* her cat pouted.

*Shut up.*

She finished her drink and slid off the barstool. She weaved unsteadily as she made her way to the ladies' room. She ducked into the stall and used the toilet. As she was buttoning her jeans, the bathroom door opened, and her cat hissed when she heard the high-pitched giggling of the rabbit shifters.

"Oh God, Tori, you were right. He is so dreamy," Lori said.

"I know, right? My shift is over in an hour. Are you up for taking the bird home?" Tori asked.

"Oh, hell, yes," Lori said. "The kids are with their dad tonight, so my night is free."

"Good. But listen, my kids will be at home, so you need to keep it down."

"Sure, no problem," Lori giggled. "But you'd better tell the bird that too. The two of us are going to knock his tail feathers off tonight."

Kat's nails lengthened, and her cat hissed angrily. She stopped herself from tearing open the stall door and showing the horny little bunnies what happened to females who tried to take what was hers.

*Not yours!*

*Yes, mine!* Her cat hissed.

"How do my tits look?" Tori asked.

"Fucking fantastic, how about mine?" Lori said.

"Gorgeous," Tori said. "Okay, we gotta get back out there. Porter will have my head if I stay in here much longer."

Kat heard a high-five and clenched her fists again as the two rabbit shifters left the bathroom. She escaped the stall and washed her hands before staring at herself in the mirror. Her cheeks were bright red, and her dark hair had started to escape the clip. She scooped it back into place with hands that trembled lightly and clipped it securely.

*Go home, Kat. You're drunk.*

Yes, that was an excellent idea. Besides, did she want to watch Ronin leave with the bunnies?

No, she didn't.

Kat pushed open the bathroom door, stopping in surprise when Ronin stepped out of the men's room. They faced each other in the hallway, and she frowned when Ronin, his voice uncharacteristically somber, said, "You've had too much to drink, Kat."

"I'm fine," she said.

He shook his head. "You've been tossing back whiskey like it's water. I think you've had enough."

She snorted. "Thanks for the advice."

"I'm serious. Let me give you a ride home and -"

"I don't think so, but thanks."

"Kat, wait." He grabbed her arm as she walked unsteadily past him, and her nostrils flared as fresh lust filled her belly.

She turned and shoved him against the wall, and he groaned when she rubbed her entire body against his.

"Kitten, what -"

"Shut up," she muttered before rubbing her face against his neck. She grabbed his wrists and pinned his arms against the wall above his head before rubbing her body against his again. She rubbed against him repeatedly until he was panting, and she could feel his erection against her belly with every slow stroke of her body against his.

She rubbed her cheeks against his face, relishing the feel of his warm breath against her skin.

"Jesus, Kat, you are killing me over here," he groaned.

She ignored him, and he made a harsh gasp, his entire body arching against hers when she licked him from the base of his neck to his mouth. She licked his lips before licking the rough stubble on his chin. She purred and turned around, sliding her body up and down his as he cupped her waist. She ground her ass against his cock, and he made another harsh groan as his fingers tightened.

"If you don't stop doing that, I'm going to fuck you right here in the hallway," he warned in a hoarse voice.

Her cat yowled with excitement, and she ground her ass against his dick again.

"I warned you, Kitten," he muttered before turning her and yanking her against his hard body. His hands gripped her ass, and he squeezed as he lowered his mouth toward hers. Before he could kiss her, Porter walked down the hallway.

"What the hell?" he said.

Kat tore herself away from Ronin as her cat hissed her disapproval. She stumbled down the hallway, shaking off Porter's hand when he reached out to steady her and hurried back to her barstool.

She sat down, her hands shaking badly, and stared at her empty whiskey glass. Jesus Christ, what was she thinking?

Ronin sat down at his table, and her hands fisted around the glass when Lori immediately joined him. The rabbit shifter's nose twitched rapidly, and she took a step back before glancing at Kat. Even through her shame, Kat felt the hard bite of satisfaction when Lori took another step back and stared in disappointment at Ronin.

"What are you doing, Kat?"

Porter was back behind the bar, and she refused to look at him. "Another whiskey, Porter,"

"No. You're cut off. What are you doing?" he said.

"I don't know what you mean."

Her cat hissed angrily. After her initial hesitation, Lori was back to pressing her ample chest against Ronin's arm and giggling madly. Another hiss escaped her mouth when Tori passed by them and dragged her hand across Ronin's broad back.

"Bullshit," Porter said as he glanced at Ronin and the two rabbit shifters. "Wolves aren't the only ones who mark, Kat."

"We don't mark like wolves," she said

"No, not usually, but you can mark if you're really riled up. Ronin's twenty feet away, and I can smell you all over him. Does he know you marked him?" Porter said.

"It was an accident, and besides, it doesn't seem to be affecting his game any," she said.

"Why the hell did you mark him? I've never seen a cat go after a bird before," Porter said. "Does he know you're a cat shifter?"

"Yes," Kat said. "And I told you – it was an accident."

"Sure, it was," Porter said with a small grin.

"It was," she insisted. "He's my employee."

"What is up with the security firm and marking their employees? First Mal and now you," Porter said. "You guys are going to get a reputation."

"Oh my God." Kat buried her face in her hands. "I am losing my damn mind, Porter."

"Maybe what you need is a wolf to distract you from your lust for birds," Porter said with a grin. "You know that little bird could never handle your claws, Kat."

She glared at him, and he held his hands up defensively. "Okay, okay. I'm just teasing. For some weird reason, I know you don't find me attractive in any way, shape, or form. I'm mostly over it."

"Fuck," Kat groaned before rubbing at her temples. They were starting to ache from the alcohol, and she started a little when a hand dropped onto her back.

"You okay, Kat?"

"Hey, Judd. Yeah, I'm good." She smiled faintly at the

bouncer. He was a bear shifter and a good guy, if not a bit of a player.

"You don't look so good," he said.

"Just a bit too much to drink. I think I'm going to call it quits," she said as Porter took her empty glass. She fumbled out her credit card and handed it to Porter as Judd rubbed her back.

"Why don't you let me give you a ride home, Kat?"

"That's nice of you, Judd, but I can't impose."

"I don't mind," the bear shifter said. His hand still circled her back as Porter frowned at him.

"Judd, she's drunk."

"I know," Judd said. "I'll behave myself, for God's sake, Porter."

"Will you?" Porter asked.

The bouncer growled at him. "What the fuck kind of guy do you think I am?"

"I know you're a good guy, but you've had a crush on Kat for a long time and sometimes -"

"Can the two of you please stop talking like I'm not here," Kat said before taking her credit card back from Porter and shoving it in her purse. "Just because I'm drunk doesn't mean I'm going to automatically fuck Judd."

Judd flushed. "I didn't think that, Kat."

"Yeah," she said, "I know. Listen, it's sweet of you to offer, but I'll take an Uber home."

"I don't mind," Judd said before curving his arm around her waist and hugging her briefly. "You should probably have someone make sure you get tucked into bed safely."

"Move your arm before I move it for you."

The terse demand made all three of them stare in surprise at the bird shifter standing next to the bar.

"What did you say?" Judd asked as his arm tightened around Kat's waist.

"You heard me," Ronin said. All trace of his usual good humour had disappeared, and he gave the bouncer a dark look. "I'm driving Kat home tonight, so do us both a favour and stop drooling on her."

"Ronin, don't," Kat said.

"Yeah, Ronin, don't," Judd repeated softly.

"Last chance, big guy," Ronin said.

Something in his voice made Judd stiffen, and he dropped his arm before taking a step toward him. "You're awfully brave for a bird shifter."

"Let's go, Kat," Ronin said. He held his hand out, his gaze never leaving Judd's.

"Hold on. Kat and I are old friends. I'm sure she'd much rather have me drive her home and tuck her into bed than a fragile little bird like you," Judd said.

"Talk about her bed again, and I'll break your jaw, you idiot mouth-breather," Ronin said.

"Oh, you just made a big mistake, little birdie," Judd said.

Kat cursed and slid off the barstool as Judd rushed Ronin. The shift was happening, her cat yowling to be free and help the bird shifter. Ronin was strong and brave, but he was a bird and no match for the angry bear. She'd seen Judd take down a thousand-pound bull without breaking a sweat.

Before she could shift, Judd, snarling under his breath, swung at Ronin. Kat's mouth dropped open, and her cat stared in silent surprise as Ronin dodged the blow easily and grabbed Judd's arm when the force of his swing knocked him off balance. He wrenched Judd's arm up behind his back, and the bear screamed shrilly as there was a loud crack.

Ronin pulled again, and Judd dropped to his knees, snarling and growling viciously as Ronin leaned over him.

"I've broken your arm, but I did make a promise to break your jaw, didn't I?"

"Ronin, stop," Kat said quickly as she staggered toward them.

"I'm going to let you go, and you're going to stay right where you are until the lady and I leave. Do you get me?" Ronin said to Judd.

The bear shifter snarled at him, and Ronin yanked his arm higher. "Do you get me?"

Judd screamed again before nodding his head. "Yes! Yes!"

"Good." Ronin dropped his arm. Judd stayed on his knees, and Ronin held his hand out to Kat. "Let's go, Katarina."

She took his hand and followed him outside. He helped her into his car and buckled her in before starting the vehicle. "What's your address?"

She recited it to him, and he drove down the dark streets as she stared at him.

"What?" He glanced at her, and she was a little relieved to see the dark anger on his face had disappeared.

"Do you have a death wish?"

"Why?" He laughed.

"Judd's a bear shifter. You're lucky he didn't kill you."

"I can handle myself," he said. "Don't you worry about that, Kitten."

"You didn't have to give me a ride home," she said.

"Like I was going to let that Neanderthal drive you home. Even I could smell his lust, and I can't smell for shit," he said.

"Judd's just a friend."

"He wants more, and if he had driven you home, he might have gotten it."

58

She glared at him. "I'm not like that."

"I know, but you're drunk, and sometimes when people are drunk, they make bad choices," he said cheerfully. "I was saving you from doing something you regret. See how nice I am? You should reconsider your decision to kick me out of the applicant pool for satisfying your heat cycle requirements."

"Why don't you satisfy those damn rabbit shifters? They were all over you," she said moodily.

"Well, according to Lori and Tori - both with an i, by the way - I am positively drenched in the scent of your sweet pussy," he paused and grinned, "cat. Oddly enough, the bunnies didn't like it."

Her cheeks flamed red. "That was an accident."

"Oh, I know," he said. "That hallway was pretty narrow, and you pretty much *had* to rub your body all over mine. Now, the licking was probably over the top, but -"

"Oh my God, shut up," she groaned before rubbing at her temple. "I'm drunk, okay? Besides, the bunnies were still all over you."

"That's true, they were," he agreed.

"So why aren't you...."

He raised his eyebrows at her. "Being the lettuce in a bunny sandwich?"

"Yeah," she muttered.

He shrugged. "Truthfully, I'm not really into bunnies. I prefer more teeth and claws."

She flushed. "I don't use my claws and teeth."

"Now I know you're drunk," he laughed. "I heard you telling that straight-laced tiger shifter that you were demanding and aggressive in the sack."

"A gentleman wouldn't bring that up," she said through gritted teeth.

"Probably not," he said. "But he also wouldn't point out that he had claw marks all over his chest for days after you fucked him."

"It's not my fault you're a bird and don't heal as well as the rest of us," she said.

He laughed. "Birds heal just fine. I was actually only clawed up for a few hours, but I thought I might get the sympathy vote in the 'heat cycle servicing pool' if you thought you'd injured me for days."

"You're not in the running. Do you understand that?" she muttered before closing her eyes. The car's interior was spinning, and she felt off-kilter and slow.

"Yes, so you've mentioned," he said before falling silent.

They rode in silence until he pulled up in front of her house. He shut off the engine, and she smiled briefly at him. "Thanks for the ride home, Ronin. I'll see you at work on – shit!"

"What?"

"I left my damn purse at the bar. It has my house keys and my cell phone in it."

"I can drive you back," Ronin said.

She shook her head. "No, it's fine. Can I borrow your phone?"

He handed her the phone, and she thought for a moment before punching the number in.

"Porter? It's Kat. Yeah, I'm fine. Listen, I left my – oh, you've got it? Thanks, Porter."

Kat smiled a little, "Yes, I'll stop by your place tomorrow and pick it up."

She listened and then laughed. "A five-minute make-out session is not going to be my thank-you. Nice try, buddy."

She laughed again. "Yeah, I know. I'll see you tomorrow. Thanks, Porter."

She ended the call and handed Ronin his phone. He frowned at her. "How close are you to the bartender?"

"Why?"

"You know his phone number by memory."

"I have a good memory for numbers," she said absently as she opened the car door. "Thanks again, Ronin. Have a good night."

She staggered a little as she got out of the car. Christ, she was drunker than she thought. Her cat purred happily when Ronin appeared and slung his arm around her waist.

"What are you doing?" She swallowed down the purr rising in her throat.

"You're locked out of your house, remember?" He tried to guide her back into his car, and she shook her head.

"I've got a secret key. I'm good. You can go now."

"I don't think so, pussy cat. You need help into the house."

"I don't," she said. "I'm not nearly as drunk as you think I am."

"No? So that's not your hand on my ass then?" he asked.

She peered behind him to see that her hand was indeed on his ass, squeezing and rubbing, and the sound of her purring was deafening in the quiet air.

She snatched her hand away, and Ronin grinned at her before leading her up the front pathway of her house. Before Ronin had touched her, it had seemed very important to maintain some control. But now? The heat of his arm around her waist, his hard hand gripping her hip, and his scent was making her cat nearly crazy, and she really couldn't remember why it was a bad idea to fuck him.

"The key is under the flowerpot," she said.

He bent and lifted the clay pot. "This is not a safe hiding spot, Kat. It's the first place a thief would – Jesus!"

He jumped when Kat's hand slid between his thighs and cupped his cock. He straightened and knocked her hand away, and she hissed angrily before taking a step toward him and falling.

He caught her with scarily quick reflexes, and she licked her lips before slurring, "You're so damn fast. Sure you're not part cat?"

He shook his head and tried to protect his cock from her wandering hands. "Yes. God, Kitten, stop doing that."

"Stop doing what?" she asked innocently. Her nails had lengthened, and she traced the zipper of his pants.

"Manhandling little Ronin," he said as he opened the front door and ushered her inside.

"Little Ronin? Oh, believe me, handsome, there is nothing little about him."

"Thanks," he said. "Which way to the bedroom?"

"Why wait for the bedroom?" She pushed him up against the wall and rubbed her body against his. "I'm a cat, remember? I'm very," she paused and licked her lips again, "limber."

She licked his throat before scraping her fangs across the stubble. He groaned, and his hands tightened around her waist.

"I want to fuck my pretty little bird," she whispered before licking him again.

He cleared his throat roughly. "I can't, Kat."

"What happened to fucking me in the hallway? Back at the bar, you were more than willing."

"Temporary insanity," he muttered.

She reached between them and rubbed his erect cock. "*Little* Ronin seems more than up to it."

He pulled her hand away. "I can't," he repeated. "Not when you're drunk."

"I'm not that drunk," she purred. "I know exactly what I'm doing."

"You don't, and I won't take advantage of that," he said.

She scowled at him, and he kissed her forehead. "Tell me where your bedroom is."

"Let me fuck you, and I will," she said.

He sighed loudly, and she made a startled meow when he bent and heaved her over his shoulder. She lifted his shirt and licked the small of his back, and he muttered a curse as he climbed the stairs. She wiggled her hands inside his jeans and squeezed his naked ass, and he muttered another curse.

"You are killing me, Katarina."

"I'd rather be fucking you, little bird," she giggled before hiccupping.

She placed warm, wet kisses over as much of his naked back as she could reach as he opened the first door in the hallway and peered in.

"Not my bedroom," she said before nipping him with her fangs.

He hissed, his back arching a little, and slapped her sharply on the ass. "No biting, Kitten."

She bit him harder in response, and he grunted with pain and slapped her ass again. She squealed before licking at the bite mark.

"You might want to tie me down before we have sex," she said as he carried her to the next door. "Sometimes I like to bite and," she traced her claws across his naked ass, "scratch."

"Yes, I remember," he puffed as he opened the door. "But since we're not having sex tonight, there's no need for restraints. Is this your room or a guest room?"

"Guest room," she said.

"Kat," he said.

"Fine. It's my bedroom."

He carried her into the room and set her on her feet next to the bed. She immediately staggered back and fell on the bed, giggling softly.

Ronin tugged off her shoes and socks, and she sat up and traced her bare foot over his jean-covered erection. "Hello, pretty bird."

He rolled his eyes and gently pushed away her foot. "Crawl into bed, Kat."

"Help me take off my pants," she said.

"Oh, hell no," he said.

"I can't sleep in my jeans," she pouted. "Help me, Ronin."

He sighed and reached for the button on her jeans. "Lie back and lift your hips."

She did as he asked, and he pulled down her jeans. She wore a blue thong and grinned when his gaze dropped to her pussy.

"Fuck me," he muttered.

"I keep trying. You won't let me," she said.

She sat up and pulled her shirt over her head. He stared hungrily at her breasts in the matching blue bra, and his hands clenched into fists.

"Can you help me remove my bra, pretty bird?" she purred.

"Not a goddamn chance, Kitten," he said hoarsely.

She squeaked in surprise when he pulled her to her feet and yanked the covers back. She clung to him, wrapping her arms around his shoulders and rubbing her pussy against his cock. He groaned, and his hands dropped to her ass. He cupped it tightly and ground his cock against her before slanting his mouth over hers and kissing her. She sucked at his tongue, purring loudly and fumbling at the button on his jeans. He tore his mouth from hers and cursed again before knocking her to the bed, swinging her legs onto the mattress and pushing her onto her back. He covered her up quickly and backed away from the bed as she sat up.

"Go to sleep, Katarina," he gritted out.

She hissed at him. "You can't leave me like this, Ronin."

"I have to," he said. He left the bedroom, slamming the door behind him. She collapsed on her back and stared at the ceiling, her body throbbing and her cat yowling with anger.

***

GOD, HIS HEAD HURT. THE LAST TWO MONTHS, THE headache, which had started as a faint pain at the bottom of his skull, had grown until his entire head felt too big and fragile – like it was a balloon that the slightest pressure would pop. He groaned and rubbed the back of his head in a desperate attempt to relieve the pain. He could feel his quills poking through his hair, and panic threaded through him as he slid out of bed and staggered to the bathroom. He shut the door and turned on the light, shading his eyes against the bright glow as he peered into the mirror.

"What is happening?" he moaned.

His quills were still pushing through his skin, and with a fierce bout of concentration that made his head throb sickeningly, his quills retracted. He blinked and leaned closer to the mirror. He could see lines of bright red threading through the whites of his eyes, and as he watched, they thickened and spread until no white remained. Fresh panic exploded within him. His quills poked through his flesh with a soft popping noise, and he stumbled back, slamming into the bathroom door as his head throbbed and ached. His body swelled, the

65

bones cracking and his flesh splitting as his muscles increased to an impossible size.

"Bart? What's wrong? Are you sick?"

He staggered away from the door as she pounded on it again. "Bart?"

Yes, he was sick. And it was all her fault. She had done this to him. She had – had fed him something that was killing him, and she needed to pay for it.

He made an inhuman roar and ripped open the bathroom door. She cried out and fell onto her butt as he loomed over her. His quills were out, and she screamed and scrambled back when a dozen of them shot out from his sternum and stuck like small spears in the carpet just in front of her toes.

"Bart! Honey, what's wrong with you?" she cried as she scooted backward on her butt. He stalked toward her, his head – *oh his aching head* – lowered as he breathed harshly through his mouth.

"You. You did this to me." His voice was garbled, and he could feel his teeth elongating. Fangs appeared, scraping against his bottom lip, and he licked away his blood.

"No," the woman gasped. "No, honey, it's me! It's Marla! Please, honey, you're scaring me."

Her soft crying slipped past the madness in his head, and he slowed to a stop, staring hesitantly at her.

"Marla?" he said hoarsely.

"Yes, honey. It's Marla," she whispered. "You – you're sick, and you need to see a doctor."

"My head hurts so bad," he mumbled. "Help me, Marla. Please help me."

"I will, honey," she said. "Just sit down, okay? Just sit down, and I'll call the doctor and -"

His eyes widened, and he snarled at her, saliva dripping from his open mouth. "You'll call the doctor? The doctor?"

He raised his arm, the quills poking out through his pajama sleeve, and she shrieked when his fingernails turned to claws. He hesitated again, staring at the crying, frightened woman below him before staring at his hands.

"Wh-what's happening to me?" he moaned before clawing at his face. Blood, black and foul-smelling, spilled down his face, and Marla screamed again.

"Forgive me," he whispered before turning and lumbering from the bedroom.

He ran out of the house, his body still swelling, as his skin turned impossibly tight, and quills shot out from his body in all directions. Snarling and drooling, his head a heavy aching mass, he ran down the street and into the blessed darkness.

———

"C'MON, BABY, DON'T PLAY SHY."

He held her hands and gave her a wry look. "I'm not being shy. We're in a public park, Sandra."

"So, what?" She tried to wiggle her hand down his pants again, and he squeezed them firmly.

"So, we have a perfectly good apartment, not five blocks from here."

"Yeah, but isn't this exciting?' She giggled and squirmed on his lap. "Knowing that anyone could walk by and see us fucking on the park bench?"

He sighed and kissed her briefly. "It's cold, it's late, and being arrested for public indecency is not my idea of a good time."

"God, Brad," she sighed, "you're such a prude."

"Yeah, I know. C'mon, it's time to go."

She slid off his lap with a small pout. "Maybe I don't want to have sex with you when we get home."

"Your choice," he said with a shrug.

She gaped at him. "You're a real dick, Brad. You know that?"

"Don't start, Sandra."

"Don't start? Don't start what, Brad? Don't start pointing out all the ways you treat me like shit?"

"Are you kidding me?" He glared at her. "Just because I won't do what you want doesn't mean I treat you like shit."

"Whatever," she sniffed. "Let's just go."

He tried to take her hand, and she yanked it away from him. "Don't touch me."

"Fine," he snapped. "Let's go."

He stalked ahead of her, and she zipped up her jacket before following him. "You know, you think you're so perfect, Brad. Well, guess what? You're not. Do you know how many guys would kill to have sex with me in a park?"

He snorted. "Then why don't you go find one, Sandra."

"Maybe I will," she said peevishly as she stumbled in her high heels. "Maybe I'll -"

She screamed when it came out of the darkness. It roared and swiped at her with its claws, and bright agony flared across her thigh as blood poured out of the ragged cut. She fell onto her ass and stared wide-eyed at the monster standing over her.

"Sandra!" Brad ran toward them, and she screamed again as the creature spun to face him.

"Get away from her! What the fuck are you -"

Brad bellowed in pain, and she had a horrifying glimpse of the needle-like quills that suddenly covered his face before the monster fell on him. Brad's screams of agony pierced the night air, and she shrieked with him as the creature tore into his stomach. Loops of intestines slithered out to land in the grass, and the beast roared in triumph before ripping out

Brad's throat. Crying and moaning, she slid backward as the creature stood and turned to stare at her.

"No," she whispered as it grinned at her. Saliva and blood dripped from its horrifyingly large fangs, and Sandra immediately shifted to her squirrel. The creature screamed in outrage when she disappeared. Her clothes held the shape of her human form for a second or two before collapsing gently to the ground.

She squirmed out of the jacket as the creature lumbered forward. It lunged for her, and she darted between its legs and, limping badly, ran for the trees. It chased after her, and she squealed thinly when its hand closed around her tail and lifted her into the air. She reared up and, squealing and chittering, sunk her teeth deep into the scaly skin of its hand. It screamed and dropped her to the ground, and she bounced to her feet before leaping for the large tree in front of her. She climbed quickly as the creature, snarling and howling with rage, clawed at the tree, shredding the bark and tearing deep marks into the wood.

She climbed nimbly despite her wounded leg and disappeared among the leaves as the creature dropped to its knees and snuffled the ground. Already it was losing interest as her scent faded, and it turned to Brad's body lying behind it. It shuffled closer and dragged Brad past the running trail that wound through the park and into a dense clump of bushes.

Sandra clung to the tree, her bushy tail wrapped tightly around her body, the pain in her thigh making her feel sick as her squirrel chittered to her in high-pitched terror.

Sirens wailed in the night, and she watched as headlights swept along the road beside the park. The creature flinched and snarled softly before loping clumsily to the far end of the park. It vanished into the trees as a police car, its siren wailing and lights flashing, pulled onto the street.

# CHAPTER 6

"Surprise!"

Kat stared at the tiny brunette holding two cups of coffee and standing in her doorway before stumbling forward and wrapping her arms around her. She squeezed tightly as the woman giggled. "Hello, Kit-Kat. Have you missed me?"

"Have I missed you?" Kat mumbled. "Oh, Bria, you have no idea."

She hugged her again, and the tiger shifter squeaked in pain. "Kat, too tight!"

"Sorry," Kat eased her grip and smiled at her best friend. "When did you get back?"

"Yesterday," Bria said.

"I thought you were extending your trip," Kat said.

"Well, I did technically extend it by about a month, and I would have stayed longer, but then Raden decided to come back here with me. My parents were a little relieved. They thought I was going to live in the jungle forever."

"Raden?" Kat asked.

"Jungle hottie with the man bun, remember?' Bria said. "Raden – my new man."

Kat blinked before shaking her head. "Right, right. Sorry – the guy you keep posting pictures of on Facebook."

"Yes, the guy on Facebook." Bria laughed. "Listen, I know I've been gone for a while, and we haven't talked that much, but you've been getting my messages about Raden, right? We've been friends for years – there's no way you've found a new bestie to replace me."

Kat didn't reply, and Bria arched her eyebrow at her. "Have you?"

"What? No, of course not. Come into the house," Kat said.

Bria collapsed on the couch with a sigh and tucked her legs under her as Kat sipped at her coffee. "I needed this. Thank you, honey."

"You're welcome. Did I wake you up?"

"Um," Kat hesitated. "She had technically been awake, but she was still in bed, nursing the mother of all hangovers and replaying over and over exactly what she had said and done to Ronin last night.

"Kat?" Bria cocked her head at her. "Tell me what's wrong, honey."

Kat sighed and took another sip of the steaming coffee. "I fucked a bird shifter, Bria."

Bria's mouth dropped open, and she leaned forward. "The hell you did."

"I did," Kat groaned before covering her face with one hand. "And God help me, it was the best sex of my life."

Bria squeezed her knee. "Start from the beginning, Kit-Kat. Tell me everything."

"OKAY, SO MAYBE YOU DIDN'T HAVE THE BEST SEX OF YOUR life with a bird," Bria said half an hour later. "It was during your heat cycle, and we always think sex during our heat cycle is the best sex of our life. You know that, Kat."

Kat rubbed her aching forehead. "Yeah, maybe."

"And you were drunk last night. People do stupid things when they're drunk. Just explain that to this Ronin when you see him at work on Monday."

"Oh God, I don't even want to think about seeing him at work tomorrow," Kat groaned. "Fuck, I am making such a mess of this."

Bria sipped at her coffee. "Is it such a big deal that you want to sleep with a bird? It's not like the guy's a weakling. He took down Judd."

"Yes, I'm sure that will make my mother very happy," Kat said.

Bria flinched. "I forgot about your mom. She'll freak out if she knows you're dating a bird. Remember that time in high school when we were hanging out with that – oh, what was she again?"

"Peacock," Kat said.

"Right, Patty the peacock," Bria said. "Your mother flipped when she came home and found Patty sitting at the kitchen table with us. Poor Patty. I think she nearly had a heart attack when your mother started hissing and spitting at her. Remember how she shifted and then started dropping feathers everywhere?"

"Yes," Kat said. "We were finding feathers for weeks afterwards, and every time we did, Mom made me scrub the entire kitchen from top to bottom to get rid of the life-threatening bird diseases."

Bria laughed before patting her arm. "It sounds like Ronin's pretty charming. Maybe he'll win your mother over."

"He's never going to meet my mother. We're not dating, Bria," Kat said with a frown.

"Just sleeping together."

"No, not that either. I made a mistake.

Bria leaned forward and studied her carefully. "Listen, all kidding aside, Kat, why does it bother you so much that he's a bird? I know there are cat shifters who do hate birds, but I also know that you're not one of them. You're the most accepting person I know. "

"It's not because he's a bird," Kat admitted. "He's my employee, and it's inappropriate for me to be sleeping with him."

"Isn't Mal dating your receptionist?"

"Yes, but it's different."

"Why?"

"Because," Kat hesitated, "because I've worked hard to gain Mal and Bishop's respect, and for the first time in my life, I feel like an equal in my career. It's what I've always wanted, Bria, and I'm not going to throw it all away for some roll in the hay."

"I know I've only met Mal and Bishop a couple of times, but they don't seem like the type of shifters who will judge you on who you sleep with," Bria said.

"Maybe not on the surface but deep down…." Kat gave Bria a rueful smile. "It's a bad idea, Bria."

Bria nodded sympathetically. "I'm sorry, Kit-Kat."

"It's fine, Bria. It's for the best. Can you give me a ride to Mal's brother's place? He has my purse and my cell phone."

"Of course," Bria said. "And I'll take you for breakfast afterward."

"Ugh." Kat shook her head. "I'm too hungover to eat."

"Nonsense," Bria said. "It'll help your stomach. Run and get dressed, Kit-Kat. I'm starving."

"Thank you for seeing me, Officer Umbert."

The officer nodded before taking a sip of his coffee. "You're welcome, Mr. Haddon."

"Please, call me Clay."

"Sorry it took so long to meet, but the wife and I were on our annual trip to Mexico. Go every year for six weeks."

Clay leaned back in his chair and sipped at his coffee before glancing at the front window of the coffee shop. "That's no problem. So, you said the coyote shifter looked odd."

The officer nodded. "Yeah, bigger."

"Have you seen a lot of shifters in their animal form?" Clay asked.

"Probably more than most humans. Part of the job, you know? And there are more shifters on the force than you'd think. Where did you say you worked again?"

"Stowe Laboratories," Clay said.

"Right," the officer said before giving him an appraising look. "And Stowe Laboratories does what exactly?"

"We study shifters and their healing abilities," Clay said.

"And why is your company interested in what happened at this coffee shop two months ago?"

"You shot the shifter in the chest, is that correct?" Clay asked.

Officer Umbert nodded. "Yes. He went down, and I thought it was over. But then he popped back up like some crazed jack-in-the-box, so I shot him three times in the head."

"So, you shot him in the chest, which maybe wouldn't be enough to kill him, but it would put him down and require a trip to the hospital, don't you agree?"

The officer shrugged. "Shifters are pretty strong."

"True, but have you ever heard of a shifter shrugging off a direct shot to the chest?"

He hesitated and then shook his head. "Nah."

"Exactly. Yet, this shifter did. That's why we're interested, Officer Umbert. Our lab wants to know what it was about this shifter that gave him such enhanced healing abilities," Clay lied. "It would give us new data for our research."

The officer sipped again at his coffee, and Clay scrolled through his phone for a moment. "Was anyone bitten or scratched during the attack?"

"Not that I know of, but I just showed up at the end. It was just luck that I was even there." The cop frowned in thought. "Although an ambulance did show up, and I seem to remember them loading someone into it."

"Do you know who?"

"No, but even if I did, I wouldn't tell you. We don't share details of cases with civilians," Officer Umbert said.

Clay bit back his grunt of frustration before staring at his phone again. "There was a jaguar shifter and a bear shifter at the scene. Is that correct?"

The cop nodded. "Yeah. They were trying to hold off the coyote shifter. I guess they were in the coffee shop when it went down the way it did."

"Were they bitten?"

"Not that I'm aware of," Officer Umbert said.

"Do you know their names? I'd like to speak with them."

"I don't, but again, even if I did...."

Clay smiled stiffly at him. "Right, no details."

---

KAT SMILED AT THE BARISTA AND TOOK HER CUP OF COFFEE with a nod of thanks. She glanced at her watch. She had

76

nearly half an hour before the office opened, and she tried to decide if she wanted to sit in the coffee shop or go to the office. It would be quiet, and she could get some work done before the others showed up.

Her stomach churned nervously. She had barely slept last night, and she was dreading talking to Ronin this morning. It had to be done, though. Not just because she needed to apologize for Saturday night, but she also needed to talk to him about his new assignment.

She took her coffee and headed for the door as a familiar face caught her attention. She slowed to a stop and studied the grey-haired man. She was confident it was the cop who had saved her life, and she hesitated only briefly before heading toward him.

She stopped next to the table, and he, as well as the dark-haired man with him, stood as she smiled uncertainly at him. "Hi, I'm not sure if you remember me, but -"

"Jaguar shifter," the cop said.

"That's right. We met a couple of months ago at this coffee shop when that coyote shifter went crazy. We spoke briefly before I gave my statement to the police, but I realized later that I never found out your name or thanked you for saving my life."

"Travis Umbert, ma'am. It's a pleasure to meet you."

"I'm Katarina Frost. Thank you for saving my life," she said before shaking his hand.

"Not sure if that's entirely accurate – you and your bear friend seemed to be holding your own – but you're welcome," the cop said.

Kat glanced at the dark-haired man. He was tall with broad shoulders and short dark hair, and he was wearing an expensive-looking grey suit with a dark blue tie. The blue in this tie matched his eye colour perfectly.

"This is Clay Haddon," the cop said.

"Nice to meet you, Mr. Haddon," Kat said before holding out her hand.

He shook it briefly before smiling at her. "Nice to meet you as well. I was just speaking with Officer Umbert about the incident with the coyote shifter."

"Mr. Haddon works for a laboratory that studies shifters and their healing abilities," Officer Umbert said.

"I was wondering if you had some free time to go over the events of that day with me. It would be beneficial to my company and our research," Clay said.

"Why would a coyote shifter who has gone mad be helpful to your company?" Kat asked.

"We believe he had some type of healing ability that hasn't been seen before," Clay said. "I can explain in more detail during our meeting. Would now work?"

"Unfortunately, no. I have a hectic day. But I could meet with you tomorrow." She handed him a business card. "Just call the number on the front and have our receptionist set up an appointment, okay?"

"Absolutely. Thank you, Ms. Frost."

She nodded to him before turning and holding her hand out to the cop. "Thank you again, Officer Umbert."

He shook her hand again, and she squeezed it lightly before leaving. She walked briskly down the sidewalk toward the office, her mind already worrying over what she would say to Ronin. She sighed and shoved the building door open before heading to the elevator. She would just keep it simple and straightforward. She would apologize, thank him for giving her a ride home, and then keep it strictly professional from now on.

CLAY CLIMBED INTO HIS CAR AND WATCHED AS KAT ENTERED a large grey building not far from the coffee shop. He studied the business card in his hand. The jaguar shifter was a beautiful woman, and he wondered briefly if he could coax her into his bed. He'd never slept with a shifter before, but her lithe body and light green eyes were highly tempting. He snorted to himself as his cell phone buzzed. Mixing business with pleasure was a bad idea.

"This is Clay."

He listened intently before muttering a curse. "Are you sure? Yeah, okay. No, I'm not far from there, so I'll head over and see what I can find out. Tell Wyatt I'll call him later."

He threw his cell phone on the seat and rubbed a hand through his dark hair before starting the car. Fuck, he hoped like hell the animal attack at Galloway Park had nothing to do with the fucking mess they were in, but he had a sinking feeling in his gut that it did.

---

"MORNING, BREN."

"Morning, Jake. What have we got?"

Bren Matthews followed the beat cop down the walking path of the park. Bright yellow police tape cordoned off an area. They moved past the crowd of civilians looking on with avid interest and ducked under it. He could see crime scene investigators, covered from head to toe in white coveralls, milling about, and Jake glanced at the coffee Bren held in his hand.

"How much of that have you had to drink?"

"That bad?" Bren asked.

Jake nodded. "That bad."

The smell hit him first, a combination of rotting meat and

dank earth, and he made a low grunt of disgust as his stomach turned over. He studied the body lying just behind the bushes.

"Jesus," he said. "What the hell happened?"

"So, this," Jake flipped open a small black notepad, "is Brad Swarmson. He's twenty-seven years old, works for First Credit Bank over on 110 Avenue, and he's a squirrel shifter."

Bren, holding his hand over his nose, leaned closer. "Are those quills?"

Jake nodded. "Sure are. Apparently, he crossed paths with a porcupine shifter. It's what tore his throat open and ripped out his insides."

Bren frowned. "Since when do porcupine shifters go on murderous rampages?" He took another look at the missing chunks of flesh on the squirrel shifter's face and torso. "Or eat other shifters?"

Jake shrugged. "Hell, I don't know a damn thing about shifters."

"What's the time of death?"

"Well, according to the girlfriend," Jake flipped over a page, "a Miss Sandra Mickelson, also twenty-seven and also a bank employee, about eleven-thirty Saturday night."

"Saturday night? It's Monday morning," Bren said. "Why the hell did she wait until this morning to report it?"

"She barely escaped with her life after being attacked as well. According to her, she spent most of Sunday hiding in that tree just over there." Jake pointed past the crowd of gawkers at a large oak tree at the edge of the park. "Several residents in the area called 9-1-1 after they heard screaming, and a patrol car did a drive-by of the area but didn't see anything."

"Why didn't the woman flag down the police?" Bren asked.

Jake shrugged again. "Like I said, she was terrified and

stayed in the tree until early this morning. Although, just between you and me, I get a serious 'I don't trust the police' vibe from the woman. You know how some of the shifters are."

"Yeah, but can you blame them?" Bren said.

"Nah, I guess I can't, but hell, we got enough shifters on the force – you'd think that would create some goodwill."

"Where is she now?"

"She's at their apartment. It's only about five blocks south of the park. I told her a detective would be over to speak with her."

Bren nodded before turning and scanning the crowd behind them.

"Think the killer might be watching?" Jake murmured.

"Maybe," Bren said. "It's happened before."

He stared at each face. Most people wore athletic wear – joggers taking advantage of the park's trails – but there were a few elderly people and more than one mother pushing a stroller. He frowned. A man was standing in the middle of the crowd. He was tall with dark hair and dressed in a dark grey suit. He stood out from the others like a beacon, and Bren started toward him when Jake called his name.

"What?" He turned to glance at Jake.

"I asked if you're going to go talk to Ms. Mickelson now or wait for the ME report."

"I'll talk to her now," he said before turning back to the crowd. He blinked in surprise. The man was gone, and he scanned the park and the street before coming up empty. Even running, there was no way in hell the guy could have disappeared that quickly.

"You see something?" Jake asked.

"Maybe, I don't know. Listen, I want to talk to the girl-friend. Can you give me her address?"

As Jake recited the woman's address, he typed it into his phone and filed away the man's face in his mental bank. It was probably nothing, but something about the guy had his instincts on high alert.

---

CLAY DUCKED DOWN IN THE DRIVER'S SEAT AS THE DETECTIVE walked past his car and climbed into a dark blue sedan parked further up the street. He started the car and followed the detective. It had been nearly impossible to catch all of the cop and detective's conversation, the babbling of the crowd had been annoyingly loud, but he had heard enough to know they were speaking to the girlfriend of the victim.

He grunted in surprise when the detective pulled over only a few blocks away. He quickly slipped his car into a spot behind a white SUV. The detective had noticed him in the crowd. He would have to be extremely careful not to attract his attention again. He took a casual look around. The street was empty – he guessed most of the neighbours were either at work or gawking at the dead shifter in the park – and he closed his eyes and concentrated before vanishing.

He materialized precisely where he wanted to - at the side of the building the detective was walking toward – and he pressed his back against the rough brick and took a quick peek around the corner. The detective had climbed the steps, and he studied the list of names next to the front door before pressing a buzzer.

After a few seconds, a woman's voice, tinny and slightly muffled, came through the speaker. "Hello?"

"Ms. Mickleson? My name is Detective Bren Matthews. I'm here to speak with you about your boyfriend. May I come in?"

There was a moment of hesitation, and then the door buzzed. Clay ducked back behind the building just as the detective's gaze turned toward him. He waited patiently before taking another quick look. The detective was gone, and he walked quickly up the steps and read the names on the list. There was an S. Mickelson listed next to a B. Swarmson in apartment 203. Satisfied, he jogged to his car and drove away.

———

"You're here early."

Kat looked up from her computer as Bishop entered her office and dropped into the chair across from her desk.

"So are you," she said.

He shrugged, and she studied him carefully. "What's up with you?"

"What do you mean?"

"It's not even eight yet, and you're not only at the office, but you're wide awake and happy. You're even less than a morning person than I am, Bishop."

He grinned at her. "Maybe I'm turning over a new leaf."

"Yeah, maybe," she said. "How's Ava feeling?"

"Oh, uh, she's a little better," he said before looking away.

"Just a touch of the flu then?"

"Uh, yeah, I think so." Bishop cracked his knuckles before changing the subject. "Mal talked to you about Ronin's new assignment?"

"Yes. We're pulling Ronin off the warehouse detail and moving him to the mall while Boris is on holiday."

Bishop shook his head. "That was the original plan, but Mal's thinking something different now."

"What?" she asked.

"You remember Mavina Sorenson?"

Kat groaned inwardly. Mavina Sorenson was a two-hundred-and-fifteen-year-old vampire who would forever look and act like a twenty-year-old. At the beginning of the year, her father had hired the firm to keep track of her after she began sneaking out of the house and fell in with a bad crowd of vamps. Like most vampires, she radiated charm and sexuality, and they'd been forced to fire one of their employees, a bear shifter named Peter when he'd started sleeping with the sexy vampire. Garth had replaced the bear shifter and, according to him, he spent most of the security detail fending off the vampire's wandering hands. He had been more than relieved when Mavina had started to bend to her father's wishes, and the security contract had ended.

"I remember her," she said as Bishop stared expectantly at her. "Did she join up with that gang of vampires again?"

He shook his head. "Nah. She took up with some other vampire for a few months. Some old-school dude, super powerful and rich, and he didn't take it very well when she broke it off. He's been following her, making some threatening remarks, and her parents are worried he's going to kidnap her or something. Anyway, Mal thought it would be a good idea to assign Ronin to her security detail."

"We should use Garth," Kat said. "He's dealt with her before and -"

"Garth flat-out refused," Bishop said with a small grin. "He said he doesn't have the willpower to resist her again."

Kat sighed. "Seriously? Garth needs to learn to keep it in his pants, or maybe he should find employment with someone else."

Bishop frowned at her. "Garth's a good employee, Kat, and I appreciate his honesty. Besides, vampires are damn hard to resist when they set out to seduce someone, and you know that."

"Yeah, I know," she said. "What about Fenton? He's got a thing for Ginger, so it'll be easier for him to resist Mavina's charms."

"Mal thinks Ronin would be best, and I agree with him. The guy's an ex-cop, good with guns, and knows kung-fu. If this vampire is as dangerous as Mavina's parents think he is, we want someone like Ronin watching over her."

"He hasn't been with us long enough to put him into this type of security detail," Kat said. "We should keep him at the warehouse until we know we can trust him."

"Mal and I do trust him, Kat. He saved Ava's life, remember?"

"I remember," she said.

"Are you more concerned that he won't be able to protect Mavina or that he won't be able to resist sleeping with her?"

She glared at him. "What do I care who Ronin sleeps with? Since you and Mal seem to love him so much, I would think you wouldn't want to assign him to Mavina. If he does sleep with her, we'll have to fire him, remember?"

"Ronin's going to get bored if we keep him on the warehouse detail much longer," Bishop said. "We need to keep someone like him around. He's an asset, and we're damn lucky to have him. We can't stick him on night security at a warehouse where nothing happens."

She didn't reply, and Bishop leaned forward. "Kat, I know you like him."

Her face flushed, and she stared out the window. "Jesus, Bishop, we're not in high school."

He laughed a little. "Yeah, I know."

"And I don't like him. He's arrogant and sarcastic and – and stupid."

Bishop roared laughter, and she hissed at him before crossing her arms over her chest. "I don't like him, Bishop."

"That night that the dragon attacked Ava and Ronin, I saw the look on your face when you thought he was dead," Bishop said.

"Yeah, because it's a hell of a lot of paperwork when an employee dies on the job," she said.

"Right, of course," Bishop said. "And the way you hugged him and ran your hands over his naked ass was because you were thankful you wouldn't have to do paperwork."

"I did not run my hands over his naked ass!" Her fangs popped out, and she growled at Bishop as her fingernails lengthened into sharp claws.

"Okay, okay," Bishop held his hands up, "I'm sorry. Listen, Ronin is our best guy for the Mavina security detail. You know that. And unless you can come up with a better reason for not wanting him on this assignment, Mal's not going to budge."

She scowled at her computer as Bishop heaved his large body out of the chair. "You'll talk to Ronin about his new assignment? Or do you want me to do it?"

"I'll talk to him," she said.

"Perfect. Tell Ronin I'll take him to meet Mavina and her family tonight."

Her scowl deepened, and Bishop grinned at her. "Want to tag along?"

She opened her mouth to say absolutely not and instead said, "Yes."

"Sounds good. We'll meet here at the office at ten tonight."

Bishop left her office, and Kat sank back in her chair. She stared at the ceiling and rubbed her forehead. She didn't care if Ronin slept with Mavina. She didn't. Hell, if he did, they'd have to fire him, and his sarcastic attitude and stupid dimple and tattoos would no longer torment her. In fact, she should be thrilled that he would be guarding Mavina. Vampires were extremely hard to resist, and sooner or later, Ronin would succumb to Mavina's charms. This was probably a good thing. So why did she have such a sinking feeling in the pit of her stomach?

# CHAPTER 7

"Good morning, Kat." Ronin stuck his head into her office and smiled cheerfully at her. "Willow said you wanted to talk to me."

"Yes, come in. Close the door."

He sat down in the chair with a lazy grace, and she folded her hands together neatly on the desk. "I had two things I needed to speak to you about. First," she forced herself to meet his gaze, "I wanted to apologize for my behaviour on Saturday night. I was extremely drunk, and the things I said and did were very inappropriate."

She waited for his sarcastic quip, but he only nodded and said, "Apology accepted."

Relief coursing through her, she moved briskly to the next point. "Second – we're pulling you from the warehouse security and giving you a new assignment. We have a vampire who needs some protecting."

"Against what?" he asked. "It seems a bit unusual for a vampire to need protection."

She nodded. "It is, but an older and more powerful vampire is harassing this vampire. It's probably nothing - her parents are a bit on the nervous side when it comes to their daughter - but Mal, Bishop, and I thought it would be best to have someone with your skill set work this assignment. In case this other vampire is actually a problem."

"Sure," he said.

"If you'd rather not take this assignment, tell me now so we can find someone else. This has the potential to be much more dangerous than our usual security jobs, and we'll understand if you'd rather stick to the warehouse," she said.

"Nah, I'll be fine," he said.

She frowned at him. "You understand how dangerous vampires can be, right?"

"I do."

"Do you?" She arched her eyebrow at him, and his dimple deepened as he grinned broadly at her.

"Are you worried about your pretty little bird, Kitten?"

"No," she snapped. "Obviously, it'll be a night shift, probably ten until dawn, but we can confirm that with the Sorenson family tonight. Can you meet Bishop and me here at the office at around ten? We'll drive to the Sorenson's house, and you can meet Mavina."

"Sure, but I'm supposed to be working the warehouse this afternoon."

"We're assigning Garth to the warehouse. He'll take your shift."

"Okay," Ronin said. "But be prepared for an angry call from Marika Belfry."

"What? Why?"

"That lizard loves me," Ronin said. "She's not going to be happy when she finds out I'm on a different assignment."

"Mrs. Belfry loves you?"

"Yes, is that so hard to believe?"

"Uh, yes," Kat said. "Mrs. Belfry doesn't love anyone but her sons."

"What can I say? I can be very charming."

She rolled her eyes and pushed back her chair. "Okay, well, unless you have any more questions, we'll see you at the office at ten tonight."

"Actually," Ronin stood and moved behind her desk, "I did have one more question."

She took a nervous step back before forcing herself to stand still. "What is it?"

He reached out and took her wrist, rubbing his thumb over her pulse, and a smug smile crossed his face when her pulse quickened. "Have you decided on who you'll be hiring for your heat?"

She glanced nervously at the closed door and tried to pull her wrist free. Ronin's grip tightened for a moment before releasing her, and she tucked her hands behind her back. "Keep your voice down. I don't discuss my personal life at the office, so unless you have a work-related question, I'm swamped."

"Here." He pulled a folded piece of paper from his back pocket and handed it to her.

"What is this?"

"Medical records," he said. "In case you decide to choose me, I thought you'd like to see I'm as clean as that tiger shifter."

"I don't need this," she said. "I'm – I'm not choosing you."

He gave her a careless little grin before heading for the door. "See you at ten, Katarina."

Kat sat down in her chair and stared at the paper in her hand before unfolding it and scanning it. She stuffed it into her purse, then pulled out the tiger shifter's business card and stared fixedly at it for a moment. Next week, her heat cycle was happening, and she needed to call Jace. He was the best candidate, and the longer she waited, the higher the chance that he would no longer be available to help her. She tapped the card against the desk before, using her office phone, calling the number. The phone rang twice and, her nerves fraying, she was about to hang up when Jace answered.

"Jace speaking."

"Uh, hi, Jace. It's Kat Frost calling," she said.

"Hi, Kat. How are you?"

The friendliness in his voice calmed her nerves, and she said, "I'm good. How are you?"

"Doing very well, thank you."

"So, I'm calling about our, uh, meeting the other night. I've thought a lot about it, and I – I'm sorry, but I won't... that is, I'm not going to be requiring your, uh, services."

"That's a shame," he said.

"It's not you," she said hastily. "I've just decided it's not for me. I – it would have been you if I had decided to, um, go this route."

His low chuckle brought heat to her cheeks. "That's good to know. Thanks for calling, Kat."

"Bye, Jace."

She ended the call and stared blankly at the phone. What the hell just happened? She had called intending to ask Jace to help her during her heat, so why the hell did she just tell him thanks but no thanks?

*Because you want the bird. Ask him to help you, Kat. He's more than willing.*

She groaned and dropped her head into her hands. She couldn't do that, but she also couldn't sleep with Jace – not when she would just be imagining he was Ronin for her entire heat. She'd just have to hope that her damn vibrator was enough.

---

"SAUL GAINED ACCESS TO THE SQUIRREL'S BODY AT THE morgue, Wyatt. The wounds are consistent with the other bodies," Clay said.

"I know. I've read the report," Wyatt said. He paced back and forth in his office, then glanced again at the monitor on his desk. "Did you speak to the squirrel shifter who survived?"

"Not yet, but I have her address. I think it's more important that we find the porcupine shifter before he infects others, don't you?"

Wyatt grimaced. "What if the squirrel shifter was bitten? You need to speak with her, Clay."

"I will," Clay said before shifting in his chair. "I'll give it a few days. A detective spoke to her this morning, and I don't want to chance running into him if he decides to ask a few more questions."

"If she's been bitten or scratched, we're running out of time," Wyatt said before running his hand through his hair. From the monitor came a low roar, and he winced before dropping into his seat and tracing his finger across the screen.

"Shh, ma chérie," he whispered. "Shh."

"It took two months for the porcupine shifter to change. We've got time."

"Each shifter is different," Wyatt snapped at him. "You know that, Clay. Squirrel shifters have high metabolisms, which means she'll change faster. We can't risk her infecting someone else."

"We've already got a shifter killing people, possibly

infecting them. That's our number one priority right now," Clay said patiently. "I have two of my men watching the squirrel. If she shows any signs of changing, they'll bring her in."

"Have you spoken with the wife of the porcupine shifter?" Wyatt asked.

"How did you find out his name?" Clay asked.

"Saul hacked into the police station's computer system. It didn't take long for him to find the information on the attack that day."

Clay shook his head. "Fuck, that was quick. Where the hell did you find Saul? The kid can't be more than eighteen."

"It's not important. Did you speak to the wife?" Wyatt asked impatiently.

Clay nodded. "After Saul texted me his name and address, I went to his home. I spoke with," he checked his phone, "Marla, and she assures me that Bart neither bit nor scratched her."

"We should bring her in anyway, test her for the virus," Wyatt mumbled as he stared at the computer monitor.

Clay shook his head. "Not a good idea. She's filed a missing person report, and the cops have already been to see her. They've already connected him with the dead squirrel shifter. She bought my story that I was a detective without asking for a badge, but that was just luck. She was too distraught to think straight. We can't just bring her to the facility without her asking too many questions that we can't answer."

"Jesus, what a fucking mess," Wyatt said.

"I'm meeting with the cat shifter tomorrow morning," Clay said. "I'll find out if she or the bear shifter were bitten. We'll drug them and bring them to the facility if they are. In the meantime, we've got men combing the park and surrounding areas for the porcupine. If he's out there, we'll find him."

"And what about the bird?" Wyatt asked.

"No luck yet," Clay said.

Wyatt glared at him. "Maybe you should be leaving this other business to your men and Saul and do what I asked you."

Clay's temper flared. "If I'm not doing a good enough job for you, Wyatt, I'm more than happy to walk away and let you find someone else to do your dirty work."

"You don't think Ronin can help. I know that," Wyatt said, "but it's not your decision to make. I need you to find him if we're to have any chance of curing her."

"It's too late to cure your wife," Clay said bluntly.

His face bright red, Wyatt stood up before ripping the phone from his desk and throwing it at Clay. He vanished, and the phone landed on the empty chair with a muffled thump. Wyatt jerked back when Clay appeared in front of him and grabbed him by the collar of his jacket.

"Don't ever do that again, Wyatt. Do you hear me?"

"I hear you," Wyatt snapped. "Let go of me."

Clay dropped his hands and took a step back. "I'm your friend, Wyatt. You need to remember that. Now, go home. Have a shower and something to eat and get some goddamn sleep."

"I'm fine," Wyatt said sulkily.

"You're not. You're falling apart, and we need you. If you believe that you can still save your wife, you need to get some fucking sleep, so you're thinking straight."

Wyatt glanced at the computer monitor before giving Clay a haunted look. "I will cure her, Clay. I will."

Clay squeezed his arm gently. "Go home and get some rest, Wyatt."

"So, how do you like living with Fenton?" Willow asked as she sat down at the kitchen table.

Ginger flushed. "I'm not living with him, Willow. He just gave me a place to stay while I cleaned up my mess of an apartment. In fact, I'm staying at my place tonight. Thanks for helping me, by the way. I know you're still trying to settle in here at Mal's, and it was great of you to spend your entire evening helping me."

"It's not a problem, honey. Besides, you and Fenton had most of it finished by the time I came by."

"It was mostly Fenton," Ginger said. "I'm still fairly useless. Do you know he even had Garth pick up a new box spring and mattress for me? He brought it by this afternoon with his truck."

"I knew Garth had asked Bishop if he could take a couple of hours off this afternoon but didn't know why," Willow said. "That was sweet of Fenton to do that. How are your ribs, by the way? You didn't seem to be wincing as much when we were throwing your ripped-up clothing in the garbage bags."

"Getting better, I think. Of course, that could just be the morphine pills Dr. Jibbens prescribed for me," Ginger said as the cat, its black fur gleaming in the light from the kitchen, rubbed up against her leg. She reached down and patted it lightly. "Which one is this again?"

"Dolly Parton, I think," Willow said. She bent and reached to pat the cat. It hissed loudly at her, arching its back, before streaking out of the kitchen. "Yep, Dolly Parton. Johnny Cash is starting to let me touch him, at least, but Dolly still hates my guts. Ungrateful brat."

Ginger glanced at her watch as Willow stood and dropped

tea bags into the two mugs sitting on the counter. "Do you need me to give you a ride back to Fenton's?"

"No. Fenton said he would drop by and pick me up after he finished running his errand."

"What's he doing?" Willow asked.

"I don't know," Ginger admitted. "He wouldn't say."

"That's weird."

"Yeah, it is a little. I mean, not that Fenton's the most talkative guy, but he usually tells me what he's doing."

Willow grinned at her. "You two having sex yet, or what?"

Ginger blushed. "Of course not."

"Because you're injured, right?" Willow said. "It's obvious you two have a thing for each other."

Ginger's blush deepened, and she traced the top of the kitchen table with the tip of her finger. "It might be because I'm injured."

Willow squeezed her hand delightedly. "I'm so glad you and Fenton are dating, honey. He's a good guy."

"We're not dating," Ginger said. "I – I don't know what we're doing. I mean, I like him, obviously, and he's attracted to me, but we barely know each other."

"That's what dating is," Willow said. "Getting to know each other."

"I guess," Ginger said. "I just wish I could read him better, you know? I don't know if he let me stay with him because he's attracted to me or because he feels sorry for me. I have terrible taste in men, and I know Fenton is different but what if I'm reading the signals wrong? What if he just wants a roll in the hay?"

"He doesn't," Willow said as she lifted the whistling kettle from the stove and poured the boiling water into the mugs. "I'm sure of it."

Ginger took the mug of tea from her. "I hope you're right. Where's Mal tonight, anyway?"

"Becky has a baseball game. Mara and Roland are out of town this week at some work conference for Roland's law firm, so Mal picked up Becky and drove her to the game."

"I'm sorry. I didn't mean to make you miss it," Ginger said.

"You didn't," Willow said. "I wanted to help you, and besides, Amos was going as well, and I figured it would be good for Mal and Amos to have some alone time together."

"I thought it was going better with Mal's grandfather?" Ginger said before sipping at her tea.

"It is. I think. He calls me by my name now instead of human, most of the time," Willow said. "I think I'm starting to win him over, but that probably has more to do with Ava's influence than mine."

Ginger gave her a curious look, and Willow grinned at her. "Mal's grandfather might hate humans, but apparently, that hatred doesn't extend toward Ava. He's very fond of her, and since Mara and Roland are practically Bishop's adoptive parents, Ava and Bishop visit them often. I guess the other night, Ava hugged him, and he didn't even freak out. I get anywhere near him, and he tenses up and gets this weird look on his face."

"Sorry, Will," Ginger said.

"It's fine," Willow said. "Eventually, I'll win him over. He doesn't stand a chance against my charm. He just doesn't know it yet."

Ginger laughed, "Isn't that the truth."

"What did the police say about talking to Robbie?" Willow suddenly asked. "I keep forgetting to ask."

A look of anxiety passed over Ginger's face. "They

dusted for fingerprints but didn't find anything, and Robbie denied it was him."

"Of course, he did," Willow said with an irritated grimace.

"I don't know. Maybe it wasn't him," Ginger said. "There were no fingerprints and -"

"So, Robbie was smart enough to wear gloves," Willow said. "He's an idiot, but even idiots have moments of brilliance from time to time."

"He said he was at a friend's house all night, and his friend confirmed it," Ginger said.

"Easy enough to get a friend to lie for you. You know it was him, don't you?" Willow said.

"Yeah," Ginger said quietly. She studied her tea as Willow squeezed her hand.

"Are you afraid to go back to your apartment, honey? The door has been repaired, but you're still staying with Fenton."

Ginger nodded. "I am. It's ridiculous, but I can't shake the feeling that Robbie will do something else. I had no idea he could be so vindictive. Just more proof that I'm terrible at relationships. Still, I can't keep staying with Fenton forever. His place is small, and I really shouldn't have sex for at least another few days. He's going to get tired of me sooner or later and -"

"Fenton isn't that type of guy," Willow said with a frown. "He's not going to force you to go back to your apartment just because you can't have sex with him."

"Do you know that for sure, Will?" Ginger asked. "I never thought Robbie would break into my apartment and destroy everything I owned and look how that turned out."

"Fenton is nothing like Robbie," Willow said.

"I know he isn't. I just – I can't trust my judgment when it comes to men," Ginger said.

Her cell buzzed, and she scanned the text, a small smile crossing her face.

"Is that Fenton?" Willow asked.

"No, my brother. I made the mistake of calling him and telling him what happened, and now he's sending me daily texts. He was going to come home, but I told him not to and that I was perfectly fine and safe."

She hesitated, "I might have told him that I had some protection detail from your security firm."

"You kind of do," Willow said cheerfully. "Fenton isn't going to let anything happen to you. Is your brother still in Australia?"

"Truthfully, I'm not exactly sure where he is, and he won't tell me. You know how he is when it comes to his job. It's so secretive, hell, I've never even really been positive of what he does exactly."

Willow took a drink of tea as Dolly Parton returned silently to the kitchen. She rubbed up against Ginger before leaping into her lap and butting her face against her chin. Ginger scratched the cat's face, and throat and Dolly purred loudly before lying down in her lap. She caught sight of Willow and hissed as her tail flicked back and forth.

Willow rolled her eyes. "I'm starting to regret the day I saved her and her brother from certain death."

Ginger laughed and stroked the cat's soft fur. "She'll come around, Willow. You're terribly hard to resist, remember?"

Willow nodded. "So true, but my charming personality seems to be completely useless with house cats."

Ginger snickered again before glancing at her watch. After helping her and Willow clean up her bedroom – the last of the apartment that was still a mess – and setting up her new bed, Fenton had left on his errand. He had said he wouldn't be long, but it had been nearly two hours since Willow had driven her back to the house she now shared with Mal, and she hadn't heard a thing from the cheetah shifter. Worry gnawed at her belly. God, she hoped nothing had happened to him.

———

FENTON STOOD QUIETLY IN THE DARK APARTMENT. IT SMELLED of stale pot and sweat, and his cheetah hissed disgruntledly. He soothed it lightly and shifted on his feet. Sunday evening, exhausted after spending the day cleaning up her apartment, Ginger had fallen into a deep sleep in his bed. He had found some evidence of her old life with Robbie when they were cleaning – a cell phone bill with his last name, a photograph of Ginger and Robbie lying in the mess on the living room floor – and he had memorized his face before Ginger had snatched the photo from him and ripped it into pieces.

Once she had fallen asleep, he had logged in to Facebook and found Robbie in less than five minutes. After only a few minutes of perusing his profile, it had been ridiculously easy to find out where the man was at that exact moment. Leaving Ginger sleeping in his bed, he had driven to the pub and found a booth a few feet from where Robbie, surrounded by his equally vile friends, was loudly arguing the merits of some online video game.

He shifted again, ignoring the sounds of the couple fucking in the apartment next to this one, and snorted quietly. Gaming held no appeal for him, and he would never understand why a grown-ass man like Robbie would be so obsessed with it when he had a woman like Ginger.

His groin stirred as he thought of Ginger sleeping in his bed, and he adjusted his dick with a grimace. It had been pure torture sleeping with Ginger the last two nights and not being able to touch her, to hear her cry his name with breathless need. His cheetah made a soft growl of agreement, and he soothed it again.

After four hours, he had followed the extremely drunk Robbie out of the pub. The loser had stumbled his way four blocks north to a run-down apartment building and hadn't even noticed the large blond man who followed him silently up the stairs. Once Fenton discovered which apartment was Robbie's, he had left, melting into the shadows of the narrow hallway as Robbie had staggered into his apartment and slammed the door. Fenton had been back in the bed next to the still-sleeping Ginger without her ever realizing he was gone.

The police had nothing to tie Robbie to Ginger's apartment, and Fenton clenched his fists as the woman next door screamed her pleasure like a banshee, and the man gave a harsh animalistic grunt of satisfaction. Ginger was still afraid, he could smell it on her, and while he was happy to have her stay with him as long as she wanted, he hated that she was afraid to go back to her apartment. The lock turned, and his cheetah growled softly as his body stiffened with anticipation.

***

ROBBIE DROPPED HIS KEYS INTO HIS POCKET AND PUSHED open the door. He set the groceries on the floor before flicking on the light. He thought about the rat he had seen scurrying in the hallway and grinned a little. He'd see if he could catch it later tonight. He couldn't go back to Ginger's apartment, the police might be keeping an eye on him despite their lack of evidence, but he could send Ginger a little present in the mail. She hated rats, and the thought of how she would react when she opened up her mail and found a dead rat made him laugh out loud. That bitch had always thought she was better than him, and fuck if he wasn't enjoying making her squirm. Tearing up all of her clothes and destroying her furniture had been a fucking blast, and he hadn't been surprised to see he had a hard-on when he was finished. If he'd been thinking, he would have jerked off on her favourite dress, but he'd already shredded it, and he'd been at her apartment long enough.

He scratched his balls absentmindedly before giving his fingers a sniff. He should probably shower before he went out but fuck it – if the bitches at the bar didn't like the way he smelled, they could go fuck themselves. A flicker of movement caught his eye, and he glanced up to see a large man, dressed all in black and wearing a black knitted cap on his head, standing in front of him. He screamed shrilly and stumbled back as the man grinned.

"What the fuck! Who the fuck are you?" Robbie snapped.

"It doesn't matter who I am," the man said.

"How the fuck did you get in my apartment?" Robbie rubbed at his chest. His heart pounded against his ribs, and he glanced uneasily at the man in black.

"You really should get a better lock on your door, Robbie," the man said.

"How do you know my name?" Robbie's unease turned into panic. "I ain't got nothing worth stealing, man."

"I'm not a thief," the man said.

Robbie took another step back. "What do you want from me?"

"What I want is very simple. You're going to stay away from Ginger. Do you understand?"

Robbie's mouth dropped open. "That fucking bitch sent you?"

The stranger made a soft hiss, and Robbie had time for one strangled yelp before the man was on him. He wrapped his hand around Robbie's throat and shoved him up against the door, squeezing firmly when Robbie tried to scream.

The stranger's pupils changed to dark slits, and a golden-coloured beard sprouted on his face. He hissed again at Robbie and then made a low chuckle of delight when the scent of urine filled the air. He glanced at the wet patch spreading on the front of Robbie's pants and released his throat. Robbie stood frozen against the door as the stranger raised his hand. He moaned pitifully when the stranger's blunt nails turned to razor-sharp claws.

"No, please," he moaned again.

"You're going to stay away from Ginger. Is that clear?" the shifter said softly.

Robbie nodded frantically, turning his face away and closing his eyes when the shifter leaned even closer, and his hot breath washed over him.

"If you go anywhere near her, if I find out you so much as say her name," the shifter reached out and traced one claw across Robbie's throat, "I'll hunt you down and slit your throat. Do you believe me, Robbie?" A thin line of blood appeared on Robbie's neck, and tears oozed down his face.

The shifter growled menacingly when Robbie remained silent. "Do you believe me?"

"Yes!" Robbie cried. "Yes, I believe you."

"Good." The shifter grabbed him by the shoulders and tossed him carelessly to the floor before opening the door and disappearing into the hallway.

Robbie, still on his knees and his breath whistling in and out of his throat, slammed the door and locked it with a trembling hand. He stared wide-eyed at the bag of groceries sitting forgotten on the floor before climbing to his feet and staggering to the bedroom.

---

"THANK YOU FOR DRIVING ME HOME, FENTON," GINGER SAID as he parked on the street outside of her apartment building.

"You know you can still stay with me if you want," he said. "I don't mind."

"Thanks, but I've intruded on your space long enough," she said.

"Two days isn't a long time."

She smiled at him. "I can't stay with you forever."

She could, he thought but didn't say. He would scare the crap out of her if she suspected that he was already halfway to obsessed with her.

She glanced nervously out the window of the car, and he squeezed her narrow thigh. "I'll walk you up."

"Thank you," she said with noticeable relief.

When they were standing in her apartment, he had installed a heavier chain across the door after maintenance had repaired it, she smiled at him. "Well, um, thanks again. Maybe we could have dinner sometime?"

"Do you want me to stay with you tonight?" he asked.

"Yes!" she blurted out before blushing. "I mean, no, that's okay. I'm good."

"I'll stay," he said.

She nodded, her relief written all over her face and coming off her in waves. He glanced into the living room. After delivering the new bed, Garth had hauled Ginger's ruined couch to the dump, but Fenton could sleep on the floor. He'd slept in worse places.

As if she read his mind, she took his hand and led him to

her bedroom. She disappeared into the bathroom, and he stripped down to his briefs before climbing into the bed. It was early, not even nine yet, but Ginger looked tired and in pain. She returned wearing a silky little nightgown that made his cheetah purr happily.

She gave him a nervous look before rubbing her hands over the material. "Willow and I did a quick shopping trip when you left on your errand."

"It's beautiful," he said hoarsely as he willed his cock to behave.

She slid into the bed next to him and hesitated only briefly before cuddling up next to him. "I know it's early," she said, "but I'm pretty tired."

He put his arm around her and stroked her back before pressing a kiss against the top of her head. "It's fine."

"Thank you for staying with me, Fenton. I'm sorry I'm such a big baby."

"You're not," he said before grasping her chin and tilting up her head. "You don't have to worry about Robbie. He's not going to bother you again."

"How do you know that?" she said.

"I just do," he said. There was no way in hell he was telling her about being at Robbie's place earlier tonight.

She gave him an intent look, her brow furrowing. "Fenton, did you – did you hurt Robbie?"

He shook his head. He hadn't hurt him, not really. Pissing your pants didn't exactly hurt. "No, of course not."

She gave him a slightly embarrassed look. "Sorry, that was a stupid thing to say."

She pressed her head against his shoulder and rubbed his chest with one soft hand. His purring started immediately, and he groaned inwardly. Fuck, it was embarrassing that he couldn't control his purring whenever Ginger touched him.

After about ten minutes, she raised her head and smiled at him. "Your purring is my new favourite thing. Did you know that?"

He shook his head and studied the glassiness in her eyes. "Love, did you take a morphine pill?"

She nodded as her hand dipped below his navel, and his hips jerked in response. "Yeah, I didn't want to, but my ribs were hurting pretty badly."

Her words were starting to slur together, and he groaned when she pushed her hand under his briefs and wrapped it around his erect cock before stroking him firmly.

"Love, we can't."

"Sure, we can," she said. "I've got no pain at all, Fenton. This is the perfect time."

She gave his cock a firm squeeze, smiling when he gasped out a choked purring noise and his pelvis thrust against her.

"Maybe we can't have sex yet," she whispered, "but that doesn't mean you shouldn't get to come."

His nostrils flared as she bent her head and flicked his flat nipple with her tongue. She stroked his cock rapidly, and he groaned before yanking her hand away.

"Fenton?" She frowned at him. "Let me make you come."

"No, love," he said hoarsely. "Not if you can't."

Her eyes widened. Her pupils were large and dark, and he would have grinned at how stoned she was if he wasn't so worried about her.

"I – you're turning down a handjob because I don't get to have an orgasm?" she said.

He nodded, and her bottom lip dropped a little. "I – I don't even know what to say to that."

He leaned over her and pressed a light kiss against her mouth as she wrapped her slender arms around his neck.

"I don't want you to leave because I can't have sex with you," she confessed hazily.

He frowned. "Ginger, I'm not going to leave."

"You might," she muttered. "Robbie didn't like it when I said no to sex."

She parted her thighs and tried to urge him between her legs. "Just fuck me quickly, Fenton. I don't mind," she sighed as her eyes drifted shut.

Fresh anger flooded through him, and for a moment, he wished he had hurt the slimy little bastard.

"Quick, honey," Ginger murmured with her eyes still shut. "I don't need to come. Just let me make you feel good."

He turned her gently to her uninjured side before curling up behind her. His erection pressed against her soft ass, and she made a low cooing noise of pleasure as he cupped one small breast through her silk nightgown.

"Please, Fenton," she muttered.

he kissed the back of her neck. "Go to sleep, love."

CHAPTER 8

"Hey, Bishop, almost here?" Kat answered her cell phone just as Ronin strolled into the office.

She frowned. "Maybe she should go to the hospital?" She listened silently before nodding. "Okay, no, it's not a problem. Don't worry about it, big guy. Tell Ava I said to feel better soon."

She ended the call. "Ava's got the flu and still isn't feeling well. Bishop doesn't want to leave her alone."

"Looks like it's just you and me meeting up with the vamps," he said with a grin.

"Right. Do you want to follow me there or go in my car?" she asked.

"I'll go with you," he said.

He followed her silently out of the office and down to the parking garage. He sat in the passenger seat and stared at the interior of the car. "Nice wheels, Kitten."

"Thanks," she said briefly. She was ridiculously proud of her bright blue Camaro. She loved driving, and the flashy sports car had been something she couldn't resist buying. She pulled out of the garage, and Ronin laughed when she stepped on the gas and the powerful car moved forward in a burst of speed.

"You like driving fast, huh?"

She shrugged. "I'm a jaguar."

He didn't reply, and they drove silently through the dark streets. She half-expected him to bring up her heat cycle again, and she was dismayed to realize she was disappointed that he wasn't. Did she want him to keep pestering her about it?

RONIN STARED OUT THE WINDOW AT THE BUILDINGS ZIPPING by. He had wanted Kat before she had thrown him to her office floor and fucked him into the best orgasm of his life, and now that want had turned into a need that was bordering on obsession. He clenched his hands into fists and held back his urge to just beg her to let him help her during her heat cycle.

So far, he had managed to keep it light and act like it was a fun game to him, but the thought of her using that damn tiger shifter to ease her need had been tearing him up inside the entire weekend. Earlier this afternoon, he had given himself a much-needed pep talk and thought he'd convinced himself that sleeping with Kat, even just during her heat cycle, was a terrible idea.

He believed it had worked until he stepped into the office tonight and saw her. Her tight skirt, long legs, and bright red top had drawn him in like a beacon and made him forget all the reasons why he shouldn't sleep with her.

He swore inwardly and folded his arms across his chest. His obsession with Katarina Frost was a dangerous one. Not only was she his boss, but if the people who were undoubtedly still looking for him found him, he'd be putting her life in danger. He couldn't have a relationship with her.

*Relationship? What happened to just helping her out once a month during her heat?*

He cleared his throat loudly, Kat glanced at him before staring out the windshield again, and he tried to relax. He was just lonely. He hadn't had sex in nearly a year until that night with Kat. He just needed to get laid, that was all.

*Oh yeah? So why didn't you take those bunny shifters up on their offer for a threesome?*

He ignored his inner voice and stared grimly out the window. It had been a mistake to come back to the city he had grown up in. Not only would it be the first place they would look for him, but a year ago, Wyatt had opened a second lab not an hour from the city. He shouldn't have been surprised by that. Both Wyatt and Lora had grown up here, just like him, and he could see Wyatt wanting to move his wife home, hoping that it would make her more comfortable.

He should have stayed away, but he'd been badly shaken by what had happened to him in the lab in New York. He couldn't hide on a damn island teaching surfing lessons for the rest of his life. He needed to feel grounded again, needed to find some type of comfort, and he had come back to the city on pure instinct. It was a big place, and even if they were looking for him, it would take a goddamn miracle for them to find him. But that didn't mean he should put Kat's life in danger. Besides, if they did find him, he'd be on the run once more, and he'd never see the jaguar shifter again. It was better just to stop obsessing about her.

Too bad that was easier said than done.

KAT GLANCED AT RONIN. HE'D LAPSED INTO SILENCE FOR THE last fifteen minutes, and he stared moodily out the window. She wanted to ask him what was wrong, but what was the point? She needed to keep her distance from him, and being friendly even in a platonic way was a bad idea.

They were in the heart of downtown now, and Kat parked the car before pointing to the building across the street. "The Sorensons live in the penthouse suite."

"Nice," he said as they left the car and quickly crossed to the building. The guard sitting behind the lobby desk took their driver's licenses and perused them carefully before making a phone call.

He handed back their licenses and pointed to the elevator. "They're expecting you."

"Thanks," Kat said.

They walked to the elevator, and she pushed the button for the penthouse.

"So, the Sorensons must have money," Ronin said thoughtfully as he stared at the lush interior of the elevator.

"They do. A lot of money."

The elevator dinged quietly, and the doors slid open. A man, wearing a dark suit with his dark hair slicked back, stood in the foyer of the penthouse. He smiled at Kat, revealing his sharp fangs. "Ms. Frost, lovely to see you again."

"Hello, Mr. Sorenson. It's nice to see you as well. This is my associate, Ronin Smith."

The vampire shook Ronin's hand as a tall and very slender blonde woman drifted into the foyer.

"Hello, Mrs. Sorenson," Kat said.

"Katarina, how are you?" she said in a sultry voice. She glanced appreciatively at Ronin, and Kat's jaguar hissed in disapproval.

"I thought Mr. King was joining us this evening," Mrs. Sorenson said.

"He had a family emergency," Kat said.

"What a shame," the woman murmured. "I do so enjoy seeing him. He's just so very," she licked her lips, "large."

"Behave yourself, my dear," Mr. Sorenson said, and she grinned at him before holding her hand out to Ronin.

He shook it as her gaze drifted over his body. "Although I must say that you make up for the lack of the bear shifter, mister…?

"Smith, Ronin Smith."

"And are you a shifter as well?"

"I am."

"What kind?" she asked.

"Bird," he said, and a soft frown crossed her face.

"Are you capable of protecting our Mavina? She is very precious to us."

"Ronin is more than capable, I assure you," Kat said. "We know how important Mavina is to you, and Ronin is our best man for the job."

"Very well. Why don't you join us in the family room? Mavina is upstairs at the moment, but she'll be down shortly."

Kat and Ronin followed the two vampires into the family room. Its large windows revealed a fantastic view of the city, and varying shades of red decorated the room. It made the room look like it was bathed in blood, and, as Kat sat down on the black leather couch, she supposed that was exactly the look the vampires were going for.

"Would you like some wine? A beer, perhaps?" Mr. Sorenson asked. "We don't carry much human drink or food, I'm afraid, but I'm certain we have something in the fridge that's suitable."

Kat shook her head. "No, thank you."

"Mr. Smith?"

Ronin declined, and Mr. Sorenson moved to the bar at the room's far end. He opened a large crystal decanter, and Kat's stomach heaved a little when he poured the dark red liquid into two wine glasses, and the smell of blood drifted to her.

The vampire handed a glass to his wife, and she brought it to her nose and inhaled deeply before taking a sip.

"Delicious," she murmured as she licked the blood from her lips.

"Freshly drawn this morning, my dear," Mr. Sorenson said before taking his own drink.

She smiled happily before sitting in the chair across from the couch. Mr. Sorenson seated himself in the second chair and stared solemnly at Kat. "As I mentioned on the phone, I'm afraid our Mavina has gotten herself into trouble again. This vampire she was seeing has begun to show very unpleasant tendencies."

"He's a brute." Mrs. Sorenson sniffed. "Why, there are even rumours going around that he's drinking from humans against their will."

She shook her head and sipped delicately at her goblet of blood. "It's vampires like him that give the rest of us a bad name."

Kat nodded sympathetically. Once the shifters had revealed themselves to the humans, the other paranormal creatures had begun to come forward one by one, despite the initial friction between the shifters and the humans. In a bid to keep peace with their food source, the head of the Vampire Coalition had made many repeated and very public announcements that vampires had no wish to harm humans and, as they had always done, would only drink from those who were willing.

Unfortunately, humans had been highly panicked by the realization that vampires existed, and there had been numerous attempts by humans in power to eradicate the vampire species.

To their credit, the vampires had repeatedly refused to engage, even when humans in the northern wilds of Canada had banded together to create a massive army and slaughtered nearly all of the vampires living in the remote wilderness. As more and more paranormals had revealed themselves, the shock over the vampires had lessened, and that, combined with the vampires keeping a low profile, had eventually produced an uneasy truce between the humans and the undead.

Of course, like in any species, there were a few bad apples. Some vampires still took blood from unwilling humans, but it had happened less and less over the years. Many humans considered vampires to be nothing more than a nuisance now - something Kat found more than a little disturbing - and an even greater number were utterly fascinated by them and their lifestyle. Before they had revealed their existence, vampires had always used their powers of seduction to feed on the humans and then wiped their memories of it. Now, vampires worldwide had very little trouble finding willing humans to feed on and didn't bother at all to wipe their memories.

Mr. Sorenson nodded in agreement with his wife. "He does. Why if that Senator Matthews finds out that we've got rogue vampires taking humans and feeding on them without their permission, his campaign to have us forced into being identified with branding marks might catch on."

Kat gave him a horrified look. "Tell me he isn't trying to pass that bill?"

"He is," Mr. Sorenson said.

"I had no idea," Kat said. "He's been trying for ages to pass a bill requiring shifters to register with the government so they can 'keep track of us', but I hadn't heard about this branding of vampires."

"He's keeping it quiet for now," Mr. Sorenson said. "But if he catches wind of some of the more brutal of my kind, I'm afraid the branding idea might start to appeal to the general public. Unlike shifters, we have not convinced the humans to allow vampires to work in their government. There would be very little resistance if the Senator pushed hard for the branding to happen."

"Wouldn't you just heal from the branding?" Ronin asked.

Mr. Sorenson shook his head. "Not when they're using ultraviolet light to brand us."

"If that bill passes, we're moving to Europe," Mrs. Sorenson said. "They're much more liberal over there."

Before Kat could reply, the door to the room opened, and Mavina walked in. She heard Ronin's sharp inhale beside her, and her cat yowled with jealousy. The vampire was undeniably gorgeous with blonde hair that fell to her waist, bright blue eyes, and a spectacular body. She wore a dark red dress that barely covered her ass, and it was more than evident that she wore no bra. Her large breasts, their nipples pushing obscenely against the silk fabric of her dress, were high and firm looking, and a slow grin crossed her face when she caught sight of Ronin. She stood in front of him in a blink of an eye, and Kat's fangs popped out as Mavina gave Ronin a lazy smile.

"Well, hello there."

Ronin stood and cleared his throat when Mavina stepped forward, and her breasts brushed against his chest. "Hello, I'm Ronin Smith."

"Ronin Smith," she said before holding out her hand. "It's so lovely to meet you."

"Nice to meet you as well, Ms. Sorenson." Ronin shook her hand briefly.

"Please, call me Mavina. Are you my new security detail?"

"I am," Ronin said.

Mavina grinned happily. "Perhaps this won't be nearly as dreadful as I thought it would be."

"Mavina, my dear, you're being rude to Katarina," her father said.

She wrinkled her nose at him before holding her hand out to Kat. "Hello again, Ms. Frost."

"Hello, Mavina." Kat touched her hand quickly before dropping it. Her claws were threatening to extend, and she wanted to claw the vampire's coldly beautiful face.

The jealousy was a seething angry monster inside of her, and she forced her fangs to retreat. What the hell was wrong with her?

"Tell me, Ronin," Mavina purred as Ronin sat down and she wedged her slender body onto the couch between Kat and Ronin, "are you a good dancer?"

"I'm sorry?" Ronin said politely.

"There's a new club that I'd like to go to this evening. I will expect you to dance with me, of course. What better way to keep me safe than by having your body against mine?"

"Oh, Mavina," her father sighed and rolled his eyes as Kat cleared her throat.

"Mr. Smith will not be starting the security detail until tomorrow evening. This is just a meet and greet, Mavina."

She ignored Kat and pouted at her father. "I need him to start tonight, Daddy. I want to go to the club."

"Ms. Frost, perhaps Mr. Smith could start this evening?"

Mr. Sorenson smiled indulgently at his daughter as she pressed the side of one perfect breast against Ronin's arm and stroked his hair.

"I'm afraid not," Kat said. "Ronin has other work this evening."

She stood and gave Ronin a pointed look. He untangled himself from Mavina's grip and stood. She rose to her feet with a grace that Kat envied and rubbed his arm. "I'm so looking forward to having you protect me, Ronin."

"It was nice to meet you, Mavina," he said.

"Oh, you as well. I have a feeling we're going to be very good...friends," she said.

———

"ARE YOU GOING TO TELL ME WHAT'S WRONG OR JUST KEEP hissing under your breath?" Ronin asked as she shut off her car.

They had spent the entire ride from Mavina's home to the office in complete silence. Her cat was a restless, pacing ball of rage inside of her, and it was all she could do to stop it from jumping Ronin. She wanted to fuck him, scratch him, mark him with her claws and teeth so that vampire bitch knew he belonged to her.

"There's nothing wrong," she snapped before climbing out of her car. She would go up to the office to get some work done. Going back home and sitting alone was not an option at the moment.

"Bullshit," he said. "Something's got the Kitten all riled up."

She glared at him and slammed her door shut. He grinned at him before sidling around the car until he stood in front of her. "Why don't you tell me? You'll feel better."

"If you fuck her, you'll be fired," she said.

"Excuse me?"

"Mavina Sorenson. If you fuck her, you will be fired, Ronin."

Anger flickered across his face. "You think I'm going to fuck her?"

"She was all over you, and you weren't pushing her away," she said. "I'm serious, Ronin. If you sleep with her, you're out of a job and -"

"I heard you the first time," he snapped. "I'm not some mindless beast who can't keep his dick in his pants, Katarina. I didn't push her away because I tried to be polite to a new client. If you have a problem with the way I treat our clients, then maybe you should fire me right now."

Her nostrils flared, and she made a low hiss. "I'll only have a problem with it if you fuck any of our clients."

"Good to know," he said. "This jealous side of you isn't very flattering, Kitten. Mavina seems like a lovely girl who's just friendly."

"Friendly?" Kat snarled. "She was practically handing her pussy to you on a platter, and you seemed more than a little interested in -"

She gasped when he lunged forward and wrapped one hard hand in her dark hair. He gripped it tightly as he pressed her against her car and shoved her legs apart with his thigh. "Let's get something straight, Kitten. The only pussy I'm interested in is this one right here."

His hand was between her legs, his fingers pressing against her clit through the fabric of her panties before she could blink. Her cat surged to the front, purring happily and more than ready to take what was hers, and his nostrils flared when her pupils turned to dark slits.

He rubbed her roughly, and she purred before grabbing

119

his head and yanking it down to hers. She kissed him frantically, rubbing her pussy against his fingers as he angled his mouth over hers and thrust his tongue into her mouth. She slid her hands up his shirt, raking her nails down his naked back as he cupped one breast through her shirt and pinched her nipple.

She hissed in pleasure and pain and then growled when he pulled his hand out from under her skirt.

"No! Give me what's mine!" She sank her claws into his back, and he grunted with pain before lifting her and sitting her on the hood of her car. She wrapped her thighs around his hips, pulling him up against her as he pushed her skirt up around her hips. He shoved the crotch of her panties to the side, and she moaned when his fingers slid into her.

"Fuck," he muttered into her ear. "You're so wet, Kat."

He thrust his fingers in and out, groaning when her pussy sucked noisily at his fingers. She bit him on the neck, hard enough to draw blood, and he made a low curse before pulling her away with a tug to her hair.

"Play nice, Kitten," he said.

She bared her fangs at him, and he grinned before licking her lips. She sucked aggressively on his bottom lip and unbuckled his belt. He palmed her breast again, squeezing it hard before unbuttoning two of the buttons on her shirt and sliding his hand under her bra. He toyed with her nipple, pinching and pulling until it was an erect bud as she unbuttoned his jeans and raked down the zipper. She pulled out his cock, squeezing it firmly and twisting her palm against the base until he groaned.

"Jesus, it's like you want me to fuck you on top of your goddamn car."

Her hand stilled, and she stared unblinkingly at him

before purring so loudly it echoed in the empty parking garage.

"You don't have to tell me twice," he muttered before grabbing her hips and yanking her forward. He reached between them and gripped his cock. Her panties had slipped back into place, and he scowled when the head of his cock rubbed against the silk material.

"Move your panties, Kitten," he demanded.

A tiny flicker of sanity went through her, and she hesitated. Ronin's hand tightened in her hair again, and he bent his head and bit the slender column of her throat. She hissed in pain, and he gave her a dark grin.

"You're not the only one with teeth, Kitten. Now move your damn panties so I can fuck you."

She yanked the crotch of her panties to the side and arched her back when Ronin pushed in the head of his cock.

"Christ, you're even tighter than I remember," he moaned as he pushed forward steadily.

She made soft meows and purrs of excitement, and when he was finally sheathed entirely inside of her, she licked at his mouth eagerly as his hands curled around her hips.

"Ready, Kitten?"

"Yes," she whispered. "Oh God, yes. Please, Ronin. Don't make me -"

"Hey! You can't do that in here."

They both froze, and Kat looked over her shoulder to see Arnie, the security guard for the office building, standing twenty feet away.

"Ms. Frost? Is that you?" He gave her a look of surprise, and her face turned bright red.

"Get lost, asshole!" Ronin snarled at him.

Arnie bristled and stood a little taller. "I certainly will not. This type of behaviour is not allowed in a public parking garage. I'm about two minutes from calling the cops, and unless you want to be arrested for public indecency, you'll get in your damn car and get out of here."

Ronin glared at him, but Kat pushed at his chest before he could say anything.

"Move, Ronin," she muttered before giving Arnie a look of embarrassment. "Sorry, Arnie. We'll, uh, leave."

Ronin pulled out of her. Her cat hissed in displeasure as Ronin stuffed his cock back into his pants. Mortified, Kat yanked her skirt down before sliding off her car.

"I'll follow you home in my car," Ronin said quietly.

She shook her head. "No, I – no, Ronin."

He sighed in annoyance as Arnie tapped one foot on the cement.

Ronin buckled his belt. "Kat, for God's sake, just let me –"

"No, I'm sorry. I have to go." She pushed past him and climbed into her car. She started it and drove away without looking at Ronin or Arnie.

# CHAPTER 9

"I swear, Willow, as soon as she found out I was a lynx shifter, she was all over me. She was grabbing me under the damn table!"

Willow laughed. "What did you do?"

"What do you think I did?" Davis leaned against the reception desk. "I told Maryanne's mother I was flattered but that I didn't date mother/daughter duos."

"Are you telling the mother/daughter story again?" Bishop rumbled as he came out of his office. "That happened two years ago, Davis."

Davis grinned. "Don't take away my glory, Bishop."

The door to the office opened, and a dark-haired man, handsome with bright blue eyes and a broad frame, walked into the office.

"Good afternoon. How can I help you?" Willow said as Bishop and Davis eyed him curiously.

"I'm Clay Haddon. I have an appointment with Ms. Frost," he said.

"I'll let Ms. Frost know you're here. Please have a seat. Can I get you a drink?"

"No, thank you," he said as Davis followed Bishop into his office and closed the door.

———

"IT'S NICE TO SEE YOU AGAIN, MR. HADDON," KAT SAID. She studied the human, more curious than she wanted to admit about why he wanted to speak with her.

"You as well, please call me Clay," he said.

"Call me Kat. You wanted to speak to me about the coyote shifter incident, is that right?"

"Yes," Clay said. "Officer Umbert said he shot the shifter in the chest but that he then had to shoot him in the head to put him down effectively. Is that your recollection of the events?"

Kat nodded. "Yes. So, your company studies a shifter's healing abilities?"

"We do," Clay said. "Stowe Laboratories works with shifters to try to unlock the secrets of their healing abilities."

"Why?" Kat asked. "What's the purpose of that?"

"Well, there are many reasons. Dr. Stowe wants to know why some shifters heal faster than others. Grizzly bears, for instance, heal, on average, ninety-three percent faster than any other shifter. Why is that? What makes their abilities so much stronger than, say, a jaguar shifter such as yourself?"

Kat shrugged. "I guess I've never really thought about it."

"There are other factors to consider as well. We know that a shifter's healing powers start to fade as they grow older. Is this because of genetics? Or perhaps food or environment is a factor. Could a shifter's healing powers be enhanced somehow? Is it possible that a sloth's healing powers could somehow be modified, so they heal as quickly as a grizzly?"

Kat cocked her head at him. "It sounds like Dr. Stowe is trying to play God."

Clay chuckled. "Not at all, Kat. What he's trying to do is discover the mystery of your healing abilities and help future generations of shifters. Imagine if he could find a way to prevent your healing powers from fading. Heart attacks, strokes, cancer – none of it would affect you. Who knows how long shifters could live if their healing powers remained intact?"

Kat frowned at him. "Still sounds to me like he's attempting to play God. Is he a shifter?"

Clay nodded. "He's a black bear shifter."

"So, to 'unlock' the secrets of a shifter's healing powers, he must be experimenting on his own kind," she said.

"Not experimenting," Clay said. "Do we have test subjects in the lab? Of course. But they're all volunteers and are well-compensated for their time."

"I still don't understand why you're interested in the coyote shifter who went mad," Kat said.

"The coyote shifter survived a direct shot to the chest. Of course, many shifters have survived being shot in the chest, but that was with immediate medical attention. At the very least, the bullet needs to be removed before the shifter can start healing. But, according to Office Umbert, the coyote shifter was down less than a minute before he recovered. That's never happened before, and Dr. Stowe wants to know why."

"It's too late. The shifter is dead," Kat said. "Any possible healing enhancements died with him. Besides, the coyote shifter looked like he was on death's door when he came into the coffee shop. There's no way he had enhanced healing abilities."

"Maybe, maybe not. However, Dr. Stowe feels that any

information leading up to the moment he died could benefit our research, which leads me to you and Officer Umbert. My understanding is there was also a grizzly shifter. Did you know him?"

Kat nodded. "Bishop King. He's a partner here at the firm."

A look of satisfaction crossed Clay's face. "Do you think we could have him join us? It would be helpful to speak to both of you."

Kat picked up her phone and buzzed Bishop's office. He joined them after a brief explanation, shaking Clay's hand before easing his large bulk into the chair next to him. Kat listened silently as Clay explained to Bishop the purpose of Stowe Laboratories.

"So, what exactly is it you want to know about that day," Bishop asked when Clay finished.

"Everything, Mr. King," Clay said. "Why don't the two of you start from the beginning."

HALF AN HOUR LATER, CLAY SAT BACK IN HIS CHAIR AND laced his fingers together over his flat abdomen. "So, the coyote shifter was bigger and stronger."

Kat nodded. "Incredibly strong. He shoved Bishop through the plate glass window after Bishop had shifted."

"He had to be on some type of steroid," Bishop said. "It's the only explanation."

"Steroids don't affect shifters like that, Bishop," Kat said. "Look at chipmunk shifters. Those guys are always popping steroids, and it doesn't affect their size when they're in chipmunk form. Besides, the guy was normal size as a human. It wasn't until after he shifted that he became so," she paused, "weird. I mean, you saw the guy's teeth, remember?"

Bishop nodded. "Yeah, something wasn't right."

Kat tapped one long nail on the top of her desk as she stared thoughtfully at Clay. "It had to have been some type of mutation or infection, or maybe a virus."

"Perhaps," Clay said.

Bishop glanced at his watch. "Are we almost done? I have an appointment."

"Yes," Clay said. "Just one more question – were either of you bitten or scratched by the coyote?"

Kat shook her head. "I wasn't."

Clay glanced at Bishop. "The coyote attacked you – were you injured, Mr. King?"

"Nah," Bishop said. "I was in my grizzly form by then, and it takes a lot to pierce through my fur and skin."

Clay stood and held out his hand. Bishop stood and shook his hand as Clay said, "Thank you for your time, Mr. King."

He turned to Kat, and she stood and shook his hand. "Nice to meet you, Clay."

"You as well. Thank you, Kat."

Clay left her office, shutting the door behind him. There was a moment of silence before Bishop said, "That was strange."

"Yes, it was," Kat said.

"You believe his explanation for why they're interested in that coyote shifter?"

Kat shrugged. "Not entirely. I think he spun a very nice story made up of half-truths."

"Yeah," Bishop grunted. "Now what?"

"I'm going to do a bit of research into Stowe Laboratories," Kat said as she sat down at her computer. "Hey, how's Ava feeling?"

"Uh, better." Bishop cracked his knuckles. "Let me know what you find out, okay?"

"You bet, big guy." Kat opened her laptop.

———

"OH MY GOD," SANDRA MOANED AS SHE STARED AT HER swollen, throbbing leg. The wound from the monster in the park was infected. Despite dousing it daily with antiseptic, thick green pus still dripped out of it. Steeling herself, she sat on the side of the tub and poured nearly half the bottle of antiseptic over the wound. It burned like fire, and she bit down on the towel to muffle her screams. After a few moments, the pain subsided to a dull ache, and she gingerly blotted the wound before taping a clean white bandage over it.

She eased her way out of the tub and hobbled into the kitchen. Her head ached, and she took some Advil before cooking her dinner. She sat alone at the table and picked at the food in front of her. She had made Brad's favourite dish – brown rice with almonds and sunflower seeds – and as she stared at her plate, tears dripped down her face. God, she missed him. If he were here right now, he'd be forcing her to go to the hospital, and she would go, despite her nearly paralyzing fear of doctors and hospitals, because he would help her be brave.

She still couldn't quite believe that he was dead, and she'd never see him again. It was only Thursday, and Brad had been dead for less than a week but still…when would her mind stop trying to convince her that he would come walking through the apartment door just like he always did?

His mother had called her tonight, crying and sobbing and drunk out of her mind, and Sandra had tried to comfort her but failed miserably. She sighed and scraped her dinner into the overflowing garbage can. It was starting to smell. Brad always took the garbage out, and she grimaced before tying the bag. She glanced out the window, and a trickle of fear went through her. Darkness had fallen, and even though the dumpster was only ten feet behind the apartment building, she was dismayed to realize that she was afraid to take out the garbage.

She had called Detective Matthews' cell this morning, and he had assured her that although they had not found the creature yet, they had combed the park and surrounding area, and he was most definitely not there. She sighed and rubbed her hand over her forehead. She had given them the best description she could, and Detective Matthews had listened carefully and didn't question her description, but even to herself, she had sounded crazy.

He said they were dealing with a sick porcupine shifter, but she couldn't – didn't know how to – articulate just how odd the shifter had looked. It was a porcupine shifter, but it wasn't, and she was terribly afraid that her stuttering, pathetic description of its strength and speed had been woefully inadequate.

She stared at the garbage and then out the window again before taking a deep breath. She was being stupid. She was perfectly safe, and it was time to stop hiding out in her apartment the moment the sun went down. She would take out the garbage, and nothing bad would happen. She'd be fine.

---

"HEY, THAT'S A GOOD SONG." THE MAN GLARED AT HIS companion as he turned off the radio.

"They've played it four times in the last six hours," the second man said. "I'm sick of this shit."

He tapped his fingers on the steering wheel before reaching between the seats and grabbing a donut from the box on the back seat. "I don't know why we're even keeping tabs on this squirrel shifter at night. The bitch doesn't leave her apartment once it gets dark."

The first man shrugged. "Boss says to keep an eye on her – we keep an eye on her."

"If she'd been bitten, she woulda turned by now," the second man said. "She's a squirrel shifter. They got metabolisms like a fuckin' racehorse."

"Horses don't have fast metabolisms, moron."

"Fuck you, Kyle."

"Sorry, I don't swing that way. Just ask your mother," Kyle said impudently.

The second man glared at him. "Talk about my mother again, and I'll -"

"What the hell is that?" Kyle leaned forward and squinted through the windshield.

"What? I don't see nothin'."

"Open your goddamn eyes, Reggie," Kyle snapped. "Over there, under the streetlamp."

Reggie ate the last of his donut before licking his fingers. "Some homeless guy. Who the fuck cares?"

"That isn't a fucking homeless dude, asshole."

Kyle opened the door and climbed out, shutting it quietly behind him. Reggie sighed before following him. Kyle stood in front of the car, and as Reggie joined him, the homeless man turned. The glow of the streetlight above him illuminated his face, and Kyle cursed under his breath.

"Holy fuck, it's the porcupine."

"Bullshit," Reggie muttered. "That's not the fucking porcupine."

"It is," Kyle hissed. "He's got fucking quills, for fuck's sake."

Reggie squinted. "I don't see 'em."

"Oh, for fuck's sake, get some fucking glasses, you twit," Kyle snapped before hauling out his cell phone.

"Who are you calling?"

"Who do you think?"

Reggie grabbed his arm. "If you call him and it ain't that porcupine shifter, he'll have our heads on poles."

Kyle ignored him and pushed a button on the screen before holding it up to his ear. The porcupine shifter had dropped to all fours and was sniffing the dirty pavement in front of him, and a shiver of fear went down Kyle's spine when the creature lifted his head and sniffed the air.

"Boss?" Kyle dropped his voice to a whisper. "It's Kyle."

He listened and shook his head. "No, the squirrel shifter is still acting normal, but I – I think we got your porcupine here. Should I call the team and," he paused and listened again, "yeah, pretty sure. I mean, it looks like him, but I -"

There was a soft pop, and Clay appeared in front of him wearing a t-shirt and worn jeans. Reggie staggered back, holding his chest as Kyle slipped his phone into his pocket.

"Where?" Clay said quietly.

"Behind you." Kyle pointed over his shoulder, and Clay turned and walked forward a few feet.

"Fuck, I hate it when he does that," Reggie muttered into his ear. Kyle shook him off before following Clay. He pulled his gun from his shoulder holster.

"Boss, is it him?"

Clay nodded.

"Do I call the team?"

Clay shook his head and held out his hand. "Darts?"

"Yeah," Kyle said before placing the gun in his hand.

The motion light behind the squirrel shifter's apartment building clicked on, and Kyle's eyes widened as the squirrel shifter, holding a garbage bag in her hand, opened the back door and stepped out into the light. The porcupine shifter turned toward the light and stared at the woman before sprinting across the street toward her.

"Oh fuck," Kyle said as Clay vanished.

The squirrel shifter froze with the garbage bag in her hand before turning toward the street. The creature, quills shooting out in all directions, raced across the street toward her. She screamed in terror and threw the bag of garbage at it before bolting into her apartment building and slamming the door shut. The creature made a roar of rage and slammed his body against the door. It shuddered under its weight, and Kyle heard the squirrel's muffled screaming even behind the thick, steel door.

The creature smashed his body against the steel door again as quills bounced off of him. There was a low whistle behind him, and he whirled around. Saliva dripped from his fangs, and he snarled at Clay.

The porcupine shifter leaped for him, and Clay shot him in the chest with the dart before disappearing. The creature roared again, staring in dumb surprise at the empty spot of pavement as Clay appeared behind him and shot him in the back. He turned and took a staggering step toward Clay before sinking to his knees. He whimpered quietly before falling forward on his face.

"Boss?" Kyle joined Clay behind the apartment building, followed by a loudly panting Reggie.

"He's down," Clay said. He handed Kyle his gun as a car approached.

"Fuck," Kyle said. "We gotta get him out of here, we gotta -"

132

He blinked when Clay gripped the creature's wrist in one hand, and the two of them vanished.

"Did I mention I fucking hate it when he does that?" Reggie said morosely.

"C'mon," Kyle glanced around nervously as the car drove past them, "we need to get back to the car before someone sees us."

---

"WILLOW, WE HAVE TO START LOCKING THE CATS OUT OF the bedroom at night," Mal said as he unlocked the office door.

It was Friday morning, and, not surprisingly, they were the first ones to arrive. Willow followed him into the office and flipped on the lights as Mal took her jacket and hung it in the closet.

"I feel so bad. They love sleeping on the bed, Mal," Willow said as she headed to the kitchenette.

Mal leaned against the counter as she started the coffee machine. He reached out and took her slender wrist, pushing up her shirt sleeve and studying the four bright red scratches that went from her elbow to her wrist.

"It's fine," Willow said. "Dolly Parton didn't mean to scratch me."

Mal laughed. "She did, and you know it."

"I didn't realize she was lying on your chest. It's my fault for trying to cuddle you," Willow said.

"Listen, you know I love Johnny and Dolly, but you're my mate, Willow. When you're hurt, it's physically painful for me."

"Really?" Her eyes widened. "You're bullshitting me, Mal."

He bent his head and pressed a path of gentle kisses against the scratches. "I'm not."

"So, what? Is it like a stomach ache or something?" Willow asked.

Mal laughed and pulled her into his arms before kissing her. "We're locking the cats out of the bedroom at night, Willow."

"They'll scratch at the door," she said.

"Probably." He bent and tasted her throat with his tongue, grinning when she moaned quietly.

"They'll destroy the curtains in the living room in protest of their exile," she said as Mal squeezed her small ass.

"We'll buy new ones," he murmured before nipping at her earlobe.

"It would be nice to sex you up without having to worry if Dolly Parton's going to attack me in a fit of jealousy." Willow's voice was breathless. "Hey, think Kat and Bishop will be late?"

"Why?" Mal murmured into her ear.

"I think maybe we should be totally inappropriate and have a quickie in your office."

He nuzzled her throat. "I like that idea."

"Good." She rubbed her slender body against his. "Let's
-"

The bell over the door jingled as it opened and a thin woman with short dark hair stepped into the office. She limped slightly, and her pale face had dark shadows under her eyes.

"Hello," Willow said as she stepped away from Mal. "How can we help you?"

The woman froze at the sound of Willow's voice. Willow glanced at Mal as the woman swallowed compulsively and, in a barely audible voice, said, "I – I'm here to see about protection."

The door opened, and Kat, followed by Bishop balancing a tray of coffees in one large hand, walked into the office. The woman screamed in surprise and darted forward, tripping over her own feet and landing on the floor with a heavy thud. She winced and grabbed at her leg as Willow hurried over and knelt beside her.

"Goodness, are you okay?"

"I'm so sorry," the woman whispered before beginning to cry.

"Oh, honey, don't cry," Willow said and patted her narrow shoulder.

"I need help," the woman sobbed. "Please, can you help me?"

"Of course, we can," Willow said as Mal knelt next to them. "What's your name, honey?"

"Sandra Mickelson."

———

"Ms. Mickelson?" Kat said as she opened the boardroom door.

"Call me Sandra." The squirrel shifter sniffed. Mal handed her another tissue as Kat brought Davis into the boardroom.

"Sandra, this is Davis. He's going to take the first shift with you."

Davis held out his hand. Sandra sniffed nervously in his direction, and her nose made a slight twitch of fear. "You – you're a cat shifter."

"Yes, ma'am, I am," Davis said. "But you're perfectly safe with me, I promise."

She made a watery sigh. "I'm sorry, that was rude of me. I just – I'm very on edge right now."

"That's fine, ma'am," Davis said. "I understand completely."

"As we talked about," Mal said as Sandra rubbed at her temples, "we're assigning two people to watch you in twelve-hour shifts. Davis will introduce you to Fenton when they do their shift change. All right?"

She nodded, and Mal patted her hand. "Don't worry, Ms. Mickelson, we're very good at what we do, and Davis and Fenton are two of our best. The porcupine shifter won't get anywhere near you."

"Thank you." Sandra stood and gave Davis a nervous look. "So, um, do I just give you the address of my apartment?"

"How about I walk you to your car," Davis said before holding out his arm. "I'll follow you back to your place and do a quick check of your apartment."

"Will – will you stay with me in the apartment?" she asked timidly.

"I can stay in your apartment or my car outside of your apartment," Davis said. "Whatever you're most comfortable with."

"I – I think in my apartment," Sandra said.

Davis smiled at her. "That sounds good. Shall we go?"

When they were gone, Mal stared at Bishop and Kat. "Is it just me, or does this monster porcupine shifter sound a lot like that coyote shifter that went crazy in the coffee shop?"

Kat nodded as Bishop scratched out a few more notes in Sandra's file before closing it. The door opened, and Willow stuck her head in. "Want me to take the file and get it entered into the system?"

"Thanks, Will." Bishop handed the file to her, and she squeezed Mal's arm before leaving.

Mal tapped one finger against the table. "There was a porcupine shifter bitten at the coffee shop, right?"

"Yes," Bishop said. "I never got his name or anything, but he was bitten."

"Did this Clay guy talk to you about the porcupine shifter?" Mal asked.

Kat and Bishop had filled Mal in on the details of their meeting with Clay and shared their suspicions that something was off with Stowe Laboratories.

"Nope," Bishop said. "But he did want to know if either of us were bitten or scratched."

"Interesting," Mal said. "So, we have a coyote shifter with super strength and size go crazy and bite a porcupine shifter. Then the same mutation, for lack of a better word, happens to the porcupine shifter."

"It has to be a virus of some sort," Kat said. "Transmitted by bites or scratches."

"What did you find out about Stowe Laboratories?" Bishop asked.

"Nothing," Kat said.

"Nothing?" Mal raised his eyebrow at her. "You always find something, Kat."

"Not this time," Kat said. "Everything that this Clay guy told us checks out. They are a research lab that studies the healing abilities of shifters. All shifters are volunteers, and I even called a couple of them to see exactly what they volunteered for. Mostly they gave blood samples and allowed the lab to injure them slightly and monitor how long it took them to heal. Neither had anything bad to say about the lab or the doctors that worked there."

"What about this Dr. Stowe?" Mal said.

"He's the lab head and a black bear shifter. He started the lab with his own money. His parents came from wealthy families and died in a car accident when he was nineteen. He inherited thirty million and moved to New York. Ten years later, he used the money to start Stowe Laboratories. Two years ago, he opened a second lab just outside our city and, from what I can tell, he works out of that one. I dug into their financial information, and everything is squeaky clean. No hidden monsters in the basement."

"Clay's explanation for why they're interested in this is pretty damn weak," Bishop said.

"I'm wondering why the porcupine shifter is stalking Sandra," Kat said. "According to her, she's never even spoken to a porcupine shifter before, so it's doubtful that they knew each other before he went crazy."

"Maybe it was just a coincidence," Mal said. "She was originally attacked close to her home. Maybe the porcupine shifter was still in the area, and it was just bad luck."

"Maybe," Kat said.

"We need to tell Davis and Fenton that if they do see this porcupine shifter, not to let it close enough to bite or scratch," Bishop said.

"We don't know for sure if it's even related," Kat said. "It could be another insane porcupine on a murderous rampage due to a completely different reason."

"Do you really think so?" Mal said.

Kat sighed. "No. They're related. It's too weird not to be."

She glanced at her watch. "I'm going to do a bit more digging into Stowe Labs, see what I can find."

"When does Ronin start with Mavina Sorenson?" Mal asked.

"Already has," Bishop said.

"And?" Mal asked with a grin.

Bishop rumbled laughter. "Ronin texted me late last night. He was at some club with Mavina, and he wanted to know if we provided a clothing allowance. I guess Mavina sliced his shirt off of him with those damn nails of hers."

They turned at Kat's loud hiss and studied her red face with interest as she said, "Why the fuck is she taking off his clothes?"

Bishop glanced at Mal before shrugging. "You know vamps, Kat. They're flirts."

"More like they'll fuck anything that moves." She hissed again.

"Ronin will behave," Mal said. "Stop worrying."

"I'm not worried," Kat snapped before standing. "Are you guys still good with me taking Tuesday and Wednesday off? I may have to leave a little early on Monday, depending on," she paused, "you know."

"Yes, it's no problem," Mal said.

She left, and Bishop grinned at Mal. "You ever think you'd see Kat so worked up over a bird?"

Mal shook his head. "No. It's weird to see her like this."

He started to stand, and Bishop cleared his throat. "Hey, Mal? I have something to tell you."

Mal sat back down, and Bishop glanced at the closed door before lowering his voice. "I wanted you to be one of the first people to know – Ava's pregnant."

"Holy shit," Mal said. He crossed the room and hauled Bishop to his feet before hugging him. "Bishop, that's great! Congratulations, buddy!"

Bishop gave him a pleased grin. "Thanks, Mal. It wasn't exactly planned, but we're both thrilled."

"I'm assuming Willow knows," Mal said. "She's been acting weird about Ava for the last week."

Bishop nodded. "She does. Ava confided in her that she thought she might be pregnant, and then after she took the home pregnancy test and we found out for sure, she called Willow."

"Huh, Willow's getting much better at keeping secrets," Mal said with a laugh.

"She knew I wanted to be the one to tell you. We wanted to wait until after Ava went to the doctor just in case the home test was a false positive or something. She's only a couple of months, so we'd appreciate it if you could keep it quiet for now. Ava's having coffee with Willow and Ginger tomorrow, and she'll tell Ginger, but we're waiting until she's twelve weeks to tell everyone else."

"I won't say a word," Mal said. "Will you tell Leslie?"

"We haven't decided yet. I haven't spoken to her since the day the dragon attacked Ava. She's called a few times, but I didn't answer. Still, she is my mom, and it is her grandbaby, you know?"

"Does Ava want to tell her?"

"She's letting me decide, said she would support me either way. But if I do tell her and Leslie freaks out and starts talking shit about the baby or me, Ava will...."

Mal grinned at him. "Tear your mother apart?"

"Yeah," Bishop said. "You know how she gets when she's angry."

Mal snickered. "My grandfather still talks about how she faced Leslie down in the living room." He clapped Bishop on the back. "You're going to be a great dad, Bishop."

"I hope so," Bishop said.

"You will be," Mal said. "I know it."

# CHAPTER 10

In his dream, Ginger was straddling him. She was naked, her small breasts bouncing lightly as she rocked against his dick, and her pale face flushed with excitement. He couldn't stop purring, couldn't stop from gripping her narrow hips and lifting her until he could feel the heat of her pussy on the head of his cock. He wanted her so badly, *needed* her, and he didn't want to deny himself a moment longer.

"Fenton? Open your eyes, honey."

He didn't want to open his eyes. He wanted to keep dreaming about Ginger and her tight little body and soft moans. He had continued to spend each night with her at her apartment, and his lust for her was nearly out of control. He muttered irritably and then twitched and purred when her soft hand stroked his chest.

She giggled - he loved it when she giggled - and patted his chest. "Wake up. I have a surprise for you."

He rubbed at his eyes and stretched, wondering at her little gasp, and blinked sleepily. He turned his head and stared at Ginger's empty pillow.

"Ginger?" he said hoarsely.

"Up here, honey," she said.

He became aware of her weight, of her soft skin against his for the first time. His cheetah growled happily when he turned his head and stared at the naked woman sitting on him.

"Fuck," he said, and she giggled again. "Ginger, what time is it?"

She glanced at the alarm clock. "Just after seven. Sorry, I'm a bit of an early riser, even on the weekends."

"Am I dreaming?" He felt extraordinarily stupid and slow, but he wasn't sure if he was awake or still asleep.

"No," she said. "Not dreaming, honey."

"We can't," he said. "Your ribs -"

"Are much better," she said. "I think as long as I'm on top, we'll be fine. I don't want any pressure on my ribs."

"This is not a good idea," he groaned as she stroked his cock firmly. Jesus, how the hell did she have such soft hands?

"It's an excellent idea," she said before slowly leaning over him and pressing her mouth against his. He kissed her gently, and she gave his cock a squeeze before thrusting her tongue into his mouth.

He traced the new scar on her jawline with his fingers before cupping her breast. She gasped and made a soft moaning noise when he teased her nipple.

"I really can't wait," she suddenly said. "I'm sorry, I just can't. You have no idea how badly I want you, Fenton."

"I think I have an idea," he murmured against her mouth. He slid one hand between her thighs and cupped her pussy. She was very wet, and he carefully pushed one finger into her.

"Oh!" She ground her pussy against his hand and kissed him again before sitting up. "Yeah, I definitely can't wait."

She leaned over carefully, holding one hand against her ribs, and opened the nightstand before pulling out a condom.

He stared in surprise at the condom, and she blushed a little. "I bought them last week. I really want to have sex with you, Fenton."

He purred in response, and she ripped the foil open and smoothed it over his cock. "God, you're big."

"Thank you," he said before giving her a cheeky grin.

She braced her hand against his chest, and he gripped her hips, helping to lift her as she grasped his cock and pressed the head against her narrow entrance. He thrust up a little, he just couldn't help himself, and she winced slightly.

He froze beneath her, his body screaming at him to enter her, and gave her a worried look. "We have to stop."

"Like hell, we have to stop," she said.

They both moaned when she pushed her body down onto his cock. Despite his size, he slid into her easily. She was dripping wet, and there was only the slightest pleasure-drenched resistance, and he made a harsh groan as his hands tightened on her hips.

"Holy fuck, that feels amazing."

"It does," she agreed breathlessly. "Fuck, you're so big. Move slow, okay?"

"I'll try," he groaned. He rocked his hips in a gentle up and down motion. Ginger gasped, and he reached up and cupped her breasts, kneading them lightly as she rode him carefully.

He was purring so loudly he could barely hear her soft moans and sighs of pleasure. She rested her hands on his chest before rocking back and forth. They moved together in long, slow strokes. Purring and panting harshly, Fenton watched as Ginger moved her hand between her thighs.

She hesitated and gave him an anxious look. "Do you mind if I, um, touch myself? I can't always climax from sex alone."

He shook his head. "I told you, love, anytime you want to touch yourself, you go right ahead."

She blushed prettily and rubbed her pussy.

"Lean back," he said hoarsely. "I want to watch you rub your pretty little clit."

Her blush deepened, but she did what he asked. He moved his hands to her pussy, stroking the soft dark curls before spreading her apart with his thumbs. He watched her fingers rub her swollen clit, his hips speeding up in response, and it only took a moment or two before she was making loud moans of pleasure and grinding her pussy on his cock. He growled, his fangs descending as she rubbed her clit furiously before arching her back and climaxing. Her pussy squeezed his cock rhythmically, and he was lost. His hands dug into her hips, and he thrust twice more and came hard. He shuddered beneath her, his hands clenching and unclenching around her hips as she stroked his chest with one hand and took harsh gulps of air. Her other hand was pressed tightly against her side, and when his brain finally started working again, he stared at her in dismay.

"I hurt you."

"No, you didn't. It's just a little tender but trust me," she leaned over and kissed him lightly, "it was so worth it."

He smiled at her before helping her ease off his body. She relaxed on the bed with a soft sigh as he disposed of the condom and curled up next to her. "That was the best morning wake-up call ever."

She giggled and cupped his cheek. "Does this mean I can convince you to stay with me again tonight?"

"Love, I'll stay with you forever," he said. His eyes widened as he realized what he'd just blurted out, and he cleared his throat. "Sorry, that was creepy sounding. I meant that I'll stay with you for as long as you need me."

She gave him a solemn look, and his heart pounded in his chest when she said, "Forever sounds about right to me, Fenton."

———

"I'M SORRY I'M LATE," GINGER SAID AS SHE SAT DOWN NEXT to Ava.

"No problem," Ava said. "We got your coffee already. Hey, I switched shifts with Bess, so I'm working with you tomorrow on your first day back."

"That's great," Ginger said. "Thanks, honey. How are you feeling?"

"Better," Ava said.

Ginger took a sip of her coffee as Willow leaned forward and studied her closely.

"What?" Ginger said.

"You had sex with Fenton," Willow announced.

"Willow! Keep your voice down!" Ginger looked around the busy coffee shop as Ava grinned.

"Well, you did – didn't you," Willow said. "Don't try to deny it. I know an 'I just had amazing sex' face when I see it."

Ginger, blushing furiously, nodded. "Yes, we slept together."

"And? How was it?" Willow said. "Everything you had hoped for?"

"And more," Ginger said.

Willow nudged Ava. "She's talking about his penis."

Ava burst into laughter, and Willow grinned at her. "What? She totally is. Ginger?"

Ginger took a sip of coffee. "I totally am."

"See!" Willow said to Ava. "I'll say one thing – shifters

145

are certainly blessed in that department. Thank God that Mal marked me as his mate. I could never go back to normal size penis after being with Mal."

"Size isn't everything, Willow," Ava said.

"Says the woman sleeping with a grizzly shifter," Willow said to Ginger. "Did you know that grizzly shifters have their own line of condoms? They're too big to fit into regular ones."

"Really?" Ginger said. "Good for you, Ava."

"As much as I'm enjoying pretending that we're teenage girls who've never seen a damn penis before," Ava said dryly, "I have some news."

She took a deep breath and smiled at Ginger. "I'm pregnant."

Ginger's mouth dropped open. "You're pregnant?"

"I am. Just a couple of months, so we're keeping it quiet for now. Only you, Willow, and Mal know at the moment."

"Oh, honey," Ginger said, "I'm so happy for you!"

"Thank you." Ava was careful not to touch Ginger's ribs when Ginger hugged her tightly.

"I can't believe it," Ginger said. "This is great."

"It is," Ava said. "And I can hardly believe it myself."

"You'll believe it when you're trying to give birth to a giant-headed baby," Willow said with a laugh.

"Will you know right away if the baby is a shifter?" Ginger asked.

Ava nodded. "Yes. Well, I won't, but Bishop says that he'll be able to smell if the baby is a shifter or not."

"That's so cool," Willow said. "Do you think Bishop will be upset if it isn't a shifter?"

"No. He says he doesn't care at all."

"What happens if it is a shifter and you're feeding it, and

it shifts?" Willow asked. "Will you have a teeny bear with no teeth on your boob?"

Ava and Ginger laughed as Willow shrugged. "Hey, it's a valid question."

"Shifters don't shift for the first time until they're two or three years old," Ava said. "And Bishop said he didn't shift until he was nearly four, so our baby might take longer as well.'

"Are you going to tell Leslie?" Willow asked.

Ava sighed. "Not sure yet. I'm leaving it up to Bishop to decide, she's his mother, but if we do and she says one word against Bishop or this baby, I'll beat her to a pulp."

Willow laughed. "Only you would threaten to beat up a grizzly shifter."

She squeezed Ava's hand before smiling at Ginger. "So, Kat and her best friend Bria are going to this club tonight, and they've invited Ava and me to go with them. We're doing a girl's night. Kat said to tell you that you were invited as well. Are you interested?"

"Oh, um…" Ginger hesitated, "well, Fenton is coming over after work tonight and, you know…."

"I do know," Willow said. "Say no more. Have fun sexing up your cheetah shifter – try not to crack another rib, okay?"

Ginger laughed. "I'll be careful."

---

"IT'S GOOD TO FINALLY MEET YOU, BRIA!" WILLOW SAID. "Kat's told me so much about you."

"It's nice to meet you too," Bria said. "Kat said you were mated to Mal?"

"I am," Willow said.

"And you're with Bishop?" Bria smiled at Ava.

"Yes," Ava said.

"I never thought Bishop would get a girlfriend. He's always so awkward around women," Bria said with a grin.

Ava laughed. "He occasionally suffers from social anxiety."

Kat barely paid attention to their small talk. Instead, she scanned the club, her long red nails tapping the table and her nostrils flaring repeatedly. The club was on the bigger side with numerous tables and an extra-large dance floor. They had sat as far from the dance floor as they could – the music was a little quieter but not by much – and ordered some drinks.

"You know, I was a little surprised when Kat invited us for a girls' night at this club," Bria said. "A club isn't usually her scene."

"Oh, it's because she knows Ronin is going to be here with that little vampire tart," Willow said.

Kat stiffened and gave Willow a sharp look. "It isn't, Willow."

"It is," Willow said as Bria laughed. "You're her best friend. I'm sure you know how badly she's got the hots for him."

Bria snickered again. "I have an idea."

"I do not have the hots for him," Kat said. "I have no idea where Ronin will be tonight with Mavina." She said the vampire's name with an angry little hiss, her jaguar's jealousy heightening her own.

"She's fibbing," Willow said. "She was at the office when Ronin called in to tell me where he and Mavina would be tonight. She read the whiteboard."

"Do they always have to call in when they're doing personal protection?" Bria asked.

"No, not usually. But Mal says the vampire that's stalking

Mavina is very dangerous, so it's better and safer for Ronin if we know where he is at all times. The other night he texted Mal seven different times. Mavina kept dragging him all over the city. But, hey, safety first, right? Mal even gave Ronin this pager thing, so if the vampire does show up, all Ronin has to do is hit a button, and it will alert Mal and Bishop, and they'll haul ass to wherever he is."

"Yeah, but does that help?" Bria asked. "If this vampire is as old and dangerous as you think, he'd be incredibly fast. He could do some serious damage in a matter of minutes."

"There's been no sign of this vampire since Mavina's parents hired us," Kat said. "I'm starting to suspect that Mavina exaggerated her claims that he was stalking her. If he were that interested in her, he would have shown up long before now."

"Maybe you're right," Willow said. "Ronin says Mavina is a terrible flirt and that she's enjoyed the company of more than one man in a club bathroom nearly every time they go out. Do you know she makes Ronin watch while she has sex with them? Says he's supposed to keep his eyes on her at all times."

"Seriously?" Ava said.

"Yep," Willow said. "I'm all for letting your kink flag fly, but that's a little too kinky for me. Anyway, you'd think if this old vampire dude were obsessed with her, he wouldn't like that she's having sex with a bunch of men that weren't him."

She grinned at Kat. "Any sign of your bird yet, Kat?"

Kat scowled at her. "Time for a subject change. Ava, when's the baby due?"

Ava's mouth dropped open. "Willow! I asked you to keep it a secret!"

"I did," Willow protested. "I didn't tell Kat, I swear."

149

Kat laughed. "Willow didn't say anything to me, and neither did Bishop, but I'm not stupid. You were sick with the," she made little air quotes with her fingers "flu, Bishop's been the happiest I've ever seen him the last week or so, and you're drinking club soda. It wasn't hard to figure out."

She leaned across the table and squeezed Ava's arm. "Congratulations, by the way. I'm very happy for you both."

"Thanks, Kat," Ava said. "We're happy too."

"Well, congratulations," Bria said. She held up her glass, and Ava clinked hers against it before they both drank. "Do you know if you're having a boy or a -"

Kat's loud hiss interrupted her, and the three women watched as Kat's fangs descended and her nails scratched gouges into the smooth wooden tabletop. They followed her gaze to the dance floor.

Mavina, wearing a skin-tight pair of jeans and a shimmering, silver top, stood in the middle of the dance floor. She had Ronin by the hand, and Kat hissed again when she rubbed her body against his before reaching for his crotch. He caught her hand and shook his head, and she pouted at him. He said something, and she rolled her eyes before turning her body and grinding her ass against his crotch.

He stepped back, and Willow snickered when the sexy vampire nearly fell on her ass. Mavina bared her fangs at Ronin, who shrugged. She flipped him the bird, turned, and sidled up to a group of twenty-something men who were staring open-mouthed at her. Within minutes she was in the middle of the group, dancing seductively, and Ronin backed away.

"Ronin! Hey, Ronin!" Willow screamed at the top of her lungs.

"Willow, don't," Kat said and then groaned when Ronin

immediately turned and nodded at them before crossing the crowded dance floor.

He joined them at their table, letting his arm brush casually against Kat's as he continued to watch Mavina.

"Hello, ladies." He scanned the club as he spoke. His body was tense and alert, and Kat refused to admit that she was a little turned on by his intensity. On the other hand, her jaguar was ready to haul him off to the nearest bed.

"Hey, Ronin. Having fun with your vampire?" Willow asked.

"Something like that," he said cheerfully. He glanced briefly at them before his gaze returned to Mavina. "What are you lovely ladies doing here this evening?"

"Oh, we thought we'd check out the club scene," Willow said. "Maybe find a handsome cat shifter for our Katarina."

Ronin jerked, and he stared at Kat before returning his gaze to Mavina. "Plenty to choose from in here."

Kat glared at Willow, who winked at her.

"I'm not looking for a cat shifter," Kat said.

"That's true," Willow said to Ava and Bria. "She prefers feathers."

Kat hissed at her as a grin broke out on Ronin's face. He was still watching Mavina and the men who surrounded her, but he couldn't resist teasing her. "I've heard a rumour about that."

Kat gave Bria a desperate look, and Bria slid off her stool and held out her hand. "Hi, Ronin. I'm Bria."

He smiled at her and shook her hand briefly. "Nice to meet you, Bria."

"Nice to meet you too."

There was a moment of silence that Ava broke. "Wow, Mavina certainly attracts a lot of attention, huh?"

"You have no idea," Ronin said. "It's been a -"

There was a light puff of wind, and Ava made a startled gasp when Mavina appeared in front of them.

"Holy shit," Willow said. "Can all vampires move that fast?"

"Actually, I'm rather slow," Mavina said as she draped her arms over Ronin's shoulders. "But slow is a good thing, isn't it, Ronin?"

"Whatever you say, Mavina," Ronin said.

"If that's slow, I'd hate to see fast," Willow said to Ava.

Mavina studied her before drifting closer. "Aren't you the prettiest little thing? What's your name?"

"Willow," Willow said and held out her hand. Mavina took her hand and raised it to her mouth. She inhaled deeply before licking the pulse in her wrist. "You smell delicious, Willow. Would you like to come home with me tonight?"

"Uh, that's nice of you to offer, but my mate is a wolf shifter, and he's not really into sharing," Willow said.

"Pity." Mavina turned to Ava. "I love your hair."

Ava gave Willow a nervous look when Mavina picked up a strand of Ava's long, red hair and rubbed it against her face. She moved a little closer and pressed her full breasts against Ava's arm. "How about you, Red? Would you like to find out what it's like to have a vampire in your bed? Or are you mated as well?"

"She is," Willow said quickly. "To a big old grizzly who *really* doesn't like to share."

A scowl crossed Mavina's face, and Bria shook her head when she started to move toward her. "In a relationship."

"You three are so boring," Mavina sighed. She glanced at Kat, but Kat kept her gaze firmly on Ronin. Mavina made a soft noise of displeasure before moving to Ronin and wrapping her arms around his waist. She rested her head on his chest and traced her fingers over the tattoos on his arm. "Hello, Ms. Frost."

"Hello, Mavina," Kat said.

"Are you here checking up on your employee?"

"No, I -"

"He's doing a wonderful job. You were right when you said he was the best man for the job. I feel so safe when I'm with him. He never lets me out of his sight, you know."

She paused and squeezed Ronin's arm. "Well, except for the other night when I blindfolded him while we were fucking."

Hot jealousy made her jaguar shoot forward. Her eyes turned yellow, her pupils narrowing into slits, and she growled loudly before lunging for Mavina. Ronin shoved the vampire away and stepped in front of Kat. He threw one arm around her waist and used his free hand to cup the back of her head.

"Let me go!" she growled.

"No," he said before pressing his mouth against her ear. "She's lying, Katarina. You know she is. You're the only one I want to fuck."

Her body shivered against his, and he loosened his hand around her waist and stroked her lower back through her shirt. "I have no interest in her. If I could, I'd fuck you right here in this club and make her watch for a change."

Another shiver went through her, and he leaned back to stare at her. "Do you believe me?"

She nodded, and he hesitated before muttering, "fuck it". He dropped his mouth to Kat's in a brief but searing kiss before releasing her so quickly she staggered a little.

He turned and ignored Mavina's glare, taking her by the arm. "Time to find another club, Mavina."

"Fine," she hissed. "And just so you know – I wouldn't watch you fuck her if you paid me to."

She stormed away as Ronin rolled his eyes and followed her.

"Ava?" Willow said.

"Yeah?"

"Is it warm in here, or am I just totally turned on by that kiss Ronin gave Kat?"

"It was pretty intense," Ava said with a small grin as heat rose in Kat's cheeks.

"What did Mavina mean when she said she wouldn't watch Ronin, uh, bone you if you paid her?" Willow asked.

"Nothing," Kat muttered.

Bria finished her glass of wine. "Ronin told Kat that Mavina was lying, and Kat was the only one he wanted to fuck. Then he said he wanted to fuck her right here in the club and make Mavina watch."

"Good gravy," Willow said before fanning herself.

"Bria!" Kat glared at her best friend, and Bria shrugged.

"I have good hearing."

"It doesn't mean you have to share a private conversation," Kat said.

"Mavina kind of spilled the beans, not me," Bria said.

Kat rubbed at her forehead, and Bria patted her arm. "Sorry, Kit-Kat. I thought the three of you were pretty close."

"We are," Willow said. "And it's pretty darn obvious that Ronin wants to have sex with Kat, so you weren't telling us anything we didn't already know. Except for that part about Ronin being an exhibitionist. That's a bit of a surprise."

"Don't be angry with me, Kat," Bria said before hugging her.

"I'm not," Kat said. "I'm just suddenly exhausted. Do you mind if I call it a night?"

"Not at all," Willow said. "After watching that kiss Ronin gave you, I am suddenly very anxious to get home to Mal."

Ava and Bria burst into laughter, and even Kat couldn't help but grin. "You're nuts, Willow."

"A little," Willow said. "Let's go, ladies. I've got a wolf shifter to bang."

CHAPTER 11

"Hello, Willow."

"Hey, Ronin." Willow smiled at the bird shifter. "Dropping off your timesheet?"

"Yes." He handed her the paper before leaning against the desk. "How are you?"

"I'm good, thanks. How's it going with that sex-tart vampire? Whew, she's something else, huh?"

"You have no idea," Ronin said. "Swear to God, it's like she has six hands."

Willow laughed. "Mal said this morning that Mavina and her family left for a vacation in Italy this week. I bet you're happy to have a break."

Ronin nodded before glancing at Kat's closed office door. "It seems kind of quiet in here for a Monday."

A small smile crossed Willow's face. "Mal and Bishop are meeting with a client and will be back in about half an hour, and Kat left early."

"Oh?" Ronin's voice was deceptively casual. "She has an appointment?"

"No," Willow said. "She won't be back until Thursday."

157

Ronin glanced at her door again. "She's gone two days? Is she on a business trip?"

"Oh, um, no, she's at home," Willow said. She might be terrible at keeping secrets, but there was no way in hell she was telling Ronin that Kat was in heat. Kat would slice her into bits.

A strange look crossed Ronin's face – a combination of anger and desire – and Willow was pretty damn sure that Ronin had already figured it out. She cleared her throat. "Ronin? What's wrong?"

"Nothing," he said with none of his usual cheeriness. "See you later, Willow."

*You know how creepy this is, right?*

*Shut up.*

*Seriously, you're sitting outside of your boss's house while she's inside fucking a tiger shifter. Go home, buddy. She doesn't want you, and you're getting more pathetic by the day.*

Ronin tapped his fingers against the steering wheel. Kat's car was the only car in the driveway, but that didn't mean shit. Her heat cycle had started, and she hadn't called him, which meant the tiger shifter was in her bed at this very moment.

Anger flooded through him at the thought of Kat fucking someone other than him, and he was out of his car and stomping up her driveway before he could stop himself.

*Stop it! What are you going to do? Throw the tiger shifter out of the house and take his place? You think that will make you feel better? Knowing that Kat will fuck you but only because you got rid of her first choice?*

He paused with his fist raised to pound on the door. Jesus, what the hell was wrong with him? He couldn't –

His head cocked, and, not caring if Kat's neighbours were watching, he pressed his ear against the door. He had excellent hearing, all birds did, and when he heard the soft moans and the low buzzing, a grin crossed his face. The sound of Kat's vibrator didn't necessarily mean the tiger shifter wasn't with her. Still, if Kat's heat had just started and the tiger already needed a vibrator to help him satisfy her heat, then she'd probably be happy if Ronin kicked him out of her house and took over. He knocked lightly and waited for a minute or two. When she didn't come to the door, he snagged the spare key from under the flowerpot and let himself into the house.

KAT TWISTED AND TURNED ON THE COUCH. HER HEAT HAD started half an hour ago, and already she regretted her choice to try to make it through on her own. Her cat begged incessantly for Ronin, and she tried desperately to ignore it as she slipped the vibrator into her yoga pants and pressed it against her clit. It sent a shiver of pleasure through her, and she moaned loudly before moving the vibrator to her wet entrance and pushing it in.

She was dimly aware of knocking, but she was already very close, and the knocking was distant and meaningless. She slid the vibrator in and out and pretended it was Ronin's hard cock. She closed her eyes as her hips rose and fell, and she squeezed her breast, circling her thumb over her nipple.

"Ronin," she moaned as her orgasm washed over. She arched her back and moaned his name again as her pussy clenched around the vibrator. She collapsed against the couch, her eyes still shut and listened to the low buzz of the vibrator.

"Fuck," she said. Desire was already starting to creep back in, and her cat hissed in anger.

*Find him! Take what is ours!*

"No," she said. "I can't."

"Can't what, Kitten?"

She screamed, her entire body jerking wildly, and nearly fell off the couch as her eyes flew open. Ronin stood at the end of the sofa, and her cat purred loudly at the sight of him.

"Wh-what are you doing here?"

I was in the area, stopped by, and heard rather alarming noises. I was worried about you," he said with a slow grin.

"How the hell did you get in here?" Redness crept across her cheeks. The fucking vibrator was still vibrating away, and her cat was purring and meowing so loudly she could barely think straight.

"Key under the flowerpot, remember?"

"I – you should go," she said. Her cat's yowl of anger turned into a satisfied purr when Ronin dropped onto her and pinned her to the couch.

"You need to go," she said.

"Did you know your crotch is buzzing?" he asked teasingly.

"No, it isn't," she lied.

"No?" His hand was down her pants and tugging lightly on the vibrator before she knew what was happening.

Her pelvis arched, and she cried out when he pulled the vibrator from her aching pussy and ran the tip of it across her swollen clit.

"Is it your heat cycle?" he asked.

She nodded, and he licked her mouth before nuzzling her

throat. "Didn't you make arrangements with a friendly tiger shifter to help you?"

She moaned as he ran the vibrator over her clit again and used his other hand to tug her shirt over her head.

"Gorgeous," he whispered before sucking one swollen and hard nipple into his mouth.

She cried out again, her hands clutching helplessly at his back as he teased each nipple with his teeth and tongue.

"Didn't you?" He lifted his head and stared at her.

"Ronin, please."

"Katarina, didn't you?"

"Yes," she hissed at him.

"So why are you alone on your couch, screaming my name while you make yourself come with a vibrator?"

She blushed furiously. "I didn't scream your name."

He grinned at her, "You will."

When she didn't reply, he licked her mouth again, pulling his head back when she tried to kiss him. "Tell me why the tiger shifter isn't here."

"He was busy."

"That sounds like a lie to me. And, if he wanted to do something else other than fuck you during your," he paused, "time of need, then he's a moron."

He studied her carefully. "Is he a moron, Katarina?"

"No," she said.

"Then why isn't he here?"

"I didn't want him."

"Who do you want?"

"You."

A satisfied grin crossed his face. "I want you too, Kitten."

"Please, Ronin," she suddenly begged, "I can't take it. I need you so badly."

He pushed the vibrator into her aching pussy, and she

made a harsh cry of need before bucking her hips against him.

"Does it feel good, Kitten?"

"Yes," she breathed.

"But you need more?"

"Yes." She lifted her head and kissed him hard on the mouth. "I need your cock, Ronin. Don't make me wait any longer."

He sat up, taking the vibrator with him, and she hissed angrily at him as she scrambled into a sitting position. He pulled his shirt over his head and dropped it on the couch. He undid his jeans and pushed them and his briefs down past his knees, smiling when she purred loudly at the sight of his erect cock.

"Hurry," she demanded as she shoved her yoga pants down her legs and threw them on the floor.

"Patience, Kitten. Here, hold this."

He handed her the vibrator, and she shut it off and tossed it on the couch as he tried to kick off his pants. She growled again before climbing on top of him.

"Patience, remem -"

He groaned when she impaled herself on his cock. She gripped his shoulders and rode him frantically as her purring grew to a deafening level. He muttered a harsh curse when her pussy clamped down on his cock, and her entire body shuddered above him. She collapsed against his chest, purring softly. He rubbed her back as she licked at his neck with her warm tongue.

"Better?" he asked.

She shook her head and bit him on the shoulder. "Don't come yet. I need more, Ronin. Do you hear me?"

"I hear you, Kitten. Take what you need." He cupped her

ass as she kissed him, pushing her tongue into his mouth and flicking it against his.

He returned her frantic kisses before moving his hands to her hips and lifting her off of him. She hissed angrily and scratched at him with her nails, and he caught her by the wrists and placed a light kiss on the palms of her hands.

"Easy, Kitten." He stood and made a grunt of surprise when she leaped onto him. She wrapped her legs around his waist as he staggered back, and she slid her hand between their bodies. His cock was back inside her warmth before he had even caught his balance, and he put one arm around her waist as she locked her hands behind his neck.

"Jesus, you're flexible."

"I'm a cat," she snapped. "Fuck me, Ronin!"

"I will," he soothed, "but how about we take this to the bedroom?"

"Yes, the bedroom is a good idea," she muttered as she rocked back and forth on his dick.

"Sweetheart, you're going to have to let me go." He grinned at her. "I can't walk with my pants around my ankles."

She hissed again and reluctantly released him, making a soft noise of displeasure when his cock slid out of her. They were only halfway up the stairs when she made a mewling, hissing noise and tripped him. He landed on the stairs with a thud, and she flipped him onto his back.

"Can't wait," she moaned. She tried to straddle him and growled when Ronin grabbed her arms. They struggled briefly, but he overpowered her and pushed her face down onto the stairs, holding her down with one hand on her back. She snarled at him, and he dodged her flailing claws before kneeling on the stair below her.

"Hands and knees, Kitten," he said as he gathered her

dark hair into a ponytail. She hurried to obey, her pussy throbbing so badly she couldn't stand it.

"Please," she said in a low voice, "please, I need it."

He didn't reply, but his hard thighs were pushing apart her soft ones, and she screamed with pleasure when he shoved his cock into her pussy. He fucked her roughly, his hand pulling her hair as he leaned over her and rested his other hand on the stair above her.

"Harder," she said.

He gave her a sexy grin before pounding into her. She purred and met each of his strokes with a hard thrust of her hips. Her claws were digging into the stairs, leaving shallow furrows in the gleaming wood, and Ronin groaned when she climaxed hard, her body shaking under his.

He eased out of her and sat on the stairs, panting as she made a soft little purr and sat up. He studied her face as she pushed her hair back. She knew what she looked like. Knew that this was the first time he saw her close to her cat form without her actually shifting. Her eyes were dark yellow, and her pupils had turned to narrow slits. Her purring slowed then stopped when Ronin's gaze dropped to her fangs. She tried to ignore the cycle of need that was already starting up in her belly again.

"What's wrong?" she asked.

"Those are some sharp fangs, Kitten," he said.

With a slight wince, she retracted her fangs. "I won't hurt you, Ronin. Don't – don't leave, okay? I won't bite, I prom-ise." Her gaze drifted to the bite on his shoulder. "I mean, I won't bite you again. I can control it."

If he left her now, she really would go crazy.

*He's mine! I'm not letting him leave!* Her cat snarled.

Ronin stood, and a jolt of pure panic went through her.

Fuck! He was leaving! Her overheated brain tried to formulate a plan.

*Tie him to the bed*, her cat said.

*Not helping!* she snarled. As appealing as the thought of Ronin tied to her bed was, when her heat cycle was over, and she could think straight again, she would let him go. He would go straight to the police and have her arrested for kidnapping and –

"I keep telling you, Kitten. I'm not afraid of a little pussy cat like you," he said.

She blinked at him, "What?"

He started up the stairs, grinning at her over his shoulder before calling softly, "Here, kitty, kitty."

She leaped gracefully to her feet and followed him up the stairs to her bedroom. He picked her up – God, he was strong for a bird – and dropped her onto the bed.

"Fuck me, Ronin," she begged.

He shook his head. "Not yet."

Her angry growl turned into a purr of delight when he spread her legs and stretched out between them.

"Don't – don't tease me, little bird," she moaned as his warm breath on her pussy sent shivers down her back. "Please, I can't wait. It hurts."

"I know," he said.

She screamed at the first touch of his tongue against her pussy. He licked her clit feverishly, his tongue warm and wet and exactly what she needed. He sucked on her clit as he pushed two fingers into her and stroked her. She arched her back, her hands fisting in his hair and rode his face to an earth-shattering climax.

"Again," she purred.

"You're the boss," he said with a small grin before lowering his mouth to her pussy again.

"Look at me, Katarina."

Kat, purring loudly, stared up at Ronin.

"Better?" he asked.

She nodded. "Yes, thank you, Ronin."

"You're welcome, sweetheart. Spread your legs wider for me."

She spread her legs as he lowered his body onto hers. He had spent over an hour with his face between her thighs, and she touched his mouth and chin with the pads of her fingers.

"You're really good at eating pussy," she said.

"Thank you," he laughed.

His laugh turned into a low moan of pleasure as he slid his cock into her. She squeezed his hips with her thighs as he made a rough thrust. The need wasn't as intense now. The multiple orgasms Ronin had given her with his mouth and fingers had eased the worst of it, but she still needed him to fuck her. He moved slowly in her, the look on his face one of tightly controlled need, and she cupped his cheek before kissing him deeply.

"I don't want it slow," she said against his mouth.

"Thank fucking Christ," he muttered.

She cried out when he propped himself on his hands above her and fucked her hard and fast. She met each of his thrusts, watching his face as another orgasm built in her belly.

"Pretty bird," she purred softly. "My pretty bird. Say it."

He didn't reply, and her cat hissed angrily. Knowing she shouldn't but unable to help it, she sank her claws into his back. "Say it, Ronin."

He grunted with pain, but his hips continued to slap against hers in a rough rhythm that made little trills of excitement spill from her lips. She purred again before raking her claws down his back.

"Mine. Say it," she growled again.

"Yours," he panted. "Yours, Kat."

His words sent her over the edge, and she scratched at his back as her pussy clenched around his thick cock. He cried out, his head falling back and his body shuddering as he climaxed. She lifted her head and bit him on the shoulder again, sinking her fangs into his hard flesh as he twitched and jerked against her.

He collapsed on top of her, and she wrapped all of her limbs around him. He buried his face in her throat, and she repeatedly licked at the bite mark on his shoulder. He moved off of her before sitting up. Kat sat up, dead tired but more than a little anxious that Ronin would leave her.

"Don't leave, Ronin. I feel okay now but in a few hours…."

She yawned hugely as he rubbed her thigh. "I'm not leaving, Kat."

"Will you stay for my entire heat cycle?" she asked as she sank onto her back and closed her eyes. "It's not over until Wednesday."

"I'll stay," he said.

She purred sleepily and curled onto her side, closing her eyes and drifting into the darkness of sleep.

---

WHEN RONIN WAS SURE KAT WAS ASLEEP, HE SLID OFF THE bed and walked to the bathroom. He stared at his back in the mirror over the sink. Puncture marks and long jagged scratches marked his back, and blood trickled from a few of them. He grinned to himself before turning on the shower. He winced as the hot water washed over his back and then smiled again. He had never been with a cat shifter before, and while he was a little unprepared for just how deeply his little Kitten would scratch, he could admit that it was a bit of a turn on when she clawed him while she climaxed.

*Your little Kitten?*

The smile dropped from his face, and he washed quickly before shutting off the shower and drying off. Kat wanted him, that was more than obvious, but if he hadn't shown up here today, she wouldn't have called him. She would have gone through agony alone, or more likely, he grimaced at himself in the mirror, she would have eventually called the tiger shifter.

He sighed and moved silently back to the bedroom. Kat was still sleeping, and he slid into the bed beside her. He turned on his side to face her, resting one hand tentatively on her hip. Her eyes popped open, they were back to her normal colour, and she made a soft trill before purring loudly. She plastered her naked body against his and pressed a kiss against his throat.

"Again?" he asked as he cupped her ass and kneaded it lightly.

"No," she said sleepily. "I'm good right now." She rubbed her face and head against him as her purr loudened. "I like to cuddle in between. Is that okay?"

He rubbed her back. "Cuddling is part of the servicing, Kitten."

Her purring stopped, and a scowl crossed her face. "Don't call it that. You're not servicing me."

"What is it that I'm doing then?" He stroked her dark hair, marveling at the softness of it.

"Fucking me," she said softly before purring again. "You're very good at fucking me, pretty bird."

He pressed a light kiss against her mouth, and she smiled briefly.

"I'm so glad you're here," she said as she rubbed her face against his chest again.

"I am, too," he said. A sated and sleepy Kat was a Kat who had her guard down for the first time since he met her. He hesitated only briefly before saying, "Why didn't you call the tiger shifter?"

"Because my cat wants the pretty little bird," she confessed sleepily. "My pretty bird," she added in a soft and dreamy voice.

"What would you have done if I hadn't shown up?"

"Called you," she admitted before yawning. "Begged my pretty bird to come over and fuck me." She cracked open one eye, "Would you have?"

"Yes. I'm here, aren't I?" he said with a slight grin.

"Why did you come over?" She was struggling to stay awake and looked ridiculously adorable.

"Willow mentioned you were taking a couple of days off. I knew what it meant," he said.

"What if the tiger shifter had been here?"

His hand tightened on her ass, and she made a soft mew of discomfort. He relaxed his grip and forced himself to sound light-hearted. "I would have kicked him out of your house."

She smiled and licked his throat. "I told him last week I didn't need his help. I would have just been pretending he was you, anyway."

He knew he was grinning smugly, but Kat's eyes were closed, and she didn't notice. "I thought I could manage it alone, but I would have broken down and called you. I need you, Ronin."

She said the last in a sleepy little mutter before her body

relaxed against him and her grip loosened. He bent his head and kissed her forehead before whispering, "I need you too, Kat."

---

HE WATCHED KAT'S FIRM ASS BOUNCE ON HIS LAP BEFORE tearing his gaze away. He'd come for sure if he kept watching. Her pussy squeezed him tightly, and he groaned, his hands digging into her hips. He was sitting on the couch with Kat on his lap. Her back was turned to him, and she braced her hands on his knees and rode him enthusiastically. She was both very strong and incredibly limber, and he watched as she lifted her body up and down before rotating her hips.

"Fuck!" His breath exploded from his lungs, and she made a throaty laugh before staring at him over her shoulder.

"Does my pretty bird like that?"

"God, yes," he panted.

It was late Tuesday morning, and Kat's heat was still going strong. He'd lost track of how many times he'd fucked her, how many times he'd eaten her pussy. She was insatiable, and he loved every fucking minute of it.

She stood and turned before straddling him and thrusting down onto his cock. She purred happily, her eyes glowing and her nails sharp claws, and he groaned loudly when she resumed her bouncing.

"I love your cock," she panted.

He made a hard little thrust, and she trilled with pleasure before licking his mouth. "It's my cock, isn't it?"

Already her nails were starting to dig into his ribs, and he nodded quickly. "Yes, Kat, it's yours."

"You belong to me," she said in a soft voice. "Say you belong to me, little bird."

"I belong to you," he said.

She purred with pleasure, and he cupped her breasts and tugged on her nipples as she reached down and rubbed at her clit.

He had discovered relatively quickly that if he disagreed with her and didn't tell her that he belonged to her, she would scratch and claw him until he did. To save his chest and back from being completely shredded, he had told her what she wanted to hear.

*Is that why? Or are you starting to think you do belong to her?*

He ignored his inner voice and tweaked Kat's nipple until she arched her back and made a soft moan of delight. He leaned forward and rubbed his rough stubble against the tip before sucking it into his mouth.

She was tightening around him, her purrs of pleasure growing more high-pitched, and he now easily recognized the signs of her approaching orgasm. He sucked harder, nipping at her with his teeth – the closer she came to coming, the rougher she liked it – and she hissed her pleasure before clutching his shoulders.

He pulled away and took her wrists in one big hand, holding them captive as she glared at him. "Let me go, little bird."

"No, sweetheart," he said. "You need to play nice this time."

She growled at him, and he just barely had time to clamp his other hand on the back of her neck to prevent her from sinking her fangs into his already bruised and bitten shoulder. Being restrained sent her desire into overdrive, and she writhed and squirmed and ground her pussy against him before moaning his name and coming all over his cock. He pumped his hips furiously as she squeezed her knees against his thighs and held on. Her full breasts bounced, and he stared greedily at them before, with a hoarse moan, finding his release. She collapsed against him, and he released her wrists and rubbed the back of her neck. She purred and kissed his chest as they relaxed against the couch.

"Good for now?" he asked.

She nodded before licking at the deep scratches on his chest. He stroked her dark hair and grinned when her stomach growled. They hadn't eaten last night, she had been too amped up to want anything but his cock, and he squeezed her ass before lifting her and placing her on the couch. She sprawled on her back and purred contently as he stood.

"Hungry, Kat?"

"Yes," she said. "Feed me, Ronin."

He squeezed her leg before walking naked to the kitchen. He peered into the fridge and wasn't surprised to see a large platter of raw meat already cut up into chunks. He had done some googling on cat shifter's heats last week and discovered that most cats ate their meat raw during their heat. He grabbed a plate and moved some of the raw meat onto it before rummaging in the fridge again. There was a container of leftover cooked chicken, and he grabbed it and set it next to the plate of raw meat before pouring them both glasses of water. He carried it into the living room and set it on the coffee table as Kat sat up and snatched the plate of meat. She ate enthusiastically, making small sounds of pleasure as he ate his chicken.

"This is so good," she said before tossing a piece of beef into her mouth.

"Glad you like it," he said.

She drank her water and sat patiently as he finished his food.

"Nap time?" he asked before drinking his glass of water.

She stretched. "I'm going to have a shower first. Will you join me?"

He nodded, and she stood and took his hand, tugging him to his feet. "Will you eat my pussy in the shower?"

"Yes."

She purred loudly and rubbed her head against his chest. He kissed the top of her head before leading her toward the stairs.

# CHAPTER 12

R onin added some oil to the pan and waited for it to
heat. It was late afternoon on Wednesday, and Kat
was sound asleep upstairs. He suspected that her heat was
finished. Her need for him over the last six hours or so had
progressively lessened, and he ignored his twinge of disappointment. He had just spent the last forty-eight hours
fucking Kat. He was tired, and his entire body ached. He
should be happy, should be looking forward to going home
and sleeping for the next twenty-four hours, but he wasn't.
Kat would kick him out the minute she woke up, and that was
that.

*She'll want you again for her next heat.*

Yeah, she probably would. But the thought of having to
go an entire month before he was allowed to touch her again
made him feel grumpy and unsettled. Kat was only using him
for her heat, which was for the best. He'd be putting her in
danger if it was anything more.

*Maybe they've given up? It's been over two years. Lora is
probably dead by now.*

Sorrow flooded through him, and he closed his eyes for a

moment. Lora had been his partner for only a year and a half, but they had grown close very quickly. Hell, he had spent more time at her and Wyatt's house than he had his own. She was a damn good cop, and their partnership was one of mutual friendship and respect.

He sighed before adding some meat to the pan. There was no point in dwelling on the past. Lora had gotten sick. He had tried to help her and failed. Then Wyatt had lost his goddamn mind and kept him prisoner for over a month. He shuddered as he remembered the pain, the horrifying feeling of losing control, and the overwhelming hunger.

*Stop, Ronin! Don't think about it, for God's sake. Do you want the nightmares to come back?*

He added some spices to the cooking meat and froze when the front door slammed. Quick and impatient footsteps tapped down the hallway.

"Katarina, you cannot keep ignoring my texts. Do you have any idea how rude that is?" A tall, dark-haired woman, who looked remarkably similar to Kat, appeared in the kitchen.

She made a soft hiss of surprise and stared at Ronin. "Who are you?"

"I'm Ronin," he said.

She sniffed the air delicately before a look of distaste crossed her face. "You're a bird."

"I am," he confirmed. "Kat didn't tell me her younger sister was dropping by."

She rolled her eyes. "I do hope my Katarina was not won over with cheesy lines like that."

"Nope," he said with a grin. "Truthfully, she finds me pretty annoying."

He was wearing just his jeans, and she studied his clawed and bitten chest and back. "Apparently not that annoying."

His grin widened, and he pointed to the teakettle. "Kat's sleeping at the moment, and I was just going to make some tea. Would you like a cup, Ms. Frost?"

She nodded. "Yes, I'll take a cup of tea."

KAT STRETCHED LAZILY, WINCING WHEN IT SENT SHOOTING pain down her thighs. She rubbed them gingerly. God, her heat had been intense this month. It was her own fault. That's what happened when you went months without having an actual partner to fuck during your heat. Now that it was over, she could feel every aching muscle. Her thighs burned, and her crotch was sore. Ronin's dick was on the large side, and it had been months since she'd fucked him in her office. Thank God he'd shown up and –

Her eyes flew open, and she stared at the empty side of the bed. Where was he? She could smell the delicious scent of cooked meat, and her stomach growled. She climbed out of bed, used the bathroom quickly, and grabbed her robe before descending the stairs.

"Ronin? You didn't have to cook...."

Her stomach dropped to the floor as she stared at her mother sitting next to Ronin at the table.

"Hello, Katarina," her mother said before taking a sip of tea.

"Mother, what – what are you doing here?"

"You were ignoring my texts," she said.

"I was busy," Kat said.

"Yes, I see that," Eleanor studied Ronin's naked chest before smiling at him. "Katarina thinks I smother her, but that's just because she hasn't had kittens of her own yet. Once she does, she'll understand the worry of a mother. Do you have any children, Ronin?"

"No," Ronin said.

"Do you like children?"

He nodded, and a pleased look came over her face. "Good. Katarina, don't just stand there like a lump. Sit down and have something to eat. I'm sure you're," she paused and stared at the scratch marks on Ronin's chest again, "starving."

Kat blushed furiously. "Mom, I don't mean to be rude, but could I drop by later to see you and Dad? Ronin and I need to, uh…."

"Oh goodness," Eleanor said. "Are you still in your heat, Katarina?"

"No!" Kat said as her blush deepened. "Ronin and I need to talk and -"

Eleanor nudged Ronin with her elbow. "We cat shifters aren't really into talking during our heats. I'm sure you noticed?"

"I did," Ronin said with a grin as Kat made a loud groan of embarrassment.

"Mom, please, can I call you later?"

"Yes, Katarina," her mother said. "I'm leaving so you and Ronin can… talk."

Ronin stood and helped her into her jacket, and she smiled at the bird shifter. "Thank you, Ronin."

"You're welcome, Mrs. Frost."

"I told you to call me Eleanor." She gave him a disapproving look.

"It was lovely to meet you, Eleanor."

"You as well, Ronin."

Kat's mouth dropped open as Eleanor leaned forward and turned her face. Ronin pressed a kiss against her smooth cheek, and Eleanor made a low tsking noise and patted his bruised shoulder lightly before turning to Kat.

"Katarina, darling, you must be a little gentler with the poor boy. He is only a bird, after all." She paused and smiled at Ronin. "No offense, Ronin."

"None taken," Ronin said.

Eleanor stopped in front of Kat and kissed her on the cheek. "Drop by the house later, Katarina." She eyed Kat's hair before smoothing it a little with her hand. "And do me a favour and run a brush through your hair, will you?"

Kat followed her mother down the hallway, grabbing her arm when she opened the front door. "Mom, what – what has gotten into you?"

"What do you mean?"

"Ronin's a bird."

"I know," her mother said. "I can smell, Katarina. Speaking of which," she sniffed delicately, "promise me you'll shower before you come by the house. You're covered in Ronin's scent, and your father will have a heart attack if he smells bird all over you."

"Dad? Dad will have a heart attack?" Kat said. "Mom, you hate birds!"

"Hate birds? Whatever gave you that idea?" her mother said. "Honestly, Katarina, the things you come up with. Now," she kissed Kat's cheek again, "I'll see you later tonight and seriously – run upstairs and brush your hair. It's a mess."

She walked out of the house, closing the door behind her, and Kat stared blankly at it before slowly returning to the kitchen.

"Hey, are you hungry? There's some cooked meat here, but there's also still some raw meat in the fridge," Ronin said. He was loading the dishwasher, and he frowned at the look on her face. "What's wrong?"

"What just happened?" she said slowly.

"What do you mean?"

"My mother hates birds, Ronin. She hates them."

"I keep telling you I'm very charming, Kitten."

She collapsed in the chair and rubbed at her forehead as Ronin said, "You should eat, Kat."

"I'm not hungry." She made herself look at him, and her face paled at his bitten and bruised skin. "God, I'm so sorry, Ronin."

"It's fine," he said with a careless shrug. "They'll heal."

"My heat is over," she said.

"Right," he said. "Well, I guess I'll go then."

He started to leave, and she grabbed his arm. "Ronin, wait."

Her stomach churned with guilt at the pleased smile on his face, and she cleared her throat. "Thank you for helping me, but you know that this is it, right? I can't – I mean, being together for anything other than my heat cycles just isn't a good idea."

"Are you asking me to help you with your next heat?" he asked.

"Yes. Will you?"

Disappointment flooded through her when he said, "Can I think about it?"

"Of course."

"I'll let you know." He grabbed his shirt from the back of the chair and tugged it over his head.

She stood and smiled tentatively at him. "Ronin, I'd like to be friends, at least."

*Not just friends*, her cat hissed grumpily.

His whole body tensed as anger flickered across his face.

"I'm sorry," she said hurriedly. "I understand that it isn't
_"

"It's fine," he said and then grinned at her. "Friends it is, Kitten."

"Are you sure?" She was a little taken aback by his sudden mood change.

"Yes. I'd better go. Bye, Kat."

He pecked her on the cheek and left the kitchen. A few moments later, she heard the front door shut, and she sank into her chair before burying her face in her hands. What the fuck was she doing?

———

"WHY THE FUCK AM I JUST READING ABOUT THIS NOW?" Clay roared. He grabbed Kyle by the front of his shirt and shook him roughly.

Kyle squealed in alarm. "What the hell are you talking about?"

Clay shoved the paper into his face. "This! Your report on the squirrel shifter!"

Kyle just looked at him blankly, and Clay could have torn the man's head off. "She went to a security company for protection. She has a goddamn bodyguard, and you didn't think that was important?"

"What's the big deal?" Kyle said. "The porcupine shifter won't be bothering her any longer, and after a few days, she'll get over her fear and fire the security. We've made sure that neither of the bodyguards knows we're watching her too."

"Get out," Clay said softly. "Get the fuck out of my sight."

Kyle gave the second man in the room a look of confusion. He just shrugged, and with a suspicious glance at Clay, Kyle scurried from the room.

"Don't you think that was a bit extreme, Clay?"

"Are you fucking kidding me right now, Saul?" Clay snapped.

Saul shrugged. "Kyle doesn't know shit about what's going on. It wasn't a red flag because he had no idea of the connection. Besides, what are the odds of the squirrel shifter going to this Burke, King, and Frost security company?"

"Obviously not as low as you think," Clay said.

"It's probably not that big of a deal. The shifters probably haven't even made the connection and -"

"They have," Clay said grimly. "That jaguar shifter is fucking smart, Saul. As soon as the squirrel started blabbing about a porcupine shifter, she would have put it together. Fuck!"

"I think we have bigger problems to worry about right now," Saul said.

"What do you mean?"

"You didn't read the entire report before you called Kyle in here and started reaming out his ass, did you?"

"No," Clay admitted.

"The squirrel shifter is limping. Kyle and Reggie were tailing her and her bodyguard yesterday morning to the grocery store, and she had a noticeable limp."

"Maybe she just strained her leg," Clay said.

Saul gave him a dry look, and Clay clawed his hand through his dark hair. "Fuck. Does Wyatt know?"

"Yes. He wants us to bring her in before she turns. Thinks this new vaccine might work if they haven't fully turned yet."

"She has a goddamn bodyguard now," Clay said. "How does he think we're going to take her?"

"You know Wyatt," Saul said. "He doesn't care how it's done. He just wants what he wants. He says it needs to be quick, says the shifter is probably on the verge of turning already."

"Jesus, what a fucking mess," Clay said.

Saul shifted in his seat. "Wyatt said to kill the bodyguards and burn their bodies."

Clay stared at him. "He wants me to kill innocent people?"

Saul gave him an uncomfortable look. "That's what he said."

"Wyatt's gone mad. You know that, don't you, Saul?" Clay said.

Saul hesitated before nodding. "Yeah, I do."

"We need to put an end to this."

"That's what we're trying to do, Clay," Saul said. "This new vaccine might work. We -"

"That's not what I'm talking about," Clay said. "If she was dead if he had nothing to cure…."

Saul stared at him in horror. "You can't possibly think that's a good idea, Clay. Wyatt's your friend. You can't kill his wife."

"This Wyatt is not my friend. The man I called a friend died the moment she fully turned. Lora's not his wife anymore and hasn't been for nearly three years. She's never coming back, Saul. Even if this new vaccine worked – do you think it would help her?"

"He'd hunt you down and kill you."

"Do you really think he'd catch me?" Clay said.

"He'd find a way. Sooner or later, you'd make a mistake, and he'd be there waiting for you."

Clay sighed and rubbed his forehead. "I have to go."

"Where are you going?" Saul asked.

"I've got a squirrel shifter to kidnap, remember?" he said.

---

"Thanks for having lunch with me today, Bria. I know it was short notice," Kat said.

"My pleasure, honey," Bria said as she sat in the chair across from Kat's desk and unwrapped her burger. "One of the good things about being unemployed – you have tons of free time. The not-so-good thing – your savings account dwindles at an alarming rate."

Kat poked at her burger before blurting out, "My heat cycle just ended yesterday."

"Oh yeah?" Bria said. "Ugh, they put a tomato on my burger. I distinctly remember saying no tomatoes."

She peeled off the tomato with a look of disgust before dropping it onto the paper wrapper and slapping the burger back together.

"I – Ronin helped me with it."

Bria stopped with the burger halfway to her mouth. "You're kidding me."

"No," Kat said. "It started Monday, and I didn't call him, but it was so bad, Bria. I couldn't stand it. I was going to call him, I knew I was going to break down and beg him to help me, but before I could, he came by the house."

"Did he know you were in your heat or did he drop by for something else?" Bria asked.

"He knew," Kat said. She dropped her head into her hands. "Oh God, Bria. It was so humiliating. I was on the couch with my damn vibrator, and I didn't hear him knock. He knows where the spare key is, so he just let himself in. I was… I was moaning his name, and he heard me."

She peeked at Bria through her fingers. The tiger shifter struggled not to laugh, and Kat glared at her. "This is not funny, Bria."

"It's kind of funny," Bria said. "What happened then?"

"What do you think happened? I fucked his brains out for the next two days."

"And?"

"And what?"

"Was he good? Did he have an appropriate amount of stamina?" Bria asked. "I only ask because, and don't say a word to Raden when you finally meet him, I have never really understood the importance of your partner's stamina when you're in heat until I started dating Raden."

"Raden's having issues?" Kat asked.

"Sort of," Bria said with a sigh. "He starts strong but kind of fizzles out near the end of the two days. I mean, I can't blame him. It's more difficult than people think, and he's never been with a cat shifter before. I think he was unprepared for just how physically taxing it is."

Kat gave her a sympathetic look, and Bria shrugged. "It's fine. We're managing. Back to you – how was Ronin?"

"Amazing," Kat admitted. "I was – well, I was pretty bad this heat, and he more than kept up with me."

"Awesome," Bria said. "So, what's the problem?"

"He's my employee, and he's a bird," Kat said. "How many times do I have to tell you that, Bria?"

"I think you're too hung up on that," Bria said. "Ronin doesn't seem like a 'kiss and tell' kind of guy, and for a bird, the guy is damn hot. Hell, even I was attracted to him after that night in the club. That dimple is adorable, and his ass? Very biteable."

Kat groaned and stared at her burger as Bria bit into hers. She chewed noisily before saying, "Tell me what's really bothering you, Kit-Kat."

"I bit him and scratched him and made him repeatedly say that he belonged to me. I told him over and over that his cock was mine and that he was mine. I even ate raw meat in front of him, Bria."

"We always bite and scratch during our heat cycle," Bria said. "He's a shifter. He'll heal."

"It was bad," Kat said. "He was covered in bruises and bite marks, and I liked seeing him that way. Liked knowing that if another woman saw the marks, she'd know he was mine."

"Uh oh," Bria said.

"Yeah," Kat said miserably. "And you haven't heard the worse part. My mother found him in my kitchen half-naked and covered in my marks."

"Shit, what I wouldn't have given to be a fly on the wall," Bria said with a laugh. "What happened?"

"I don't know. I was sleeping, and when I came down-stairs, she was sitting in the damn kitchen with him having a cup of tea. She told him to call her Eleanor and let him kiss her on the cheek."

"Your mother let a bird kiss her?" Bria's half-eaten burger was forgotten.

"Yes! And she didn't even seem upset that I was having sex with a bird. She just told me to brush my hair and shower before I dropped by to see her and Dad."

"Damn, that Ronin really is a charmer, isn't he?"

Kat took a swig of water as Bria popped a French Fry into her mouth. "So now what?"

"What do you mean?"

"I mean," Bria glanced at the closed office door before lowering her voice, "are you going to keep fucking Ronin?"

"No," Kat said quickly.

"Not even during your heat?"

Kat flushed. "I asked him if he would help me with my next heat, and he asked if he could think about it."

"Ooh, that doesn't sound good," Bria said.

"No, it doesn't, but I can't blame him. I was aggressive and demanding, and, like you said, helping a cat through her heat is harder than most guys think. Hell, we don't even give a damn about their pleasure. It's all about us during our heat, and I've known guys who can't handle that. But then I told him that I at least wanted to be friends, and he said yes, no problem."

Kat rubbed at her forehead again. "I shouldn't have clawed him so much, and I definitely shouldn't have made him say he was mine, but I couldn't help it, Bria. I knew what I was saying, could hear the words coming out of my damn mouth and knew it was a stupid thing to do, but I had no control over it. And every time he said he belonged to me, it made me so damn hot I practically burst into flames."

She pushed back her chair and paced the small office. "I spent the last two days having sex with Ronin, and all I can think about is getting him back into my bed. What the hell is wrong with me?"

"You're in love with the bird," Bria said.

Kat stumbled to a stop. "No, I'm not. I don't even know anything about him. I don't even know what kind of bird he is! It's not like we did any talking the last two days."

Bria laughed. "That's not your fault. We want only three things during our heat – fucking, sleeping, and eating. Pretty sure most guys don't mind. But I've never seen you act like this over a guy before, so I'm standing by my 'you love him' theory. Congratulations."

"I don't love him, Bria. I don't," Kat said softly.

Bria just shrugged and bit into her burger. "Whatever you say, Kit-Kat."

*THIS IS A VERY BAD IDEA, RONIN.*

It wasn't. Kat had said she wanted to be friends, and friends showed up unexpectedly at their friend's house with Greek food all the time. It was a friendly thing to do.

*Oh yeah? So, you're at her house just to feed her Greek food? It has nothing to do with the fact that you've spent all goddamn day thinking about her naked body? Christ, man, it's been less than twenty-four hours since you fucked her. Have some self-control.*

*"It's been twenty-seven hours, and I have plenty of self-control. I just want to check on her and make sure she's not too sore.*

He knocked loudly before his inner voice could reply. He could hear Kat's footsteps, and he held up the bag of food when she opened the door. "Hey, Kitten? Hungry?"

"Ronin, what… what are you doing here?"

"I picked up some Greek food for dinner, and it's way too much for one person to eat. Figured I'd stop by my friend's house and see if she wanted some. Do you like Greek food?"

She blinked before slowly nodding. "Yes."

"Good. Invite me in," he said.

He waited with his heart pounding in his chest, sure she would just shut the door in his face, but to his surprise, she stepped back. "Come in, Ronin."

He followed her into the kitchen and set the bag on the counter before opening the cupboard that held the plates. She grabbed some cutlery, and he ripped open the bag. "You haven't eaten yet?"

"No," she said. "I just got home from work."

"How was work today?"

"Good," she said. "Busy. What, uh, what time are you meeting Mavina tonight?"

"Didn't Willow tell you? Mavina and her family are in Italy until Saturday."

He thought he saw relief on her face before she turned away. "No, she didn't mention that."

"You didn't wonder why I could stay your entire heat cycle?" he asked.

She shrugged. "I didn't think about it, to be honest. I didn't care."

He dished some food onto the plates as she opened the fridge. "What would you like to drink? I have water, juice, and beer."

"I'll take a beer," he said.

She bent over, and he stared at her ass in her tight yoga pants before looking away. Friends don't ogle their friends' asses, he reminded himself.

"Ronin?"

"Yeah?"

"How are your chest and back?" she asked.

"Just fine," he said. "Don't worry about it, Kat."

"I shouldn't have scratched you so deeply. " She bit at her bottom lip, and he fought the urge to lean over and suck on it.

"I didn't mind. How are you doing?" His gaze flickered to her crotch. "Are you sore?"

She flushed prettily before shaking her head. "I was last night and this morning, but I feel fine now."

"Good. Let's eat," he said.

She joined him at the table, and he held up his beer. "To being friends, Kat."

"Friends," she echoed softly before clinking his beer bottle with her own.

## CHAPTER 13

"Seriously, Ronin, you have to tell me how you got my mother to like you," Kat said.

After dinner, they'd grabbed two more beers and moved to the living room. Kat tried desperately not to think about how she had fucked Ronin on this very couch and wondered if he was doing the same thing.

"I can't reveal my secret for winning over mothers, Kat," he said with a grin. "It's taken me years to hone that skill."

She laughed and took a drink of beer. "Well, congratulations. I can honestly say it's the most impressive feat I've ever witnessed."

"Are you close to your family?" Ronin asked.

She nodded. "Yes. We're not attached at the hip or anything, and sometimes my mother drives me crazy with her incessant, 'find a man and give me grandkittens' talk, but I love her to death."

"Do you want kids?" he asked.

"Eventually," she said.

"Is that why you don't take the drug to curb your heat?"

She stared at him in surprise. "You know about that?"

"Yes. After I offered to help you out with your heat, I did some research."

For some reason, she blushed. "Again, I'm sorry for clawing you so badly and for making you say that, uh, stuff I did."

He just shrugged. "Do you have siblings?"

"Yes, I have an older sister and a younger brother."

"I didn't take you for a middle child," he said. "You've got the bossiness of an oldest kid."

She gave him a mock scowl. "There are only fourteen months between my sister and me, and half the time, I act like the oldest sibling."

"Ahh, you're the responsible one, huh? Why am I not surprised by that?"

She rolled her eyes. "My sister is great, just a little impulsive."

"And your brother?"

She laughed. "He's great too, just *really* impulsive. How about you? Do you have any siblings?"

"Nope, an only child here."

"Surprise, surprise," she said.

He laughed. "I have the 'spoiled only child' vibe, don't I?"

"Maybe," she said. "Do your parents live here?"

"They used to," he said briefly. He couldn't tell Kat that his parents were forced into hiding, and he hadn't spoken to them in over two years. After escaping from the lab, the first thing he had done was call them. His mother was the same as him, and if Wyatt found her...

He shuddered, and Kat touched his arm briefly. "Hey, you okay?"

"Yes," he said. "How long have you been a partner at the security firm?"

"Just over three years," she said. "I started working for Mal and Bishop in the IT department, doing some research work."

He grinned. "You mean hacking."

"Maybe," she said. "Anyway, after six months, they asked if I wanted to buy into the company and become a partner, and I said yes."

"That's impressive," he said.

She smiled at him. "Thanks. Why did you leave the police force?"

He stared blankly at her for a moment, almost tempted to blurt out the truth in a moment of madness. He didn't want to lie to Kat.

"Ronin? Is something wrong?"

Was that concern in her voice or just wishful thinking on his part?

"No," he said. "I had a partner, her name was Lora, and we were close."

"Lovers?"

The jealousy in her voice was easy to spot this time, and he was ridiculously happy about it.

"No. She was married to a good guy. We got along well. Anyway, Lora got sick, and I tried to help her, and I failed. She died, and after that, I couldn't go back to working as a cop. It was too difficult. So, I taught surfing instead."

"That's quite the difference," she said.

"I enjoyed it. But I couldn't bum around on the beach forever, so after a couple of years, I came back here and applied for a job with your firm."

She studied his face intently, and he looked away, afraid she'd see the truth in his face. She touched his arm. "Ronin, what -"

He drained the rest of his beer before standing. "It's

getting late. I should go. Thanks for having dinner with me, Kat."

She stood and caught his hand. "Ronin, wait."

He stared at their hands before linking his fingers with hers. He could almost see the desire shuddering through her, and she licked her lips as she gazed at his mouth.

"Kat," he said, and she lunged forward and smashed her mouth against his.

He kissed her hungrily, his hands threading through her hair as he slid his tongue into her mouth. She sucked on it, and he groaned before pressing his erection against her. "I want you so much, Kitten."

"Ronin," she said, "I know I said we should only be friends, but I've been thinking about the last couple of days, and I know I wasn't... attentive to your needs. Maybe we should spend one more night together so I can concentrate on you this time."

He reached down and cupped her ass, squeezing it roughly. "I was more than satisfied, Kitten, but I like the direction you're going with this."

She laughed softly, and he kissed the tip of her nose. "One more night sounds good to me."

"Come with me," she said. He followed her up the stairs to the bedroom, and she tugged at the hem of his t-shirt. He raised his arms, and she pulled it off of him before gasping in surprise. His skin was smooth, with no trace of her marks remaining.

She ran her fingers over his skin. "What the hell?"

"I told you I would heal," he said.

"Ronin, you're a fast healer," she said. "You – you're as fast as a grizzly at healing." She studied him closely. "What kind of bird are you?"

"I told you – just a mutt," he said with a grin. "Now, at

the risk of sounding embarrassingly impatient, let's get you naked."

They helped each other undress, and when she stood naked in front of him, he made a low groan of appreciation. "Fuck, your body is amazing, Kitten."

He pulled her toward the bed. "Lie down. I've been dreaming about eating your sweet pussy all day."

She shook her head and pushed him into a sitting position on the bed. "No, it's about you this time, remember?"

She kneeled in front of him, pushing his legs apart, so she was on her knees between them. He muttered a low curse as she stroked his cock with her warm hands. "I'm not going to argue."

She grinned up at him before bending her head and licking his shaft with her warm, wet tongue. He inhaled sharply, his hands tightening in her hair, but before she could slide her lips around him, he pulled her head up.

"No fangs, Kitten," he said.

She laughed. "I'll be good, Ronin."

She sucked him into her mouth, tracing the ridge with her tongue before sucking hard. She kept her teeth away from him and kissed and licked the head of his cock before taking more than half of him into her mouth.

"Fuck," he said in a low moan, "you're being a very good kitten. Suck harder, sweetheart."

She did what he asked, and the silken glide of her hot mouth made his hips thrust uncontrollably. He watched the up and down slide of her mouth, sizzling bolts of raw lust flickering in his veins, as his world boiled down to the feel of her wet mouth and the touch of her soft hand stroking the base of his cock. She sucked and caressed and licked his throbbing cock for nearly ten minutes until he was moaning loudly and so close to coming he could feel his balls tightening.

"Kitten, stop!" he said hoarsely.

She ignored him, her head bobbing rapidly up and down. With a low curse, he pulled her off his cock. He held her hair, preventing her from taking him into her mouth again, and she hissed at him.

"Mine! I want it – give it to me!"

He hauled her to her feet and pushed her onto the bed. She purred loudly, her anger forgotten as he moved between her thighs.

"Yes, fuck me," she demanded.

He eased into her, a little worried that she was sore despite what she had said. He groaned at the familiar grip of her pussy. She cried out and let her thighs drop open as he propped himself up on his hands above her and moved slowly back and forth. Her hands gripped his hips, and he waited for her to sink her claws in. She squeezed him roughly but didn't claw him. Disappointment rolled through him as she licked at his mouth.

"Please, little bird," she murmured.

He bent his head and sucked on one nipple, rolling it between his lips until it was an erect bud, and she made soft noises of pleasure. He switched to the other one and pulled on it with his lips before licking the tip of it.

She stroked his back, tracing her nails across his flesh but not breaking the skin. He lifted his head and studied the golden colour of her eyes as she met each of his slow thrusts with a short pump of her hips.

"So good," she whispered.

"Yes," he agreed before dropping to his forearms. It pressed his chest against her breasts, and he relished the vibration of her purring as her warm breath brushed his cheek.

He kissed her slowly, sliding his tongue against hers as she wrapped her arms around him and clung tightly to him.

"Keep looking at me, Kat," he said when they broke apart. She stared obediently at him as he pressed a soft and tender kiss against her mouth.

"Mine," she said in a possessive voice before embarrassment flickered across her face. "I'm sorry."

He brushed his mouth against hers. "Yours."

Her purring turned up a notch, and she squeezed his hips again. "Harder, Ronin."

"Whatever you want, sweetheart," he said before thrusting hard. She cupped his face and kissed him repeatedly as their lovemaking turned rough and urgent. She still kept her claws to herself, and he realized he was desperate to feel her mark him.

He slowed down, barely moving inside of her, and grinned when she hissed and raked her claws down his back. The sting made him flinch, and her eyes widened.

"Shit, I'm sorry."

"Don't be. I like it when my Kitten marks me with her claws," he admitted hoarsely.

Her pupils turned to narrow slits, and she growled at him. "My pretty bird. Say it."

He just grinned at her, and her fangs descended with a soft pop. "Say you belong to me, Ronin."

Her nails sunk into his back, and he made a harsh groan of pain before fucking her roughly. She mewled with pleasure. "Say it, little bird."

He could feel her pussy tightening around him, her nipples were hard points against his chest, and he ground his pelvic bone against her clit. She screamed as she climaxed and sunk her fangs into his shoulder. The feel of her smooth teeth sinking into his flesh made him come hard, and he bucked against her as her pussy milked him eagerly.

"I belong to you," he rasped as she pulled her fangs from his shoulder.

"Always," she said. "Always, Ronin."

"Yes, always," he groaned as his orgasm continued to wash over him. He collapsed against her, and she licked the bite mark until he rolled off of her onto his back. They panted in unison, their legs tangled together as Kat stared up at the ceiling.

"Ronin?" Kat said hesitantly as a thick curtain of awkwardness blanketed them.

"That got a little weird, huh?" he said.

She nodded. "I'm sorry. I meant not to bite or scratch or um, make you say -"

"I should go," he said.

She winced and tried to touch his arm. "Ronin, you don't have to leave. I know that was intense, but I won't let it happen again."

He climbed out of bed and dressed quickly. As much as he wanted to stay the night, it was a terrible idea. It would make it that much harder to be only friends with her. "It's fine, Kat. Really. I just, you know, don't normally spend the night in a friend's bed."

"Oh, right. Of course," she said as she wrapped the quilt around her naked body.

He hesitated before leaning over and pressing a brief kiss against her mouth. "Bye, Kat."

"Bye, Ronin."

FRIDAY MORNING, MAL WAS STUDYING A FILE AT HIS DESK when he heard the front door open, and the scent of his mate drifted to him. He smiled and closed the file before starting toward the door. He'd gone to an early-morning meeting, so he hadn't driven in with Willow this morning. Before he could open his half-closed door, he smelled another scent, and he groaned inwardly. Like a little kid hiding from his parents, he peeked around the edge of the open door at Willow and Marika standing in reception.

"Marika, it's so good to see you," Willow said. "It's been forever."

The lizard shifter gave Willow a brittle smile. "It's nice to see you too, Willow. Where is your wolf shifter? I need to speak with him."

"He had a client meeting this morning, but I'm sure he'll be back any minute. Can I get you a cup of coffee?" Willow asked as she flicked on the lights.

Mrs. Belfry shook her head. "No, thank you."

Mal needed to go out there. Marika liked Willow – well, as much as she could like anyone who wasn't related to her – but it wasn't exactly manly of him to be hiding out in his office.

"Why didn't you invite me to your wedding, Willow?" There was a note of displeasure in Marika's voice. "I distinctly remember you saying you would."

"Oh, we're not married yet," Willow said. "Of course, we would invite you, Marika."

Marika stared at her in surprise. "That boring wolf bit you months ago, did he not?"

"He did," Willow said.

"Then what on earth are you waiting for?"

"It's kind of complicated," Willow said.

"Because of his grandfather, I imagine," Marika said.

"Actually," Willow said. "Amos is starting to be rather pleasant to me."

"Then what's the problem?" Marika said impatiently.

"There isn't a problem, exactly," Willow said.

"Oh, for God's sake, just spit it out, Willow."

Willow laughed. "Secretly, I'm waiting for Mal to ask me to marry him."

"Ask you?" Marika raised one nearly non-existent eyebrow at her. "I don't quite know how to break this to you, Willow, but your wolf shifter has marked you. You're his mate whether you like it or not."

Willow laughed again. "I know, but it's human tradition for the man to buy a ring and get down on one knee and formally ask, you know?"

Marika sighed. "Humans and their silly traditions."

"I suppose it is kind of silly," Willow said, "but I still really want it to happen that way."

"Does your wolf shifter know this?"

"I – well, no, I guess he doesn't."

"Then perhaps you should tell him," Marika said. She glanced at her watch. "Do you think he'll be much longer? I have a hectic schedule today, and I -"

Mal grabbed a file from the credenza and pushed open the door to his office. "Willow, is that you? Can you photocopy -"

He paused and smiled at Marika. "Mrs. Belfry, what a pleasant surprise."

"Indeed," Mrs. Belfry said. "How are you, Mr. Burke?"

"Very well, how are you?"

"Fine," she said. "I'm here to speak to you about the security at the warehouse."

Mal frowned. "Is there a problem?"

"Yes," she said. "I want the bird back."

"I'm sorry?" Mal blinked at her as Willow headed to the kitchen to make coffee.

"I want the bird back," she repeated.

"I'm sorry, Mrs. Belfry, but we needed Ronin on another assignment."

"What assignment?" she asked.

"We have a vampire client who -"

"Ugh. Vampires are the worst," Marika's long, forked tongue flicked out in disgust. "Such wretched creatures. Wouldn't you agree, Mr. Burke?"

"Well, I, uh...."

"I like them," Willow said as she returned to her desk. "I find them quite fascinating."

Marika's snort of derision turned into a hiss of delight when the office door opened, and Ronin walked into the office. "Mr. Smith!"

"Mrs. Belfry," Ronin stopped in front of her and kissed her rough cheek. "How are you?"

"Very well," Marika gave him a wide grin, and Mal stared in surprise at Willow when the lizard shifter hooked her arm around Ronin's and leaned against him. "I was just telling Mr. Burke that we want you back at the warehouse. We miss you."

"That's very kind of you," Ronin said, "I miss your butterscotch cookies."

Marika giggled like a girl. "I have an entire tin of cookies waiting for you in my office."

"You're making it very hard to resist," Ronin said with a flirty little grin.

Willow, her mouth open, stared wide-eyed at Mal as Marika turned her gaze to him. "Well, Mr. Burke, will Ronin be returning to the warehouse?"

"I'm sorry, Mrs. Belfry, but we need him on his current

assignment."

She sniffed angrily, and Ronin patted her arm. "Perhaps we could have coffee sometime, Mrs. Belfry, and catch up."

"That leads me to my next point," Marika said. "Koren's birthday is Wednesday, and I'm throwing him a party that evening. I will expect you," she pinned her gaze on Mal, "as well as your mate and your associates to be there. Let Mr. King and Ms. Frost know they're welcome to bring guests."

She squeezed Ronin's arm. "You will also be there, Mr. Smith."

"I would love nothing more," Ronin said, "but unfortunately, I'm working that night."

She hissed under her breath before glaring at Mal. "Surely, Mr. Burke will give you a night off."

"I wish I could, Mrs. Belfry," Mal said, "but Ronin is the only one available to keep an eye on our client."

Mrs. Belfry sighed loudly. "Bring your vampire with you, Mr. Smith."

"Oh, um, I'm not sure…." Ronin glanced at Mal for help.

"Mrs. Belfry, our client is a vampire and -"

"I'm well aware of that, Mr. Burke," Marika snapped.

She smiled up at Ronin again. "I will not take no for an answer, Ronin. Bring your wretched vampire with you, but I expect you to keep her from snacking on my guests."

"Yes, ma'am," Ronin said.

She kissed Ronin's cheek before holding out her hand to Willow. Willow squeezed it lightly and kissed Marika on the cheek.

"It was good to see you again, Marika."

"You as well, my dear. We'll see you on Wednesday night. The party starts at seven, don't be late, please."

"We won't," Willow said.

"Mr. Burke." Marika nodded to Mal before leaving the

office.

"Well, someone has a crush," Willow laughed as Ronin grinned at her.

"Ronin, can you keep Mavina well-behaved?" Mal asked.

Ronin shrugged. "I can try, but no promises. That chick is crazy." He paused. "Maybe I shouldn't bring her. She'll be happy to go – she's all about the parties – but I don't have to mention it to her."

Mal shook his head. "No, bring her. If you don't, Marika Belfry is likely to terminate our contract just because she's pissed you didn't show up at the party."

Ronin turned to Willow. "I got your email, Willow. What did I do wrong on my timesheet?"

"Oh, right. Come over here, and I'll show you," Willow said.

Mal watched as Ronin followed Willow to her desk. A small smile crossed his face. His mate wanted a proposal, and he was determined to make it happen.

---

"REMEMBER," CLAY STARED AT THE GROUP OF FIVE MEN standing in the shadows of the building. Like him, they were dressed all in black, and each of them carried a gun. "We move in, dart the squirrel shifter, and move out. There's a lynx shifter in the apartment with her. Doven, you'll dispatch him."

"Dart or bullet?" Doven grunted.

"Dart only," Clay said. "He'll be fast, and he's armed, so be quick."

"Not a problem, boss," Doven said.

Clay glanced at the dark sky. It was just after three in the morning, and the street was silent and empty. "Watch your backs in there. She hasn't turned yet, but if she bites or scratches you, you will turn, and I will kill you. Understand?"

The men nodded, and Clay vanished before reappearing on the other side of the locked door of the lobby of the building. He eased it open, and the five men followed him silently up the stairs.

SANDRA, HER LEG ON FIRE AND HER HEAD THROBBING SO painfully she wanted to vomit, staggered into the bathroom. She eased up the leg of her pajama bottoms and made a harsh cry before turning and vomiting blood and bile into the toilet.

"Oh God," she moaned weakly. "What is happening?"

Her leg was swollen to twice the size, pus dripped in a steady stream from the wound, and her squirrel was screaming and chittering away.

"Shut up! Shut up! Shut up!" she shouted before slamming her fist into her temple. It sent a wave of unbearable pain through her entire body, and she vomited again as there was a knock on the bathroom door.

"Ms. Mickelson?" The lynx shifter's voice was concerned. "What's wrong?"

"Go away," Sandra moaned. "Just go away!"

She vomited a third time as agony gripped her entire body.

HIS HEART BANGING AGAINST HIS RIBS, DAVIS LEANED CLOSER to the bathroom door and sniffed delicately.

"Shit," he muttered under his breath before covering his nose and mouth with his hand. There was a horrible stench of rot and decay drifting out from the bathroom, and he knocked again on the door. "Ms. Mickelson? Sandra, open the door."

The high-pitched chittering noise coming from within the bathroom set his teeth on edge and made his lynx hiss loudly. He jerked and stumbled back when there was a loud thud, and the door shuddered against the frame.

"Sandra?" he said. "Open the door and come out of the bathroom."

There was no reply, and fear trickled down his spine at the sudden silence. Something was very wrong with the squirrel shifter. She'd been pale and shaky all night but insisted she just had a case of the flu. She hadn't smelled like she had the flu. She'd smelled like she was rotting from the inside out. He pulled his phone out of his pocket.

His lynx snarled and hissed again, and he tried to calm it as he quickly phoned Mal. He waited impatiently for the wolf shifter to answer.

"Mal? Hey, it's Davis. Sorry to call so late, but there's something wrong with Sandra Mickelson. She's sick, I think, and won't come out of the bathroom. I'm going to call an ambulance."

He listened for a moment. "Yeah, I think it's that bad. I don't -"

The bathroom door opened, and he stared at the squirrel shifter. "Just a minute, Mal." He took a cautious step forward. "Sandra? How are you feeling?"

His lynx hissed and spit, and the hair on the back of his neck stood up. The squirrel shifter was twice her normal size, and his eyes widened when she suddenly lurched into the hallway.

"Holy fuck!" he shouted. The monstrosity standing before him was the squirrel shifter, he could smell her scent under the smell of decay, but all resemblance ended there. Her eyes were bright orbs of red, and her front teeth had lengthened until they protruded well below her chin. She snapped her jaws at him as dark fur grew on her face. Her body swelled, he could hear her bones cracking, and he made a startled shout when her long, bushy tail snapped around his leg like a snake and yanked him off his feet.

His phone fell from his hand, and he scrambled backward. His clothes were starting to rip as his lynx surged forward. He hissed at the creature, and she screamed angrily before chittering in a loud squeal that made his lynx whimper in sudden fear.

"Fuck!" he snarled as his fangs popped out. "Get the fuck away from me!"

She reached for him, but before she could tear into his rapidly shifting body, the door to her apartment burst open. Five men, dressed head-to-toe in black, rushed into the room, and the squirrel forgot about Davis and turned on them. She leaped forward, nothing more than a blur in the dark, and latched onto one of the men. She knocked him to the floor and buried her teeth in his neck before ripping out a mouthful of flesh. Blood sprayed in an arc, coating her face and the thighs of the men standing in horrified shock in front of her. She chittered triumphantly before lapping at the blood still spraying in the air.

Davis flinched when the remaining four men raised their guns and fired at the squirrel shifter. Sandra screamed before staggering back. She turned to flee, but her gaze fell on Davis, and she growled loudly before dropping to all fours and rushing toward him. He could see the bright red darts sticking out of her face and chest, and he scrambled back as a man roared, "Again! Hit her again!"

They fired a second time. Sandra arched her back, her legs collapsed beneath her, and her head hit the floor with a hard bang as she slid along the floor. Her skull bumped against Davis' legs, and he made a snarl of disgust at the smell radiating from her.

A man stepped in front of him, and Davis stared up at him before frowning. "You. I know -"

He flinched, his hand reaching up to touch the dart in his neck as he stared groggily at the gun in the man's hand.

"Fuckin' shot me," he slurred before slumping onto the floor.

---

WHAT A FUCKING CLUSTERFUCK THIS TURNED OUT TO BE. Adrenaline coursed through Clay's veins as he stared at the lynx shifter. "Goddammit. How's Doven?"

"Dead," one of the men said, and Clay swore again.

"We need to move quickly." Clay bent and grabbed the squirrel shifter's arm before vanishing. He reappeared less than thirty seconds later and glared at his men. "She's in the back of the van. Move. I could hear fucking sirens already. The neighbours must have dialed 9-1-1."

"What about him?" One of the men pointed at the unconscious lynx shifter. "He acted like he knew you."

"I'll take care of him. Go, you idiots, before they set up fucking roadblocks," Clay snarled.

They ran quickly and quietly out of the apartment, and Clay pulled a second gun from his shoulder holster and checked the clip. This one held bullets rather than darts, and he rested it against the lynx shifter's forehead as his finger tightened on the trigger. He hesitated and closed his eyes before shaking his head.

"No," he said. "No."

He holstered his gun and grabbed Doven's arm. He and

the dead man vanished as footsteps sounded in the hallway outside of the apartment.

***

"DAVIS?" BISHOP RUSHED INTO THE EMERGENCY ROOM. IT was just after five in the morning, and the ER was remarkably quiet for a Saturday.

"He's fine," Mal said. "Still a little groggy from the tranquillizer, but he'll live. They're doing some tests on him right now, just to make sure everything's good."

He squeezed Willow's hand. "You should go home, honey. Go back to bed and get some sleep."

Willow shook her head. "No, I'll stay. I called Davis' sister in California, and she's waiting for me to call her back once the tests are finished."

Kat, her dark hair in a messy bun and her face free of makeup, came hurtling into the ER. "Is Davis okay?"

"He's good," Mal said. "Just groggy."

"What the hell happened?" Bishop asked.

"Let's go to the cafeteria and grab a coffee. I'll tell you everything Davis told me," Mal said.

***

"WAS DAVIS BIT OR SCRATCHED?" KAT ASKED.

It was half an hour later, and she stared at her untouched coffee as Mal shook his head. "No. He says he wasn't, and the doctors examined him and couldn't find any marks on him."

"Thank God," Kat breathed.

"How did Davis even know it was this Clay guy," Mal asked.

"He was at the office when Clay came in to meet with Kat," Bishop said. He tapped one large knuckle on the top of the table. "So, Davis was certain that Sandra killed one of the men."

Mal nodded. "When Davis' phone went dead, I drove to Sandra's apartment. The police were already there, and they weren't letting anyone into the building. I spoke with the neighbour who was the first to go into Sandra's apartment, and he said that he found Davis unconscious on the floor as well as a massive amount of blood on the floor and sprayed on the walls."

"Where the hell was the body then?" Bishop said. "Maybe, Clay and his men could have smuggled Sandra out without anyone seeing them but Sandra *and* a dead body? No way."

"Maybe they had more men waiting for them outside," Kat said. "They moved their dead guy while Clay and the others moved Sandra."

"Maybe," Bishop said doubtfully.

"What doesn't make sense," Mal said, "is why Clay left Davis alive. Davis is sure that Clay realized he knew him. Why didn't he kill him?"

"Because they're scientists who work in a lab and not murderers?" Willow said. "For all we know, they could be doing something to help Sandra right now. If they wanted her dead, they would have just killed her right there, wouldn't they have? According to Davis, they just knocked her out, so obviously, they want to help her. I think we need to give this Stowe Laboratories the benefit of a doubt. Kat hasn't found anything suspicious about them."

Mal gave her a small smile. "Look at you being the voice of reason."

She wrinkled her nose at him. "All I'm saying is that we

ELIZABETH KELLY

shouldn't jump to any conclusions about this Clay guy or Stowe Laboratories until we have more evidence. I didn't get any funny feelings from Clay when he was at the office."

"Will, just because you see ghosts doesn't mean you can sense when people are bad," Kat said gently.

Bishop shrugged. "I don't know - she knew that snake shifter Royce was rotten."

"Thank you, Bishop," Willow said before turning to Kat. "I have excellent spidey senses, remember?"

Kat grinned at her as Mal said, "Do you still have Clay's card, Kat?"

She nodded and rummaged through her purse before pulling it out.

"Call him. Let's see what he has to say."

She called, and they waited patiently before she ended the call. "Straight to voicemail."

"Surprise, surprise," Bishop said. He suddenly stiffened and stared across the cafeteria before growling, "What is he doing here?"

They turned to see Bren Matthews ambling across the cafeteria toward them. Willow smiled and stood as he approached.

"Detective, it's nice to see you again."

He shook her hand. "Nice to see you as well, Ms. Tanner."

"Oh please, call me Willow," she said.

"Only if you call me Bren."

Willow quickly introduced Mal and Kat to Bren as Bishop glared at the detective.

"Mr. King," Bren said. "Nice to see you again. How's Ava doing?"

"She's good. She's living with me now, and she's pregnant with my cub," Bishop blurted out.

Willow choked on her swallow of coffee as Bren said, "Congratulations. Tell Ava I said hello, would you?"

Bishop nodded as Bren sat next to Willow. "So, I just spoke with your employee, Davis Wendle. Sandra Mickelson hired your firm to protect her from what she believed was a porcupine shifter stalking her. Is that right?"

Mal nodded, and Bren waited patiently. When no one said anything, he smiled briefly. "Your employee was as closed-mouth as the rest of you about details of this morning."

He leaned forward. "Last week, I had a very mutilated, very dead squirrel shifter in the park not five blocks from Ms. Mickelson's house. He was, in fact, Ms. Mickelson's boyfriend. The ME tells me that it was a porcupine shifter who killed him, although he's never heard of a porcupine shifter deciding to eat his fellow shifters. However, Ms. Mickelson did corroborate his theory."

He tapped his fingers on the table. "Now, Ms. Mickelson is missing, your employee is in the hospital with a potent sedative running through him, and there's an unsettling amount of blood - human blood - in Ms. Mickelson's apartment."

He leaned back and smiled at them. "Who wants to start explaining first?"

Mal glanced at Bishop and Kat. Bishop shook his head, but Kat said, "I think we need to tell him, Mal."

"No, Kat," Bishop snapped.

"Cool it, big guy," she said. "He might be able to help us get into Stowe Laboratories."

"Stowe Laboratories?" Bren said.

"It's kind of a long story," Kat said.

"I have nothing but time, Ms. Frost."

"So," BREN SCRATCHED HIS CHIN THOUGHTFULLY, "YOU believe that it's some kind of virus that's mutating the shifters?"

"We don't know for sure," Kat said. "But we do know that if you're bitten or scratched, you get infected."

"It appears that way," Bren said. "But Ms. Mickelson never mentioned that the porcupine shifter had injured her."

"Maybe she was afraid," Willow suggested. "Lots of shifters still don't trust humans."

Bren nodded. "You're probably right. What do you think the odds are that Stowe Laboratories caused the virus?"

"Maybe," Kat said. "That's a possibility that we hadn't thought of. It makes sense, though. If they were experimenting on shifters, trying to enhance their healing abilities, it's possible they accidentally created the virus or infection. And it would explain why they're so desperate to round up anyone they think is infected. If this got out to the general public, they'd be ruined."

"I think we should drive out to Stowe Laboratories on Monday morning to try to talk to this Clay guy," Bishop said. "It's doubtful he'll return any of your calls, Kat."

"I'll go with you," Bren said.

"No thanks," Bishop grunted. "We can handle it ourselves."

"Hold on, Bishop," Kat said. "It would be helpful to have Detective Matthews with us. He could get a warrant and -"

"Afraid not," Bren said. "We have no real evidence that Stowe Laboratories is even involved."

"We spoke to Clay. I have his business card," Kat said.

"Still not enough to convince a judge to give me a warrant. Plus, it takes days even to get one. The paperwork alone will take a week."

"That's fine," Bishop said. "Kat and I can go alone."

"I think I should still go with you," Bren said. "Sometimes flashing a badge opens more doors than a bear shifter with a security company."

Bishop growled softly, and Kat placed her hand on his arm. "He's right, Bishop. You know he is."

Bishop didn't reply, and Kat glanced at her watch. "Maybe we should go out there this morning?"

"It's Saturday, Kat," Mal said. "I doubt anyone of importance is there. Hell, for all we know, the lab could be empty."

"They have Sandra there," Willow said. "Someone would be around. We need to make sure she's okay, Mal. We told her we'd keep her safe."

Mal took her hand and squeezed it gently. "I know, Willow, but it's like you said earlier – if they wanted to kill her, they would have done it at her apartment."

"I guess," Willow said. "But what if they're torturing her or something?"

There was silence, and she leaned against Mal as Bren handed his card to Kat. "If anything happens between now and Monday, give me a call, okay? Otherwise, I'll meet you at your office, say around seven, Monday morning?"

Kat nodded, and Bren said goodbye before leaving.

"I don't like this," Bishop said grumpily. "We don't need that guy coming with us and -"

"Bren's a good guy," Willow said. "You just don't like him because he likes Ava."

Bishop blushed. "That isn't it at all, Willow."

"No? Then why did you tell him that Ava was pregnant? You're keeping that quiet, remember?"

Bishop's blush brightened, and he cleared his throat. "Uh, maybe don't tell Ava that I did that, okay, Will?"

She laughed. "Your secret's safe with me, big guy."

CHAPTER 14

The soft but insistent knocking woke Kat from her dream. She sat up, pushing her hair from her eyes and staring blearily at the alarm clock. It was just after five on Sunday morning, and she had only fallen asleep a couple of hours ago. She had tossed and turned restlessly for hours, hoping Ronin would call and ignoring her urge to text him. She hadn't spoken to or seen him since Thursday, and her cat was driving her crazy with its incessant yowling to go to him.

She didn't know why she had hoped he would call her Saturday night. Mavina was back in town, and he was working. That thought had sent fresh anger and jealousy flooding through her, and she had given up on sleep entirely and spent a few hours doing more research into Stowe Laboratories.

She had finally admitted defeat around three – she hadn't found a single bit of evidence that they were anything more than they claimed to be – and stumbled to bed. She fell asleep quickly, but her sleep was filled with jumbled images of Ronin, naked and in her bed, his raspy voice whispering in her ear as he had pinned her to the bed and pushed his cock into her aching core. She had been so close and –

There was another soft rap on her front door, and she groaned before climbing out of bed and grabbing her robe. She tightened the belt, staggered down the stairs, and peered groggily through the peephole. Her eyes widened, and her cat made a hiss of alarm as she unlocked the door and yanked it open.

"Ronin! Oh my God!" She stared in terror at him as he pushed past her and shut the door.

"Why are you – fuck – I need to call 9-1-1," she said.

"Whoa, wait, Kitten!" Ronin grabbed her arm, leaving a bloody handprint on her robe. "I'm perfectly fine."

"Perfectly fine?" Kat stared at him. "You – you're covered in blood, Ronin."

Covered was an understatement. Bright red blood drenched the bird shifter. It coated his hair and skin, and his clothes dripped blood onto the floor.

"It's not my blood," he said.

"Whose blood is it?" she asked in alarm.

He grimaced. "Mavina made me go to some vamp rave last night. They sprayed blood from the goddamn ceiling."

She made a soft sound of disgust, and he nodded. "Yeah, it's pretty gross. Mavina invited me back to her place to shower and clean up, but I didn't think that was such a great idea."

She couldn't stop her low hiss of anger, and Ronin grinned at her. "I got some weird looks from other drivers as I drove home. Your place was closer than mine, and I figured I'd stop and see if I could use your shower before someone called the cops."

He ran his hand through his hair, more blood splattered to the floor, and he winced. "Sorry, I'm making a mess. I guess it wasn't such a good idea to -"

"It's fine," she said. "Hold on a second."

216

She left the hallway and returned with a black garbage bag. "Come on, let's get you into the shower."

He followed her up the stairs, cursing under his breath. "I'm getting blood everywhere."

"It'll clean up," she said. She silently thanked God that she had wood floors and not carpet as she led him into her bathroom.

She helped him ease his shirt over his head and dropped it into the garbage bag as he peeled off his socks and unbuttoned his pants. He shoved them and his briefs down his legs – the blood had soaked through his clothing, and his entire body was tinged in red – and she added them to the garbage bag before turning on the shower.

"Sorry to wake you up, Kitten," he said.

"I wasn't sleeping," she said.

He reached out to touch her face before thinking better of it. "You do look a little tired."

She gave him a small smile. "I haven't been sleeping well."

"Me either," he said quietly.

There was a moment of awkward silence as the small bathroom filled with steam.

"I should get in the shower," he said.

"Yes," she said.

He glanced at her body before clearing his throat. "Maybe you should get in the shower with me. Wash my back for me."

"I could do that," she said.

Her hands trembling slightly, she opened her robe and slid it off her shoulders. She was naked beneath it, and Ronin inhaled sharply as his eyes roamed over her body.

"The shower, Ronin," she said a bit unsteadily, and he nodded.

She followed him into the shower, grimacing a little when he ducked under the spray and blood poured off of him.

She handed him the shampoo, and as he washed his hair, she squirted a generous amount of body wash onto the pouf before washing his back, ass, and legs. He rinsed his hair and scrubbed his face clean before turning to face her. She rinsed the pouf, added more body wash, and scrubbed his chest and arms until his skin was back to its normal colour. She traced the tattoos on his chest and placed a light kiss on the one that covered his left shoulder. He moaned softly, and she hesitated before, using the soap and just her hands, gripping his cock. He was already erect, and she rubbed and massaged him lightly before carefully washing his balls. He groaned, leaning back against the shower wall and closing his eyes as she rinsed him clean.

"All clean," she said hoarsely.

His eyes popped open. "Maybe I should return the favour."

She shook her head when he reached for the pouf. "Not with that. That's going straight in the garbage."

He smiled a little before lathering his hands with the soap. "Turn around, Kitten."

She turned and rested her hands on the wall, supporting her trembling body as his strong hands kneaded her shoulders before he ran them over her back. He washed her ass, squeezing and stroking it firmly before moving to her legs.

Her pussy throbbed, and her nipples were hard as glass by the time he tapped her lightly on the back. "Face me, Kat."

She did what he asked, moaning when his erection rubbed against her wet abdomen and arching her back when his soapy hands cupped her breasts. He cleaned them carefully, lingering on her nipples, and she moaned again as he pinched and pulled them. When his hand slid between her legs, she widened her legs and pressed herself eagerly against his fingers. He didn't breach her entrance, and she hissed at him.

"Let's rinse off the soap," he rasped.

He rinsed her quickly, and they stood quietly for a moment, staring at each other through the steam.

"Nice and clean," he said.

She nodded but remained still. "Ronin, I…"

"Kat," he whispered, and then she was in his arms, and he was kissing her, and she didn't care that they were only supposed to be friends. She wanted him desperately, and her pussy was dripping wet and aching maddeningly.

"Please," she said. "I need you."

"I need you too," he muttered into her ear.

"Now. Don't make me wait," she demanded.

"Whatever you say, Kitten." He lifted her and pressed her against the shower wall as the hot water sprayed over their bodies. She wrapped her legs around his hips and wiggled her hand between them, gripping his cock and guiding it into her.

"God, Kat," he groaned. "You're so wet already."

"I was dreaming about you," she whispered into his ear. "Dreaming about you in my bed, kissing me, touching me, fucking me."

He thrust his pelvis against her, and the bolt of pleasure made her cry out. "Fuck, yes, just like that."

They fucked hard and fast, their tongues tangling together as he pumped in and out of her, and she nipped his bottom lip. "Mine."

"Yours," he said, and she purred happily before reaching between their bodies. She rubbed her clit, her soft meows and purrs of pleasure echoing off the walls as she brought herself to orgasm.

He groaned and pumped furiously. Her wet body slapped against the shower wall, and when she sank her claws into his back, he climaxed with a loud shout. He groaned again, twitching and shaking against her as her pussy milked the last of his seed from his cock.

"Fuck," he panted. "Do you have any idea how fucking better my orgasm is when you claw me like that? I seriously had no idea I was into pain during sex."

She laughed and kissed his throat before wiggling against him. "Put me down. The water's starting to get cold."

She shut off the water, and they stepped out of the shower. They dried off quickly and walked naked into the bedroom. Ronin cleared his throat. "Well, thanks for letting me use your shower. I'll talk to you later?"

She scowled at him as she pulled back the covers on the bed. "You don't have to leave."

A look of happiness crossed his face before he shook his head. "I should go. You didn't sleep well last night, and I haven't slept at all. We both should probably get some rest and -"

"My bed, little bird. Now," she said.

A grin broke out on his face. "Yes, ma'am."

He spooned her in the bed, and she purred happily when he cupped her breast.

"I love your purring," he whispered into her ear. She squeezed his arm and pressed her ass against his groin.

"Cut that out, Kitten," he said. "We both need some sleep."

She yawned and rubbed his arm as he pressed a gentle kiss against her neck.

"It scared the hell out of me when I saw you covered in blood," she said.

He kissed her neck again. "Sorry. I probably should have called first."

"I thought you were hurt, and it made me realize that…."

She stopped before she said something that would freak him out.

"Made you realize what?" he asked.

"That my pretty little bird may not be quite as tough as he says he is," she said.

He laughed and nipped her lightly on the throat. "Don't you worry, Kitten. I'm plenty tough."

It was his turn to yawn, and she smiled when he buried his face in the back of her neck. "I'm suddenly very tired."

"Go to sleep, Ronin," she whispered.

"Hmm," he murmured sleepily as his body relaxed against hers.

*He's ours now, forever*, her cat growled happily.

She was too tired to argue.

---

BISHOP GLANCED IN THE REARVIEW MIRROR. BREN, SITTING IN the back seat, talked on his cell phone and paid no attention to them.

He eyed Kat sitting next to him. "So, you dating Ronin now or what?"

She jerked and shook her head quickly. "No, of course not. Why would you think that?"

"Maybe because you reek of his scent?" Bishop sniffed in her direction, and Kat flushed.

"He uh, he dropped by my place yesterday because Mavina took him to some rave where they sprayed blood all over everyone. He was getting weird looks from other drivers, and my place was closer, so he stopped to use my shower."

"Right," Bishop said. "So, he just used your shower and headed on home, huh?"

"Yes," she lied.

What had actually happened was a six-hour nap, followed by sex, another three-hour nap, more sex and then a second shower. They had made dinner together, eaten, watched some TV, fucked on the couch, and then Ronin had showered again, dressed, and left for work. He had an extra set of clothes in his car, and she didn't know whether to laugh or hiss angrily when she discovered it was because Mavina had a bad habit of slicing his clothes off his body.

A small grin crossed her face as she remembered Ronin's low laugh at the look on her face. "Don't worry, Kat. She's wily and super-fast with those damn nails of hers, but I've kept her from getting an eyeful or handful of little Ronin."

"You know you don't have to hide it if you're dating Ronin, right?" Bishop said.

"We're not dating," she said. "We're just friends – who have sex." She dropped her face into her hands.

"So, what? It's no big deal."

"He's our employee, Bishop."

"Mal's having sex with Willow, and she's our employee."

"It's not the same."

"It is."

"It isn't," she insisted. "It's different for men. I've worked hard to get where I am, and I don't want you and Mal thinking differently about me."

"We don't," Bishop said in surprise. "Kat, we asked you to be a partner in the firm because you're smart and good at what you do. Dating Ronin doesn't change any of that."

"Doesn't it?" she said.

"No," he said. "We don't care what you do in your personal life, Kat. It doesn't change our opinion of you – personally or when it comes to how well you do your job."

"You mean that, don't you?" she said.

"Yes. We'd be lost at the firm without you, Kat."

"Thanks, big guy," she said as Bren ended his call.

"How much longer?" he asked.

"We're here," Bishop said as he turned off the main highway. He drove for a few minutes down a winding, tree-lined road. Kat leaned forward and studied the large grey building as they rounded a final corner.

"God, it looks like a prison," she said.

A ten-foot chain-link fence surrounded the building with barbed wire lining the top of it. Wide metal gates with a small security booth blocked visitors from entering, and Kat pulled out her ID as Bishop stopped in front of the entrance. He rolled down his window as the security guard stepped out of the booth.

"Can I help you?"

"We're here to see Clay Haddon," Kat said as she passed him her identification. He studied it carefully before glancing at Bren in the back seat.

"Do you have an appointment?"

"No, but if you call Mr. Haddon, I'm sure he'll want to see me," Kat said.

The guard handed her back her ID. "No entry without an appointment."

"Just call him," Kat repeated.

The guard shook his head. "Come back when you have an appointment."

Bren rolled down the back window and showed the guard his badge. "I'm afraid we need to speak with Mr. Haddon."

The guard studied his badge before shrugging. "As I said, no appointment, no entry."

"I need to speak with him regarding an ongoing police investigation," Bren said. "He has information that will be helpful to the case. Why don't you open up that gate and let him know we're on our way? Impeding a police investigation is a serious offense."

"Do you have a warrant?" the guard asked.

Bren hesitated, and the man smiled at him. "The only way you're getting past this gate is with a warrant or an appointment. Have a nice day."

He returned to the booth and shut the door. Bishop sighed loudly. "Well, that was very helpful. Thank you, Detective."

Kat frowned at him. "He tried, Bishop."

"Yeah, I know," Bishop said. He threw the truck into reverse and turned around before driving away.

———

"Now what?" Bishop asked as he drove back to the city.

"I don't know," Kat admitted. "We can't -"

Her cell phone rang, and she dug it out of her purse before glancing at Bishop and Bren. "It's Clay Haddon."

She pressed the answer button and then the speaker button. "Hello, Clay."

"Hello, Kat. How are you?"

"Very interested in knowing what you're doing to Sandra Mickelson," Kat said. "We were just at the lab, but your guard refused us entry."

"Sorry about that," Clay said. "They're a little overzealous when it comes to security."

"We're not far," Kat said. "We can turn back and meet with you."

"I'm afraid that's not going to work," Clay said. "I'm not at the lab at the moment."

"Of course, you're not," Kat said. "Where's Sandra Mickelson?"

"She's at our lab. We're trying to help her, Kat."

"Are you?"

"Yes," Clay said. "Our doctors are already working on a vaccine that we hope will help her fight the virus."

"So, it is a virus," Kat said.

"We think so," Clay said cautiously. "Kat, I can assure you that we are not harming Sandra Mickelson. We suspected that the porcupine shifter had injured her, and while I admit that our methods of taking her were a little unorthodox, it was necessary to protect my men. How is your employee, by the way?"

"Considering he was shot with a powerful sedative, he's fine."

"Yes, please give him my apologies. I may have panicked a little," Clay said.

"You don't seem like the panicking type to me, Clay. We want to see Sandra Mickelson. She's our client, and we need to know that she's safe."

"I told you, she's perfectly safe."

"Why are you doing this?" Kat asked. "You study shifters' healing abilities, not try to cure viral mutations."

Clay cleared his throat. "I wasn't entirely truthful with you earlier, Kat. The main focus of the lab is to study shifter healing abilities, but over the last few years, Dr. Stowe has also started studying mutations and viruses in shifters."

"Why?"

"I'm afraid I can't say."

"What do you think will happen when I go to the media over this? When I accuse Stowe Laboratories of holding a shifter against her will," Kat said.

"There's no need for that, Kat," Clay said.

"Good, then you'll meet us at the lab?"

"I'm currently out of the city, but I'm back Thursday

night. I'll stop by your office Friday morning, and we'll talk. If I can't convince you that she's fine, I'll drive you to the lab myself and show you."

"Not good enough," Kat said.

"This is what I'm offering. You can take it or leave it and go to the media," Clay said. "It's your call."

Kat glanced at Bishop, who shrugged before nodding.

"Fine. See you Friday morning, Clay." She ended the call and stared at Bishop and Bren. "Well, that went better than I thought."

"We need to get into that lab," Bren said. "If mutated shifters are running around and it's their fault, we need to shut the place down before they do something worse."

"We'll get into the lab," Kat said confidently. "I don't care how Clay spins the story on Friday morning, he's not convincing me of anything until I see Sandra Mickelson."

"I'll meet you at your office on Friday," Bren said as he checked his phone.

"Probably not a good idea," Bishop said. "Clay may be willing to let Kat and me into the lab, but a detective – not a chance."

"Bishop's right," Kat said when Bren started to protest. "We'll take a look at the lab and then call you to let you know what we found out."

Bren frowned. "Something isn't right about this. You can feel it, can't you? The two of you going there alone could be very dangerous."

Bishop nodded. "Yes. But I don't think we have much choice, Detective."

"What are you doing, Clay?" Saul asked as Clay stuck his cell phone in his pocket.

"I can handle it, Saul."

"Can you? You were supposed to kill that bodyguard, remember? If you had, none of this would be happening. We need to go to Wyatt."

He started to stand. Clay grabbed him by the front of the shirt and shoved him against the wall. "You keep your fucking mouth shut, Saul. You hear me?"

Saul, his eyes wide with fear, nodded. "Yeah."

Clay glared at him before releasing him. "Sorry. I'm a little on edge."

"You can't bring them here. You know that, right?"

"Yes. Don't worry, I'll think of something. Wyatt doesn't need to know about it. I'll smooth things over with the shifters and convince them that they don't need to come to the lab."

"What's happening to you? You had very specific orders from Wyatt, and since when have you not followed orders? People can't know about this. It would have been better if you had killed the guy and -"

"That shifter was innocent," Clay said. "I don't kill innocent people, Saul."

"Is that it? Or are you just done with killing?"

"Maybe I am," Clay said moodily before vanishing.

# CHAPTER 15

"Willow! Mother mentioned you would be coming to the party. Give the birthday boy a hug." The lion shifter held out his arms, grinning cheekily at Mal as Willow stepped forward and hugged him briefly.

"Happy Birthday, Koren," she said.

"Thanks, Willow." He glanced at her bare left hand. "Still not married, huh? You know, it's not too late to try a lion shifter on for size."

Mal growled and tugged Willow away from Koren before glaring at him. Koren laughed and elbowed his golden-haired brother. "Wolf shifters, they can't take a joke, am I right?"

Keegan shrugged, his eyes lighting up when Ava and Bishop joined them. "Ava! You're looking lovely."

"Thank you, Keegan," Ava said. "How are you doing?"

"Can't complain." Keegan stepped forward to hug her and stopped when Bishop snarled at him.

"Really?" Keegan said with a grin.

Bishop didn't reply, and Ava held out her hand. Keegan rolled his eyes before shaking it.

"Hello, kitty," Koren suddenly murmured, and Willow

stifled a giggle when he gave them all a nod before walking rapidly across the yard. Kat had just arrived, and Willow had to admit that she looked stunning in a short, dark red dress that hugged her full breasts.

Keegan smiled at them. "If you'll excuse me, I told Mother I would ensure that the DJ didn't play any of that 'dreadful hip-hop' as she calls it."

"Man, Marika sure knows how to throw a party, huh? I would have thrown up a few streamers, some balloons and called it a day," Willow said.

The massive backyard was decorated to the hilt. The colour theme was yellow and blue, and there were close to two hundred large clusters of blue and yellow balloons, tied to metal stakes shoved deep into the ground, scattered around the yard. Near the house, a large table nearly overflowed with food. A DJ's booth was to their right, and behind them, a gigantic blue corkboard balanced on an equally large easel. Hundreds of photos of Koren plastered the corkboard, each one pinned carefully with a bright yellow pin. Yellow and blue lights had been added to the koi fountain in the middle of the yard, and a banner hung from the roof with the words, "Happy Birthday, Koren" written on it in a bold, blue font.

"Koren has a lot of friends," Willow said. Hundreds of people were mingling in the yard, and she watched them silently for a few minutes before turning to Mal. "Do you think we'll play pin the donkey later?"

"Knowing Koren, it's more likely to be spin the bottle," Mal said.

Willow laughed and squeezed Mal's waist as Bishop said, "I'm surprised there isn't a huge table of presents."

"I was talking with Mrs. Belfry earlier, and she said Koren asked that donations be made to the food bank in lieu of gifts," Ava said. "The lion shifters aren't all bad, Bishop."

"Should we go and rescue Kat from Koren?" Willow asked Mal.

He grinned at her. "Maybe she's enjoying talking with him."

"Maybe," Willow said. She glanced at the setting sun. "Hey, did you remember to tell her that Ronin and Mavina will be here tonight?"

Mal and Bishop gave each other identical guilty looks, and Willow poked Mal in the side. "You were supposed to warn her."

"I told Bishop to do it," Mal said.

"And I said no, I wouldn't," Bishop said. "You think I want Kat pissed at me? She's all possessive and weird about Ronin now."

"It's going to be much worse when he shows up, and she has no idea," Willow said. "One of you go over and tell her."

"Not it," Mal and Bishop said in unison.

Willow laughed. "Chickens. Both of you are chickens."

"Why don't you tell her?" Mal suggested.

Willow grabbed Ava's arm. "Gosh, I'd love to, but we're starving and need to grab some food. Isn't that right, Ava?"

"Sure," Ava said.

"Be good while we're gone," Willow said with a grin to Mal before leading Ava to the buffet table.

---

"Since when did you become friends with a vampire?" Keegan appeared in front of Kat, and she smiled at him as Koren's hand wandered from her hip to her ass. She pushed his hand away and arched her eyebrow at him.

"Sorry, Katarina, I just can't resist you," the lion shifter said with a grin.

"Koren," Keegan repeated, "when did you start hanging out with vampires? Not that I'm complaining, but Mother is going to lizard out when she sees her."

"I have no idea what you're talking about, brother," Koren said as his eyes drifted to Kat's breasts.

"Look," Keegan said impatiently.

Koren and Kat followed his gaze, and Keegan stared at Kat when she growled.

"Holy shit," Koren breathed. "I have no idea who she is, but I call dibs."

Keegan grinned at him. "We'll see who she goes home with tonight." He raised his head and inhaled deeply. "Why is she with a bird shifter?"

"What the hell are they doing here?" Kat said.

"You know them?" Keegan asked.

"The bird shifter is an employee, and the vampire is a client," Kat said. "They should not be here. I don't know who invited them but -"

"I invited them, Ms. Frost."

The three of them turned to see Marika Belfry, wearing her customary dark, high-necked dress, standing behind them.

"It's good to see you again, Mrs. Belfry. Thank you for inviting me to Koren's birthday party." Kat forced herself to smile at the lizard shifter.

"It's nice to see you as well, Ms. Frost," Marika said.

Ronin's scent grew more potent, and Kat clenched her hands into fists as Marika's face lit up, and she smiled broadly. "Ronin. You made it."

"I did," Ronin said. He stepped around Kat, and a light-ning bolt of lust rocketed through her when his bare arm brushed hers. He pressed a kiss against Marika's leathery cheek. "You're looking lovely this evening."

Keegan's and Koren's mouths dropped open as their

mother blushed and giggled softly. "Thank you, Ronin. You know my sons, Keegan and Koren."

Ronin shook each of their hands. "Happy birthday, Koren."

"Thanks," Koren's gaze had already returned to Mavina, and the vampire gave him a coy smile before holding out one pale hand.

"Hello, I'm Mavina."

Koren took her hand and pressed a kiss against her knuckles. "I'm delighted to meet you, Mavina."

She smiled, revealing her sharp white fangs, before looking him up and down. "And what kind of shifter are you, Koren?"

"I'm a lion shifter."

"You must be brave and strong then," she giggled as Keegan pushed his way in between them and took her hand.

"My name is Keegan. I'm Koren's older and *bigger* brother."

Marika made a loud snort. "Honestly, I can practically see the blood draining from your brains."

Her sons had the decency to blush before Koren held out his arm to Mavina. "Why don't I introduce you to a few of my friends."

"I'd like that," she cooed. She took his arm before holding her other hand out to Keegan. "Will you join us, Keegan?"

"It would be my pleasure," he said in a low growl.

"I swear," Marika sighed as the two lion shifters escorted the vampire across the yard, "vampires are the worst."

She took Ronin's arm. "Come, Ronin, I want you to meet a few of my closest friends."

"I'd love to, Marika, but unfortunately, I'm working tonight. I need to keep my eye on Mavina."

"Nonsense," Marika said, "the vampire is perfectly safe here. Now I must insist that you come with me."

She tugged Ronin toward a large group of older women, they were mostly lizard and snake shifters, as Kat tamped down her laughter.

---

"I'VE MISSED YOU."

Ronin's low voice spoke directly into her ear, and a warm shiver went down Kat's spine. It was nearly four hours later, and the party was winding down. Well, she supposed, technically, it was over. The only party guests left were her, Mal and Willow, Ava and Bishop, and Ronin.

*And Mavina. Don't forget Mavina.*

She stared at the vampire. The two lion brothers were flanking her, and as Kat watched, Koren leaned down and pressed a light kiss against her mouth as Keegan squeezed her firm ass.

"I've missed you too," she admitted as Ronin stepped closer until his chest brushed against her back.

She hadn't seen him since Sunday, and her cat purred happily when his large hand gripped her hip. "I thought maybe I'd bring you dinner tomorrow night before my shift starts."

"I'd like that," she said.

"I would too."

She took a quick look around. Marika was talking with Mal, Willow, Ava and Bishop. She leaned back against Ronin, making a startled noise when she felt his erection press against her ass.

"Ronin," she tried to sound disapproving, but it came out sounding more like a moan of need.

"What? I told you I missed you," he murmured before kissing her neck.

"You're working," she said.

"I'm watching her," he said.

It was true. Ronin's tongue was tracing the curve of her ear, but his gaze was firmly on the vampire who, Kat thought dryly, any minute now would probably start humping the lion brothers.

"Maybe I could stop by tomorrow morning before you go to work," Ronin said. "I can bring you breakfast in bed. Do you like donuts?"

She smiled. "Not for breakfast."

"Hmm, well, I need to feed you something for breakfast," Ronin said teasingly. "I can't have my kitten going off to work hungry."

"I'm sure we can think of something," Kat said before pressing her ass against his erection.

His breath hissed in her ear, and she made a low purr.

"Well, Koren and Keegan certainly don't share their mother's hatred of vampires, do they?" Willow's voice came from her left, and Kat could have cheerfully strangled the woman as Ronin raised his head and dropped his hand from her hip.

Ava was with Willow, and she gave Kat a little grin. Kat cleared her throat as Willow smiled at her. "Don't you think?"

"I'm sorry, what?" Kat said.

"The lion brothers seem to have a thing for vampires." Willow jabbed her thumb at them. "If their mother wasn't here, I think they'd be banging her by now."

She grinned at Ronin. "I'm fairly certain you're going to have to watch Mavina being tag-teamed by the lion shifters tonight."

"Gross," Ronin said.

"Hopefully, you won't be asked to join in on the hair braiding afterward," Willow said.

"What?" Ronin gave her a blank look.

Willow laughed. "You don't want to know."

"Do you think they'll let her bite them?" Ava asked.

"Oh, probably," Willow said. "Those lion boys are kinky. Koren will probably ask her to give him birthday bites."

"More like birthday spankings," Ava said, and Willow gave her a look of delight before raising her fist.

"Nice one, Ava."

Ava laughed and fist-bumped her. "I wonder if -"

A shadow flickered by them. A tall vampire with long, black hair appeared in front of the lion shifters and Mavina.

"What the hell?" Willow said.

The vampire hissed, and Mavina screamed as he grabbed Koren and lifted him off his feet. "You dare to touch her!"

He threw Koren across the yard. The lion shifter landed in the fountain, water spraying everywhere as Keegan roared in anger. He shifted to his lion form and leaped at the vampire. The vampire laughed and caught the lion, digging his hands into Keegan's thick mane before tossing him aside. Keegan slammed into a tree and fell to the ground, his back legs scrabbling weakly at the grass.

Ronin darted across the yard as Mavina, her eyes glowing and her fangs bared, backed away from the vampire. "Leave me alone!" she snarled.

"You're mine, you little whore!" the vampire shouted.

He reached for her and screamed angrily when Ronin tackled him. They landed on the ground with a hard thud, and Ronin punched him twice in the face before the vampire threw him off easily.

"She's mine!" he snarled at the bird shifter.

"Ronin!" Kat's terrified scream drew the vampire's attention. He stared at the three women before grinning.

"I'll kill all of you for keeping her from me. Starting with your pathetic women."

He was standing in front of them before Kat could even think of moving. Dimly she was aware of Bishop's angry roar and Mal's loud barking as the vampire reached for Willow. The vampire grunted in surprise when the wolf shifter leaped onto his back and clamped his jaws around his neck. The vampire screamed and grabbed the wolf's head, tearing Mal away as blood sprayed from the wound in his neck. He threw Mal across the yard as Willow screamed shrilly and ran toward the fallen wolf.

The vampire backed away and clamped his hand across his neck. He stared at the bright red blood on the palm of his hand before laughing. "You think you can defeat me?"

The wound was already beginning to heal, and Ava made a terrified moan as Kat, her body swelling and hair sprouting on her cheeks, bared her fangs at the vampire.

"You don't frighten me, shifter," the vampire snarled. He cocked his head and stared at Ava's bright red hair.

"You have beautiful hair," he said. "Perhaps I will keep you as my pet. Mavina and I will need something to feed on."

Ava stumbled back, her eyes darting to the left as the vampire grinned. "You should be frightened, my pet. I'm not going to be gentle. In fact, I -"

There was a low growl to his left, and the vampire turned as the giant grizzly rose to his back feet. He towered over the vampire, and for the first time, a flicker of fear crossed his face. Bishop roared and swiped his paw across the vampire's throat, tearing deep gouges into his soft skin. Blood sprayed out in a heavy arc, and the vampire made a gurgling noise before clamping his hand over his throat. He staggered back, his eyes bulging, and collapsed face down on the ground.

"Holy fuck," Kat said as Bishop dropped to all fours and lumbered to Ava.

He sniffed at her hair and nudged her with his big head. She stroked the fur on his broad shoulder. "I'm all right, honey."

Kat stared around the yard. Mavina was helping Koren out of the fountain, and Marika was kneeling next to Keegan by the tree. He shifted to his human form, and with a strength belied by her small size, she heaved her son to his feet and threw her arm around his waist before leading him toward the others.

Mal had shifted to his human form, and he cupped Willow's head, scanning her body anxiously.

"I'm fine, Mal. I'm fine," Willow said. "I'm not hurt. Are you okay?"

Bishop changed to his human form with a soft pop and put his arm around Ava before resting his hand against her belly. She leaned against him and smiled faintly as Mal and Willow joined them.

"Everyone okay?" Mal asked.

"Is he dead?" Willow asked.

Ronin crouched next to the vampire. "Yeah, I think Bishop pretty much tore his head -"

The vampire flipped to his back and hissed before grabbing Ronin's throat. He leaped to his feet as Kat, growling viciously, ran toward them.

He yanked Ronin in front of him and stared at Kat. "Come any closer, and I'll tear out his throat."

The vampire stared balefully at Bishop. "The next time you try to kill me, you should be certain to fully remove my head from my body."

His hand tightened around Ronin's neck, and the bird shifter made a low choking sound as his face turned red.

"No, don't," Kat said quickly. She raised her hands and shook her head at Mal and Bishop when they joined her. "Just – just calm down. No one has to get hurt here."

"No one has to get hurt?" The vampire laughed before massaging the rapidly closing wounds on his throat. "That bear shifter nearly took my head, but no one has to get hurt?"

He loosened his grip enough to allow Ronin to take in some ragged breaths before staring at Mavina. "Come to me."

Mavina shook her head, and the vampire snarled before shaking Ronin. "I'll kill you for trying to keep her from me. Did you think that would go unpunished?"

"Let him go," Kat said. "He was only watching her because I asked him to. I'm the one to blame."

"Be quiet, Kat," Ronin choked out.

"So, I should kill you then?" the vampire said.

"Yes," Kat said. She took a few steps forward, shaking off Bishop's hand. "I'm the one you want," she repeated. "He's no one, just a hired hand. It's my fault you can't be with Mavina."

She moved closer until she stood directly in front of Ronin and the vampire. She glanced at Ronin, and he gave her a pleading look. "Kat, do not do this. He can kill me. It won't matter. Please trust me."

She ignored him and held out her hand to the vampire. "If anyone deserves to die, it's me."

Her cat was yowling and hissing to be free - she wanted to protect her mate - and Kat controlled it grimly as the vampire stared at Ronin and then her.

"You both deserve to die," he said.

He released his grip around Ronin's neck and, his hand a blur, raked one razor-sharp nail across the bird shifter's throat. Kat screamed in horror as a thick spray of blood spurted out from Ronin's throat and drenched her face and upper body. Ronin fell to his knees, and Kat screamed again as he pitched forward face-first into the grass.

"Your turn," the vampire said. He reached for her as she stared in horrified shock at Ronin's body. She could hear Mal and Bishop running up behind her, but she couldn't tear her gaze from Ronin. The vampire's cold fingers brushed against her throat. His nail began to tear and then stopped. His eyes widened, and he made a small grunt of surprise before ripping open his shirt. The tip of a metal stake, covered in thick, black blood, stuck out from his chest.

He touched it lightly. "What -"

His body exploded into ash, covering Kat and Mal and Bishop, and the three of them stared at the ash-coated Marika standing in front of them. She held a metal stake in her hand. The balloons attached to it floated gently in the breeze behind her, and a look of disgust crossed her face before she dropped the stake to the ground and wiped her hands on her filthy dress.

"And that is why I loathe vampires," she said.

There was a second of silence, and then Kat, screaming Ronin's name, dropped to her knees beside the fallen bird shifter and heaved him onto his back.

"Ronin, look at me. Honey, hang on. You'll be okay." She clamped her hand over Ronin's throat, only a trickle of blood flowed from it now, and stared into his face. His bright green eyes were horrifyingly empty, and she lifted her head and screamed.

"No!" she shrieked and clutched at his shirt before pressing her mouth against his. "No, please, Ronin! No!"

"Kat." Bishop's warm hand rubbed her back. "Kat, I'm sorry. He's gone."

She screamed again before leaping to her feet and staring wildly around the yard. Her gaze fell on Mavina, and the vampire took a step back as Kat's eyes glowed and her fangs descended.

"You," she snarled, "this is your fault!"

She leaped for the vampire with terrifying quickness, but Bishop was faster. He grabbed Kat's arm and yanked her into his embrace. He wrapped his arms around her and held her tightly as she clawed and scratched his naked back. He roared in pain but held on grimly when she sank her fangs into his chest and tore out a chunk of flesh.

"Get her out of here!" Mal shouted at the lion brothers. Their faces pale, they hurried Mavina into the house as Kat screamed and growled and tore at Bishop's back. She was starting to turn, her dress ripping as her body swelled.

Bishop shook her hard. "Kat! Stop! Control it, Kat."

Her anger suddenly popped like a balloon, sorrow and despair replacing it. She collapsed against Bishop, the fur fading from her cheeks and her eyes returning to their normal green colour. She panted harshly as tears rolled down her cheeks. Her jaguar made a mournful howl that sent fresh sorrow radiating through her.

"Ronin," she whispered before staring up at Bishop.

Bishop brushed her hair back from her face and pressed a kiss against her forehead. "He's gone, Kat. I'm so sorry."

Her face crumpled, and he pushed her head against his broad chest, rubbing her back and speaking quietly to her. Kat barely heard his low words of comfort. Ronin was dead. She would never hear his voice again, never feel the touch of his warm skin. He was gone.

"Hey, guys?" Willow's voice was soft and hesitant. "Is it just me, or is Ronin starting to smoke?"

Kat pushed away from Bishop and stared at Ronin's body.

Wisps of smoke drifted up from his motionless body, and she cried out and staggered back when his body burst into flames.

"What the hell?" Bishop said.

The flames licked at the night air. The heat was tremendous, and Kat made a moaning cry as Ronin's body burned. There was another burst of flame and heat, this one so bright and hot it made her eyes water, and she took a step back as the fire flickered and died. A large pile of ash was all that remained of Ronin's body, and she stared at the others in shock.

"Mal?" Willow whispered. "What just happened?"

"Oh my God," Ava said in a low voice. She raised a trembling hand and pointed at the ash. It rippled slightly, and, as they watched, it rippled again, and there was a flash of red and gold.

"Holy shit," Mal said as the scarlet bird rose out of the ash. It was large, taller and broader than an ostrich with a tail rivalling a peacock's, and bright red and gold plumage. Its beak and talons were dark gold, and it shook itself, ash sprinkling down from its plumage before spreading its long wings and flapping them gently. More ash fell, and the bird stepped delicately out of the pile of ash before staring at Kat. She studied the familiar bright green eyes and stumbled forward. She stroked his bright plumage with a trembling hand, and the bird brushed his beak against her cheek.

She closed her eyes and whispered, "Ronin."

There was a low popping noise, but she kept her eyes tightly closed as hope bloomed in her belly. When his warm hand cupped her face, she shuddered all over and opened her eyes.

"Hello, Kitten," Ronin said.

She started to cry, and he pulled her into his embrace. "Don't cry, Kat."

She hugged him fiercely, and he pressed kisses all over her face before finally kissing her mouth. She returned his kiss frantically, her hands digging into his warm back as he stroked her hair.

He released her mouth and grinned at her. "Miss me, Kitten?"

"I love you," she said.

His eyes widened, and he kissed her again before resting his forehead against hers. "I love you too."

"You're a phoenix," Marika Belfry said with soft wonderment.

Ronin stepped away from Kat, holding her hand tightly, and smiled at the lizard shifter. "Yes."

She touched his face with one rough hand. "I knew there was something special about you, Mr. Smith."

She studied him quietly before dropping her hand and turning to the others.

"Well, it's not the worst party we've had here. But I'm tired, and I think it's time to call it a night," she said briskly.

She took Kat's hand and squeezed it. "Take your bird home, Ms. Frost. I'll have my boys escort that dreadful vampire home."

CHAPTER 16

"We should talk, Kat," Ronin said as she sat down on the bed.

As soon as they had arrived at her house, Ronin had led her to the shower. They had showered together, washing away the ash and the blood that covered them, but he had shaken his head when she'd tried to touch him and kiss him.

She nodded. "Yes, but not now."

"Kat -"

"I need you," she said simply.

He hesitated, and she stood and unwrapped her towel, dropping it to the floor. He stared hungrily at her naked body before looking away.

"We need to talk," he repeated.

"We will," she said before holding out her hand.

He took her hand and kissed her palm as she untucked the towel around his waist. She pushed him onto the bed until he lay on his back and straddled his thighs. His cock was hardening, and she bent over him and took it into her mouth, sucking firmly as he groaned. She darted her tongue over the slit, relishing the taste of his precum before licking the thick vein on the underside.

"Kat," he moaned, "please."

She licked and teased until his hips thrust uncontrollably, and he begged softly. She smiled at him, stroking his thighs with her nails before she sat up and scooted her body forward. She planted her knees on either side of his head and smiled down at him.

"My pretty bird," she said.

"Yes," he said. His warm hands gripped her thighs, and she cried out with pleasure when he pulled her down to his mouth. His tongue licked at her swollen clit, and she ground her pussy against him. He sucked her clit into his mouth before flicking it with the tip of his tongue, and she purred loudly as she rested her hands on his stomach and thrust her pelvis against his mouth. She was close to coming, and she pulled away before he could bring her to her release. She wanted - *needed* - him to be inside of her when she came. She ignored his grunt of disapproval as she slid down his body. He helped her guide his cock into her warm wetness, and she purred again as he filled her.

"So good," she whispered as she rocked back and forth.

"Yes," he moaned. "Faster, Kitten."

She moved faster as he cupped her full breasts and played with her nipples. He moved one hand to her clit and rubbed it firmly, and she moaned his name, sinking her claws into his chest as fire coursed through her veins.

"I can't wait," she gasped. "It feels so good, Ronin, it feels -"

Her back arched, and she came hard, her pussy tightening around his dick. Ronin shouted hoarsely, and she ground herself against him as he came with a wild thrusting of his hips. She collapsed against his warm body, resting her head on his as he rubbed her back.

"I love you," he said.

She lifted her head and smiled at him. "I love you too."

She poked him with her claws when he grinned and said, "Of course you do. I'm irresistible, Kitten."

She crawled off of him, and they climbed under the covers. He reclined on his back, and she threw her leg over his and rested her head against his chest again as he stroked her naked hip.

"So, you're a phoenix," she said.

"Yes."

"I thought they were extinct."

"There aren't many of us left," he said. "And the ones who are do everything they can to avoid detection."

He squeezed her hip. "I'm sorry I didn't tell you."

She shook her head. "You don't need to be sorry. It's not something you should be sharing. If humans found out about phoenixes, hell, if other shifters found out about you… it would be awful."

He didn't reply, and she smoothed her hand over the tattoos that covered his chest. "That's how you survived the dragon's fire. Ava was right. You were burned to a crisp that night."

"Yes. After I was reborn, I was going to slip away because I knew that Ava had seen what happened, but I couldn't leave."

"Why not?" she asked.

"I saw you," he said. "I saw you staring at those burning trees, and I knew you thought I was dead. The look on your face tore me up inside. I didn't want you to believe I was dead."

He kissed the top of her head. "Also, I really wanted to

sleep with you, and it would have been hard to do that if you thought I was dead."

She laughed and kissed his chest. "I really wanted to sleep with you too."

"I know," he said. "You practically molested me right there in front of everyone."

She pinched him in the ribs, and he winced before squeezing her naked ass. "Gentle, Kitten. I'm a fragile little bird, remember?"

She suddenly stiffened before lifting her head and staring at him. "The night that the dragon attacked us at Mal's house. I was dying, wasn't I?

He nodded, his face paling, and she took a deep breath. "I don't remember much - I didn't want to remember, and I convinced myself that what memories I had weren't real – but I remember you holding me." She touched his face. "I remember you crying."

He closed his eyes for a moment. "The dragon broke your back and paralyzed you. A phoenix's tears can heal so…."

He frowned when she started to cry. "Kat, sweetheart? Don't cry."

"You saved my life," she said. "You saved my life, and I was so – so mean to you."

He burst out laughing and hugged her tightly. "I like my mean little pussy cat, remember?"

She cupped his face and kissed him. "Thank you for saving my life, Ronin."

"You're welcome, Kat," he said.

She buried her face in his throat, and he stared silently at the ceiling. He needed to tell her about Wyatt and the lab, needed to tell her that being with him put her in danger, but it had been a long day, and they were both tired.

*Later*, he thought. *I'll tell her later.*

"HOW'S RONIN DOING?" MAL ASKED.

"Perfectly fine," Kat said. "He said he could come back to work."

Mal shook his head. "The guy died two days ago. I think we can wait until Monday. We'll put him back at the warehouse for now. Now that the vampire is dead, Mavina's parents ended the security detail on her."

"If they ask us to provide security again, I think we should say no," Bishop grumbled. "They aren't paying us nearly enough for the kind of shit that went down at Koren's party."

Kat glanced at her watch. The three of them were standing in reception, and she tensed when the door opened.

"Hey, Willow?" Fenton frowned at the piece of paper he held. "The insurance screwed up my dental claim again, and I -"

He stopped and stared at the three shifters standing by the desk. "Oh, hey. What's going on?"

"Just waiting for someone," Kat said.

Willow stood and took the piece of paper from Fenton before scanning it. "Oh, for the love of Pete," she sighed. "Your insurance company is the worst, Fenton."

"Tell me about it," he said. "Although I think I may have messed up this time and given them the wrong information."

"Here, come with me to Mal's office, and we'll check your personnel file. Maybe it's an incorrect policy number," Willow said.

Fenton followed Willow into Mal's office as Bishop glanced at his watch. "Do you think Clay will show up? It's almost noon."

249

Kat shrugged. "He'd better. I'll go to the media if I have to, and he won't -"

The door opened a second time, the bell over it jingling softly, and Clay walked into the office. He was dressed casually in jeans and a grey t-shirt, and he looked tired and out of sorts.

"Hello, Clay," Kat said.

"Hi." Clay gave the three of them a brief smile. "Sorry, I'm late."

"Why don't we talk in my office."

The three men followed Kat into her office. "Clay, this is Malcolm Burke."

Mal shook Clay's hand as Kat closed her door. Clay was still standing next to her, and he gave her another brief smile. "So, before we get started, I wanted to -"

The door to her office opened, and Ronin stuck his head in. "Hey, Kitten, I'm here to take you for lunch. I thought we'd hit the deli down the...."

He trailed off, and Kat watched as he stared at Clay, and a look of anger and fear crossed his face.

"You," Clay breathed.

---

FEAR SIZZLING THROUGH HIS VEINS, RONIN REACHED FOR Kat. His fingers brushed against her arm before she was yanked up against Clay. Clay placed a gun at her temple, and she froze as Clay barked, "Any closer, bear shifter, and she's dead. Move, Ronin."

"Let her go, Clay," Ronin said. "You don't need her."

"Move," Clay repeated.

Ronin backed into reception, and Clay prodded Kat in the back. "Walk."

She walked out of her office, Clay right behind her. He pointed the gun at Bishop and Mal. "Over with the bird, please."

They joined Ronin as Clay put his arm around her waist and pressed the gun against her temple again.

Kat stared at Ronin, and he returned her look unblinkingly as Clay studied them both.

"You know better than to let anyone get close to you, Ronin," Clay said.

"I didn't. She means nothing to me," Ronin said.

Clay's slight smile was tinged with weariness. "No? Then you won't care if I shoot her?"

His finger tightened on the trigger, and Ronin took a step forward, holding his hands out and shaking his head. "Wait! Clay, just wait a minute."

Clay smiled again. "You love her."

"Ronin, what's going on? How do you know Clay?" Kat's voice was remarkably steady, and Ronin felt a surge of love for the jaguar shifter.

"You didn't tell her?" Clay said. "I suppose you thought you were protecting her."

"How did you find me?" Ronin asked.

"Oh, you'll love this part," Clay said. "I didn't find you. I was just here to speak with Ms. Frost. You showing up is an ironic twist of fate."

"I can't help him," Ronin said. "I tried – it doesn't work."

"I know," Clay said. "He's gone mad."

"Then why are you helping him?" Ronin asked.

"He's my friend," Clay said.

"I was his friend too, and you saw what he did to me."

"He thinks it'll work this time," Clay said.

"Do you?" Ronin asked.

"Does it matter what I think?" Clay said. "I'm sorry,

Ronin, I am. I'm taking Ms. Frost to the lab. I expect you to join us. I'll let her go when you do."

He glanced at Bishop and Mal. "Just you, Ronin. Not your new friends, not the cops, just you – or she's dead. I don't want to kill her, but you know I will."

"You don't need her," Ronin said quickly. "Let her go, and I'll come with you right now."

Clay hesitated, and Ronin took a step toward them. "You don't need to involve Kat in this. I'm the one he wants. Let her go, Clay, please."

Clay stared steadily at him before nodding. Relief flooding through him, Ronin gave Kat a faint smile. "Everything will be fine, Kitten."

"I'm not leaving you," she said. "If he's taking you to that lab, I'm going with you."

"No, you're not," Ronin said. "I love you, Kat. Don't come after me, okay?"

"Fuck that," Kat snapped, and despite his fear, a small smile crossed Ronin's face.

Clay squeezed her waist. "Listen to him, Kat. You don't want to see what he'll do to the man you love."

There was a flicker of movement behind Clay. Ronin could see Fenton slipping out of Mal's office and crouching to the ground as he prepared to jump. He didn't make a sound, but Clay stiffened before looking over his shoulder just as Fenton leaped for him.

"NO!" Ronin shouted as Clay vanished, taking Kat with him.

"What the fuck!" Bishop said as Fenton, a growl of surprise erupting from his throat, landed on the floor in front of Ronin.

"He's a goddamn teleport!" Mal said.

"Fuck!" Ronin shouted. He ran for the door and scowled

at Bishop when the bear shifter grabbed him by the arm and shoved him against the wall.

"Let me go!" he snarled.

"Not a fucking chance," Bishop growled. "Not until you tell us what the fuck is going on."

Willow came out of Mal's office. "Mal? How – how did he just disappear like that?"

"He's a teleport," Mal said grimly as he joined Bishop. He stared at Ronin, his eyes glowing bright green.

"I have to go!" Ronin said. "Wyatt's insane, and he'll hurt Kat if I don't go to the fucking lab. Is that what you want? For Kat to die?"

Bishop roared with anger and slammed Ronin against the wall. "I get that you love her, but Kat's our friend, and she is just as important to us as she is to you. Now start talking, Ronin, or I'll rip open your guts and show you what your intestines look like."

———

HER STOMACH ROLLING AND SO DIZZY SHE COULD BARELY see, Kat fell to her knees and vomited on the floor. Clay grabbed her arm and hauled her to her feet. She staggered, and he steadied her.

"It can be a bit disorienting the first few times. Take some deep breaths. It will help."

She coughed and wretched again before wiping her mouth with her hand. "What the fuck did you do to me?"

They were in a small office with a desk, a credenza, and two leather chairs. Holding her arm, Clay led her toward one of the chairs. The floor was moving like she was on a boat in the middle of a storm, and she stumbled and nearly fell. Clay threw his arm around her waist and half-carried, half-dragged her to the chair. She sank into it, closing her eyes and breathing in deep gasps of air as Clay watched silently.

"What did you do to me?" she asked again as the room slowly stopped spinning.

"I'm a teleport," he said. "I can move from one -"

"I know what it means," she said irritably. "Where are we?"

"Stowe Laboratories," Clay said. He moved to the credenza as Kat eyed the closed door.

"I wouldn't suggest trying to escape," Clay said as he poured amber liquid from a crystal decanter into two glasses. "The building is huge and quite maze-like. It'll be impossible for you to find your way out before my men or I find you."

She glared at his broad back. "I move fast."

He laughed. "Yes, I imagine you do, but believe me – you're not faster than a teleport."

He held the glass out to her, frowning when she didn't take it. "It's just scotch. Drink, Kat. It will help."

She took it from him and drank the scotch in one large swallow before dropping the glass on the floor. It shattered, and Kat smiled at Clay. "Oops."

"How long have you been dating Ronin?" he asked.

"None of your fucking business, Clay," she said. "Why are you after him?"

"I can answer that."

Kat spun in her chair and stared at the man standing in the doorway. He was big and broad with dark hair, and she sniffed at him. "Dr. Wyatt Stowe, I assume?"

"Yes," he said. "I'm afraid I don't know your name."

"Katarina Frost. She's dating Ronin," Clay said before tossing back his drink.

"Really?" Wyatt said in surprise as he crossed the room

and sat behind the desk. "Can I assume that Ronin will be here soon?"

"Yes," Clay said shortly.

"Excellent work, Clay. And quite brilliant of you to use his girlfriend as leverage."

"I had no choice," Clay said.

"Why are you after Ronin?" Kat repeated.

"It's a long story, Katarina," Wyatt said.

She stared silently at him, and he glanced at the monitor sitting on the desk before stroking his fingers across the screen. "Ma chérie," he whispered.

He took a deep breath and leaned back in his chair. "Did you know that Ronin used to be a police officer?"

"Yes," Kat said.

"My wife was a police officer as well. She and Ronin were partners."

"Lora," Kat said.

Wyatt jerked in his chair and glanced at the monitor again. "Ronin told you about her?"

"A little. He said she got sick, and he tried to help her and failed. He said she died."

"She is not dead," Wyatt snarled. "My wife is still very much alive, and if Ronin had been her friend, he would not have left her to suffer the way she has these last two years."

He rubbed delicately at his temples before rummaging in the desk drawer and taking out a bottle. He shook four tablets into his hand and chewed them down, grimacing at the taste, before pouring himself a glass of scotch. He sipped at it as Kat glanced at the door again.

"Two and a half years ago, my wife contracted a virus. She's a bear shifter, and this virus attacked her system repeatedly as it tried to heal, tried to eradicate the threat. Bear shifters have the fastest, most effective healing ability of every living shifter, but as quickly as she healed, the virus moved at an extraordinary rate. Within three months, one infected cell had become millions. Her immune system, her healing ability, shut down completely, and she turned."

"Turned into what?" Kat asked.

"A monster," Wyatt said. "But still, my wife, Ms. Frost. I had spent nearly my entire life studying a shifter's healing ability. What made it work the way it did, why some shifters heal faster than others, and I knew that I could find the cure for my wife's virus."

"How did she get the virus?"

Wyatt shook his head. "I don't know. And frankly, I've stopped caring. She has the virus - she needs to be healed. That's all that matters."

"So, you used Ronin to try to heal her," Kat said.

"Yes. Lora had been on sick leave for a long time, and I could no longer keep it a secret from Ronin. That's when he told me he was a phoenix. He tried healing her with his tears, and when that didn't work, he volunteered to let us do testing on him."

Clay made a soft snort, and Wyatt gave him a cool look of disdain.

"What kind of testing?" Kat said.

"We took blood, other samples, and tried to use his DNA in a vaccine of sorts. Unfortunately, Ronin grew tired of helping and chose to leave. He believed he could do nothing to help my wife. He abandoned her, Kat. He was her friend, and he left her to suffer."

"I don't believe you," Kat said. "If Ronin thought there was any chance of helping her, he would have stayed."

"You're wrong!" Wyatt suddenly shouted. Kat watched as his body swelled and thick fur grew on his cheeks. Fangs descended with a soft pop, and he bared them at her as he growled viciously. "He's a coward, and I will never forgive him for leaving her like this!"

He swung the monitor on his desk around, and Kat inhaled sharply. A creature, monstrous in size with fangs that protruded past its chin, paced restlessly back and forth in a thick iron cage. Bedding and blankets were torn to shreds and littered the floor of the cage, and she flinched when the creature wrapped its massive paws around the bars and shook them angrily. It roared, saliva spraying from its mouth, before biting at the bars.

"That is my wife," Wyatt said. "My Lora. I have watched her suffer for the last two years while searching for Ronin. Your bird shifter flies free while my Lora lives in a cage."

He swung the monitor back to face him, stroking the screen softly with his fingertips, before studying Kat. "Perhaps Ronin will abandon you as he abandoned my wife."

Kat didn't reply, and Wyatt stood. "If Ronin isn't here by sunset, kill her."

"Wyatt, you can't be serious," Clay said. "Her partners know she's here. If we kill her, they'll go to the police, they'll -"

"Then kill them as well!" Wyatt roared. His nails turned to thick claws, and he swiped them across the top of his gleaming desk, gouging deep marks into the smooth wood. "You'll do what I tell you to do, Clay! Do you hear me?"

"I hear you, Wyatt," Clay said.

Wyatt growled at him again before his body returned to its normal size. He straightened his jacket and smoothed back his hair. "When Ronin arrives, bring him straight to the lab."

"What do you want me to do with her?" Clay asked.

"Put her in a cage," Wyatt said.

He stalked out of the room, and Kat hissed at Clay when he walked toward her. He showed her the gun tucked into his shoulder harness. "Don't make me shoot you, Kat. Stand up."

"Did Wyatt really just let Ronin leave the first time?" she asked.

"No. He was keeping Ronin prisoner, and he escaped," Clay said.

"How?" she asked.

Clay smiled a little. "Your bird shifter is very clever."

"How did Lora infect the coyote shifter?" Kat asked when Clay didn't elaborate.

"She didn't. A doctor, a hyena shifter, worked in the lab with Wyatt. Her name was Millie. She got too close to Lora and was scratched but didn't tell anyone. Wyatt sent my men and me to bring her in when she didn't come to work for a few days. We assumed she infected the coyote shifter you saw in the coffee shop that day. She had already turned by the time we got to her place. She killed three of my men and infected five others before I could kill her."

"What happened to the infected men?" Kat said.

"I killed them," Clay said.

A shudder ran down her back, and she gave Clay a look of horror. "Why would you do that? If Wyatt's right and he can find a cure -"

"There is no cure," Clay said. "If your phoenix couldn't heal them of this virus, nothing can. Wyatt's wife is dead. He just refuses to accept it."

"So, the coyote shifter infected the porcupine shifter who in turn infected Sandra," Kat said.

Clay nodded, and Kat scowled at him. "So, you killed Sandra?"

"No," Clay said. "The porcupine shifter tried to attack her again. We think it was only bad luck that he found her again, and we sedated him and brought it back to the lab. When

Sandra turned, we sedated her and brought her to the lab as well."

"Why didn't you kill Davis?" Kat asked.

"Wyatt has gone mad," Clay said.

"I know. I can smell it on him," Kat said. "Why didn't you kill Davis?"

"Because I'm not the monster you think I am." Clay's voice was bitter. "Let's go, Kat. Your bird will be here soon, and since I highly doubt he'll come alone, I have work to do."

CHAPTER 17

"How many men does this Clay guy have?" Mal asked.
Ronin had just finished telling them everything, and he paced restlessly back and forth in the reception area.

"A lot," he said. "And he'll probably have more now that the infection has spread."

"Is he a scientist like Stowe?" Bishop asked.

"No. He's an old friend of Wyatt. Wyatt brought him in just before I escaped the lab. I don't know why. But he's fucking dangerous and not just because he's a teleport. I overheard a few of the other doctors talking about him. He's good with weapons, he has hand-to-hand combat skills, and he's fucking smart. He's a mercenary for hire."

He raked his hand through his hair before glancing at his watch. "I have to go."

"We need a plan," Mal said. "You can't go alone, Ronin."

"I have to, or they'll kill Kat."

"Are Clay's men shifters or human?"

"A little bit of both," Ronin said. "Most of them are just as dangerous as he is."

"Okay," Mal said, "here's what we do. We drive out to the

261

lab, and you drop off Bishop and me a few miles from the lab. We'll shift and wait until dark, then break into the lab and get both you and Kat out of there."

"And me," Fenton said. "I'm going too."

Mal shook his head. "It's too dangerous, Fenton. We can't ask you -"

"Kat is my friend, and I'm going with you. End of story," Fenton growled.

"A fence surrounds the lab with barbed wire at the top," Bishop said. "We'll need to snip the wire. Are the grounds patrolled at night?"

Ronin nodded. "Yes, but only by a few men. They have security, but it's not exactly a fortress. The real issue will be once you're inside. The building is large, and Clay will have his men positioned in the lab. He'll be expecting trouble."

"So, you'll tell us how to get through the building to the lab, and we move quickly and quietly," Mal said. "If we wait a few hours before we go in, it might catch them off guard."

"You'll need to kill them," Ronin said gravely. "Do you understand that? Clay will give his men orders to kill, not capture."

"We know," Bishop said as Willow put her arm around Mal's waist.

"Mal? Maybe we should go to the police and -"

"No," Ronin said. "If we go to the police, Wyatt will kill Kat."

"Bren," she said suddenly. "We should at least talk to Bren. He knows a bit about what's going on and -"

"No!" Ronin shouted. "Jesus, Willow, are you listening to me? Wyatt is just as dangerous as Clay. He's – he's unstable, and he'll stop at nothing to try to cure his wife. If a bunch of cops show up at the lab, he'll kill Kat!"

"Okay," Willow said. "We won't tell Bren."

The door opened, and they all froze guiltily as the topic of their conversation walked into the office. Bren stared at them curiously. "What's going on?"

"Oh, hey, Bren," Willow said. "What are you doing here?"

"I came to see if Kat talked to Mr. Haddon this morning."

"She did," Bishop said.

"Good. Can I speak with her?" Bren asked.

"She's not here. She's at a client's," Bishop said. "I'll get her to call you later."

"Or you could just tell me what happened," Bren said pleasantly.

Bishop glanced at Ronin before shrugging. "We spoke with Clay, he explained that they were trying to help Sandra, and we were happy with his explanation."

"So, you're going to the lab?" Bren said.

"No. We don't need to. I told you, we were happy with his explanation," Bishop said. "If you'll excuse us, Detective, we have a hectic day and -"

"I'm Bren Matthews," Bren ignored Bishop and held his hand out to Ronin. "I don't believe we've met."

"Ronin Smith," Ronin said shortly.

"He's one of our employees," Bishop said. "I'm not trying to be rude, but we're busy. I'll have Kat give you a call later, okay?"

Bren studied each of them before nodding briefly. "Sounds good. Have a nice day."

He left the office, closing the door softly behind him. Willow gave Mal a nervous look. "Do you think he believed us?"

"No," Mal said. "But we can't worry about that now. We need to get moving."

"I need to speak to Ava first," Bishop said.

"We don't have time," Ronin said.

"I'll call Ava," Willow said quickly before glancing at Fenton, "and Ginger and have them come to the office right now."

She hurried toward reception, stopping to pat Ronin's arm. "Don't worry, Ronin. We'll get her back."

---

"PLEASE BE CAREFUL, BISHOP," AVA SAID.

Bishop stroked her long red hair before placing a gentle kiss against her mouth. "I will, baby. Don't worry."

"Promise me you'll come back to me, come back to us," she said as she placed her hand on her stomach.

"I promise." He rubbed her belly and rested his forehead against hers. "I love you, Ava."

"I love you too, Bishop."

He hugged her, burying his face in her hair and breathing in her scent before bending and pressing a kiss against her stomach. Behind them, Ginger clung to Fenton. He rubbed her back and whispered into her ear and, blinking back tears, Ginger nodded before kissing the cheetah shifter.

"Time to go," Mal said.

Willow had both arms wrapped around his waist, and he smiled at her when she refused to release him.

"If you die before we're married, I will never forgive you, Malcolm Burke," she said.

He kissed her and gave her another small grin. "I'm not going to die, Willow. But if I do, I'll just hang around as a ghost."

"Not funny," she said in a quiet voice.

He grimaced and hugged her hard. "I love you, Willow. I'm not going to die."

"I love you too, Mal," she said. "Please let me come with you."

"No," he said. "You stay right here, Willow. Do not go anywhere near that lab. If we're not back by tomorrow morning, call Detective Matthews and tell him what's going on but stay away. Promise me."

"I promise," she said.

He tugged her hands from around his waist and stared at her crossed fingers. She scowled and uncrossed them before saying, "Fine, I promise, Mal."

He kissed her again and cupped her face. "I love you."

"I love you too."

---

"Hello, Ronin."

"Where's Kat?" Ronin glared at Clay.

"She's safe. Pat him down."

"We did. He's clean." The massive blond man standing next to Ronin said.

"Pat him down again," Clay said.

Ronin lifted his arms and waited impatiently as the man patted his body down. "I want to see Kat."

"Wyatt's waiting for you in the lab."

Ronin's face paled slightly. "I want to see Kat first."

"Yes, I imagine you do. Let's go," Clay said.

Ronin hesitated before following Clay down the hallway. The blond man followed, and the three men entered the elevator. Clay pushed a button, and it carried them down to the basement level. The doors opened, and Ronin faltered when he saw the wide double doors that led to the lab.

"Keep moving, Ronin," Clay said before prodding him in the back.

He took a deep breath and stepped out into the hallway. Clay pressed a plain white card against the control panel next to the door. The light turned green, and he shoved the doors open. The blond man pushed Ronin into the room.

"Ronin, so good of you to join us," Wyatt patted the hospital bed. "Hop on up here, and we'll get started."

"I want to see Kat," Ronin said.

Wyatt cocked his head at him. "But of course you do."

There were four other men in the room, all wearing white lab coats, and Wyatt motioned to the man closest to the door at the far end of the room. The man disappeared, and Wyatt smiled at Ronin before laying out several surgical instruments on a small tray next to the bed. "Are you not even going to ask about Lora?"

"Lora is dead," Ronin said.

Wyatt growled at him. "Lora is most certainly not dead. In fact, now that you've come back to us, I'm certain she'll be feeling like herself in no time."

"It's not going to work, Wyatt," Ronin said. "There is no hope for her."

"Don't say that!" Wyatt shouted. "She can be cured. *You* can cure her. I just need to find the way."

The door opened, and Kat stumbled into the room. "Ronin!"

She shook off the grip of the man holding her and darted across the room. She flung her arms around him and kissed him repeatedly.

---

WHEN THE MAN LED KAT INTO THE ROOM AND SHE SAW Ronin, relief and despair coursed through her.

"Ronin!" She shook free of the man and ran across the

room, hugging Ronin tight before kissing him. "You shouldn't have come."

"Are you kidding? I couldn't let my Kitten have all the fun." He tried to give her a cocky grin, but she could see the fear in his eyes.

She kept her arms wrapped around his waist as she turned to Wyatt. "What are you going to do to him?"

Wyatt laughed. "Surely, you're not that stupid, Ms. Frost."

He finished laying out his tools and picked up a large syringe filled with a dull red liquid. "You've seen your love, Ronin. It's time to get started."

"Let Kat go, and as soon as I know she's safe, I'll help," Ronin said.

Wyatt laughed. "Do you believe you still have a choice? You know as well as I do that I cannot let Ms. Frost leave here. Unless that is, you help me find the cure. Once Lora is saved, I'll let the both of you go with a substantial amount of money. You can spend your life with her, wherever you'd like, without a care in the world."

"We had a deal," Ronin said. "I come to the lab. You let her go."

"I didn't make that deal," Wyatt said.

Ronin glanced at Clay.

"Clay had no right to make that deal. He's just the hired help." Wyatt sighed impatiently before gesturing at Clay. "Take Ms. Frost so we can get started, please."

Clay moved toward them, and Ronin stepped in front of Kat. "Clay, take her out of here. Please."

Clay hesitated, and Wyatt said, "I have your brother, Clay."

He stiffened and swung around. "What did you say?"

"Do you think I'm stupid?" Wyatt said. "Did you think I

haven't noticed your growing distaste for the job I pay you to do? Three weeks ago, I took your brother as, let's call it, insurance that you would finish the job. You'll do what I say, or you'll never see -"

He jerked as Clay vanished before reappearing in front of him. He slammed Wyatt onto the bed and snarled at him. "Where is my brother?"

"Kill me, and you'll never find out," Wyatt growled. "Let me go."

His face twisting, Clay released him, and Wyatt pushed off the bed before smiling at him. "Your brother is safe. Although, the man I gave him to has been enjoying using your brother's abilities for his own gain."

"You fucking asshole! I'm going to kill you." Clay shouted.

"Careful," Wyatt said. "I'm the only person who knows where your brother is. Remember that, Clay. Help me, and I'll release your brother. Easy as that."

Clay drew his gun and pressed it against Wyatt's shoulder. "How about I pump you full of holes? Not enough to kill you, just leave you in agony until you tell me where my brother is."

"I'll never tell," Wyatt said in a sing-song voice before grinning at Clay.

Clay's finger tightened on the trigger before he turned and stalked toward Ronin and Kat.

"Clay, don't," Ronin said.

"I have to," he snarled before yanking Kat out of Ronin's grip.

"Take her behind the glass," Wyatt said. "Let her watch."

"No!" Ronin said quickly. "She doesn't need to watch this."

"I think she does," Wyatt said. "Go on, Clay."

"Ronin!" Kat's nails turned to claws, and she raked them across Clay's face. He grunted in pain and shoved the gun against her temple.

She hissed at him as her body swelled and her eyes turned dark yellow.

Wyatt laughed. "Better calm your kitty-cat down, Ronin. If she shifts, I'll have Clay kill her."

"Kat, stop," Ronin pushed Clay away and cupped her face, his fingers stroking the fur that was growing on her cheeks. "Stop, sweetheart. It'll be okay."

"Ronin," she whispered, and he bent his head and kissed her.

"I love you," he said.

"I love you too." She blinked back her tears as Clay took her arm in a hard grip and yanked her toward a door next to a large window. He shoved her into the room and locked the door behind them before flipping a switch next to the window. Kat stared through the glass, her body trembling, as Wyatt's voice drifted out of speakers set in the walls.

"Undress, please, Ronin."

Ronin stripped off his clothes, and Wyatt gave him a pleased look. "Excellent. Hop up on the bed, make yourself comfortable."

Ronin hesitated. He glanced at the two armed men standing next to the double doors before eyeing the group of obviously nervous scientists."

Wyatt held up the syringe. "You know what this is, don't you, Ronin."

"Yes," Ronin spat.

"You don't cooperate, and I'll inject this into your precious cat shifter instead of you."

Ronin paled and glanced at the observation window. Kat

pressed up against the glass, and he gave her a small smile before walking toward the bed.

He laid down, staring at the ceiling as Wyatt and a second doctor strapped his arms and legs down with wide leather bands.

"Camera on, please," Wyatt said. He squeezed Ronin's arm before smiling at him. "This is going to sting a bit."

He slid the needle into Ronin's arm and injected the liquid. Ronin continued to stare at the ceiling as Wyatt leaned over him. "Don't fight the change. It'll be easier and faster if you don't."

"What did he just inject him with?" Kat asked Clay.

"Lora's blood," Clay said. "He wants him infected so he can take samples of his organs and tissues."

"What the hell for?" Kat said. "How is that going to help?"

"The samples that he takes will heal. Not as quickly as Ronin regenerates, but they will eventually heal. Wyatt hopes to use them to create a vaccine to heal his wife."

"He's done this before," Kat said.

"Many times," Clay said grimly. "He hasn't unlocked the secret to Ronin's healing abilities, but he's confident he will."

"If he hasn't done it by now, he's never going to -"

Ronin made a sudden harsh cry of pain. His body arched, the muscles in his arms and thighs bulging as he strained against the restraints. Kat watched in horror as his body swelled and feathers sprouted from his skin. Ronin screamed in agony, and she made a soft yowl in response.

"Ronin!" As the leather restraints snapped, she banged on the glass, tears ran down her face, and Ronin fell off the bed. He jumped to his feet, and she heard his bones crack as they stretched to impossible lengths. More feathers were sprouting across his back, and he fell to his knees, his back bowing, as his entire body rippled. He screamed, the shrill cry of an animal in agony, and she pounded on the glass again.

He snapped his head toward the sound, and she shrieked in horror. Ronin's eyes were blood red, the pupil a small circle of black in the sea of red, and his face was starting to change. His jaw was lengthening as his beak appeared, and she stared in terror at the large, jagged teeth that grew out of it. He snapped his beak and made a predatory cry of hunger before turning to face Wyatt.

The bear shifter stared calmly at him, and Ronin, his arms turning to wings, leaped for him. A gunshot rang out, and Kat screamed when Ronin flew backward. She stared at the small dark hole was in the middle of his forehead. His eyes stared lifelessly at the ceiling as one of the guards lowered his weapon and returned to the far side of the room.

"Quickly!" Wyatt shouted. "We must move quickly!"

The group of scientists heaved Ronin's body onto the table. Feathers floated everywhere as Wyatt and two others sliced and carved into Ronin's body.

"I need a large sample of his brain," Wyatt snapped as he sliced Ronin's abdomen open. Moving quickly, he yanked out a large reddish-brown organ and dropped it into a silver pan.

"Liver," he said. He pulled out Ronin's large intestines and sliced off several pieces as Kat made a moaning gasp of dismay. When the bone saw started, she stumbled back and screamed breathlessly when she felt Clay's solid body behind her. The scientist was cutting into Ronin's skull, and when Clay turned her and yanked her against his chest, she buried her face into his shirt. She threw her hands over her ears, trying to block out the sound of the bone saw, as Clay put his arms around her and rubbed her back almost soothingly.

"He's starting to smoke!"

"Goddammit! Did you get the brain?" Wyatt shouted.

Unable to help herself, Kat tore away from Clay and turned back to the glass as the scientist with the bone saw shook his head. "No, I haven't got through the skull yet."

More smoke drifted from Ronin's body, and Wyatt shook his head. "We'll get it on the next go."

He shoved Ronin's body to the floor, and Kat swallowed down the bile that rose in her throat as intestines and blood splattered across the floor.

"Get these to the freezer," Wyatt barked. "I need to stop the healing process until I can observe all of it."

The smallest scientist placed the pans of various organs on a small cart and rolled it out of the room as Ronin's body burst into flames. Wyatt winced and took a step back as the flames licked the ceiling for a moment.

They snuffed out, leaving a few burn marks on the ceiling, and Kat watched the pile of ash anxiously. It began to ripple after less than a minute, and the phoenix rose from the ash. He shifted to his human form and immediately ran to the glass that separated them.

He rested his hand on the window, and Kat pressed her hand against the glass. Tears ran down her cheeks, and he gave her a brief smile, his voice muted by the glass. "I'm okay, Kitten."

"Ronin," she said. "I'm sorry. I'm so sorry."

"Not your fault, sweetheart," he said. "I love you."

"I love you!" she shouted and pounded on the glass when he turned and walked back to the bed.

"Help him!" Kat shouted at Clay. "For God's sake, help him!"

"I can't," Clay said. "I'll never see my brother again if I do."

Sobbing, Kat turned back to the glass as Wyatt smiled at Ronin. "Let's try this again."

"FASTER, FENTON," MAL SAID IN A LOW VOICE.

The cheetah shifter nodded and continued to snip the chain link fence with the bolt cutters. When he had a section big enough for Bishop to slide through, he dropped the cutters and squeezed through the fence.

Bishop and Mal followed him and the three shifters crouched on the ground as they studied the large grey building. Night had fallen, and the sky was clouded over, but all of them could see easily in the dark.

"Okay," Mal said, "we hit the east side of the building. Ronin says there's only one guard at that door. We can -"

He stopped as Bishop turned and sniffed the air. The bear shifter studied the dark woods just beyond the fence as Mal said, "What is it?"

Bishop sniffed again. "I think I can smell the -"

"Hyenas!" Fenton said with a low hiss.

Mal turned and growled as the pack of hyenas, there were seven of them, came out of the darkness. Fenton had already shifted to his cheetah, and with a low snarl, he raced toward the pack. Mal and Bishop shifted, their clothing shredding and falling to the ground, and the wolf and the bear charged for the pack.

Three of the hyenas leaped at Bishop. He batted the first one away with a low roar and a swing of his arm as the second one latched onto his throat. It sank its teeth in, trying to puncture through the thick fur, and Bishop growled before digging his claws into the hyena's ribs. It squealed in agony and released him, and Bishop punched his paw through the hyena's abdomen. He yanked out a fistful of intestines as the hyena made another squeal of pain before going limp. Bishop threw him to the ground and bared his fangs as the third hyena, hanging off of Bishop's lower leg like a dog, bit through to the bone.

The bear shifter tore him off with a soft snarl and threw him to the ground before stomping on the hyena's head. His skull cracked, and brains burst from the back of it as Bishop dropped to all fours.

Mal had a hyena pinned to the ground, and he tore into the hyena's throat as Bishop slammed his large body into the second hyena ripping at Mal's side. The hyena bounced off the fence before scrambling to his feet. He yipped in terror and tried to dodge around the giant grizzly.

Bishop caught him easily and slammed him to the ground before wrapping his large jaws around the hyena's head and ripping it from his body. Blood gushed out, and Bishop dropped the hyena's head as there was a bloodcurdling howl of pain. Fenton had torn open a hyena's stomach, and he ripped out his intestines and stomach with a muffled growl as the hyena's back legs scrabbled weakly on the ground.

Mal barked sharply, and Fenton raised his head, his eyes gleaming in the dark. The two remaining hyenas turned and ran, and Mal and Fenton raced after them. Bishop made a low chuff as the cheetah quickly overtook the hyena and leaped onto his back. He tore into the back of his neck as the hyena stumbled and fell to the ground.

Mal was closing in on the remaining hyena, and Bishop chuffed again before stiffening. He raised his snout and inhaled deeply as a growl rose from deep within his chest. There was an answering growl from behind him, and he swung around. The grizzly standing behind him was on his back feet, and he roared with anger before delivering a blow to Bishop's chest. His razor-sharp claws cut through the fur, and blood spurted from Bishop's chest as he was knocked off his feet.

Dazed, Bishop shook his head and tried to roll to his side as the grizzly stood over him and roared again. Before he could gain his feet, the grizzly fell on him, pinning him to the ground and baring his fangs. He snarled loudly and lowered his face toward Bishop's throat. A gun's muzzle jammed against the grizzly's temple, and the gunshot made Bishop's ears ring. Half the grizzly's head disappeared in a spray of blood, brains, and fur. It remained perfectly still, blinking at Bishop with its remaining eye before slowly tipping over and landing with a ground-shaking thud.

Bishop stared at the man standing over him as Mal and Fenton joined them. They both shifted, and the man grinned at him.

"Evening, boys." He holstered his gun and stared up at the sky. "Looks like it's going to rain."

Bishop shifted, grunting with pain as the slashes on his chest burned, and glared at the detective. "I knew I smelled you before those fucking hyenas went after us. What the hell are you doing here?"

"Thanks for saving your life, you say?" Bren said. "Don't mention it, big guy. It was no trouble at all."

"I had it under control," Bishop snarled as he struggled to his feet. He touched the slashes as Mal squinted at them.

"How bad are they?"

"I'll live," Bishop said before rubbing at the bite on his leg.

"What are you doing here, Detective Matthews?" Mal asked.

"You didn't believe that I fell for your bullshit story back at the office, did you? I'm a detective, remember? You don't pass the yearly detective exam if you can't tell when people are lying." He grinned at them before glancing at the building again.

"The real question is, what are you three – four if I count your employee, Mr. Smith, who disappeared into that building hours ago and hasn't appeared since – doing here?"

"How did you even know we were here?" Fenton asked.

"I followed you from the office. Frankly, it wasn't that difficult," Bren said. "I watched you be dropped off in the woods about three miles from here, continued to follow your employee, and made myself comfortable in the woods for a few hours. I figured you guys would show up eventually, and – look at that - you did. I wasn't expecting you to cut through the chain-link fence of private property so before I arrest you all for trespassing and," he studied the bodies of the dead hyenas, "murder, maybe? It did kind of look like self-defense, so I'll cut you some slack on that one - why don't you explain what's happening here?"

"It'll take too long," Bishop said.

"I'll accept a summary," Bren said.

Bishop stared at Mal, who shrugged. "Briefly – the guy who runs this place, Wyatt Stowe, is some kind of mad scientist whose wife is infected with a virus that turns shifters into monsters. Ronin's a phoenix, Stowe believes that Ronin can heal his wife even though Ronin tried years earlier and failed, and Clay Haddon kidnapped Kat to get Ronin to cooperate. He told Ronin to come alone and that if we or the police showed up, they'd kill Kat. They're both in the lab, and we're going to rescue them."

Bren stared thoughtfully at them for nearly a minute before nodding. "Okay."

"Okay?" Fenton said. "You believe us - just like that."

"Do I have time not to believe you?"

Mal shook his head. "No. We need to get in there."

"All right, let's go."

"You're not coming with us," Bishop said. "You'll just get in the way."

"Really? Because I seem to remember that I was pretty helpful not five minutes ago when that bear was about to rip out your throat," Bren said.

Bishop growled at him, and Mal placed a restraining hand on his arm. "He's right, Bishop. It'll be easier with him."

He stared at Bren. "You can't call for backup. If the police converge on this place and we haven't found Kat yet, they'll kill her."

"Then I'll wait until we find her," Bren said. "Let's go."

## CHAPTER 18

"How many times will he do this?" Kat moaned as Ronin's body burst into flames. Ash covered the lab floor, and blood and gore coated the doctors.

She had lost track of time, of how many times Wyatt had injected Ronin with the virus and then killed him. Her cat yowled in misery as Clay shook his head.

"He's never infected him this many times in a row before."

"Please help me stop him," Kat said. "Please, Clay. I know you're a good guy. You would have killed Davis if you weren't."

"I'm not a good guy," Clay said harshly. "Thinking that I am is a very dangerous -"

He paused and held his hand to his ear as he listened intently. "Where are they?"

He dropped his hand and stared at Kat. "Your friends are here." He vanished before she could reply, and she immediately ran to the locked door. She studied the panel next to it. Maybe she could short circuit it somehow. She ripped the cover off and stared at the mess of wires as, through the glass, the phoenix rose from the ashes once again.

———

"THIS ISN'T QUIET OR QUICK!" MAL SHOUTED AS HE SKIDDED around a corner in the hallway. Gunfire erupted, bullets sinking into the walls where his head had been only moments before.

"How many in this group?" Bren asked.

"Four shifters, two humans," Fenton said.

Bren bent and yanked a gun from the holster around his ankle. "Which of you is the best shot?"

"I am," Mal said.

Bren handed him the gun. "Is shooting while you're buck naked going to affect your aim?"

Mal shook his head, and Bren stared at Bishop and Fenton. You two shift and take out the other shifters. Mal and I go first. We'll take out the humans. Ready?"

Bishop and Fenton shifted, and Bren gave Mal a grim look as footsteps thudded down the hall toward them. "Don't miss."

———

KAT HISSED AND YANKED HER HAND AWAY FROM THE PANEL as the shock went through her. She cursed under her breath and stared through the glass, panic coursing through her when she saw Ronin shift to his human form and fall to his knees.

"No," he moaned weakly. "No more."

"Get him on the table," Wyatt said to the guards. They flanked the fallen shifter and hauled him to his feet as Ronin groaned and leaned heavily against the one on his left.

"Move," Wyatt snapped.

"No," Ronin said again. "Please, Wyatt, I can't take anymore."

Wyatt frowned. "You're fine, Ronin. Don't -"

His eyes widened when Ronin suddenly head butted the guard on his left. As the man's nose broke and blood gushed down his face, Ronin yanked the gun from his hand and shot him in the chest. He turned and elbowed the second guard in the stomach as the man fired. The bullet ricocheted off the bed, and the other scientists screamed and bolted for the door as Wyatt's body swelled. Ronin grabbed the guard's wrist and twisted. He bellowed in pain but refused to drop the gun. He threw himself against Ronin, and the two men fell to the floor as another shot rang out. Kat stared wide-eyed through the glass as Ronin, covered in blood, shoved the dead guard off of him and leaped to his feet.

"Ronin! Watch out!" Kat screamed as Wyatt, in his bear form, swiped his giant paw across Ronin's back. The blow drove him to his knees, and blood poured from the deep gashes on his back.

"Ronin!" Kat screamed again and pounded uselessly on the glass. She could see torn muscles and tendons trailing from the gashes, and Wyatt roared in triumph before reaching into one of the gashes and snapping Ronin's spine. The bird shifter screamed in agony, his flailing legs going still, and collapsed face-first on the floor.

Wyatt shifted to his human form and crouched next to Ronin. "Did you think you could save yourself? You're only a bird, Ronin. Now stop being so difficult and -"

An alarm went off, braying loudly, and Wyatt frowned before moving to the computer. He typed rapidly on the keyboard and stared at the monitor before making a harsh moan and staggering back.

"Ma chérie," he whispered before running from the lab.

"Ronin!" Kat shouted through the glass. "Ronin, look at me!"

Ronin raised his head and smiled weakly at her. He was horrifyingly white, and blood poured steadily from his back. "Hey, Kitten," he said. "Be right with you."

He pulled himself forward with his arms, his legs dragging uselessly behind him, and she watched in horror as he picked up the gun.

"Oh, Ronin," she whispered as he raised the gun to his temple and fired. Blood and brains splattered across the room, and she couldn't stop the hoarse scream that pealed from her throat.

"Oh God, please, please," she moaned as she paced back and forth in front of the glass. Her cat yowled and screamed as she watched Ronin's dead body. When it began to smoke, tears flowed down her cheeks. She clenched her hands into fists and waited for the phoenix to rise.

---

"ARE YOU SURE THIS IS THE RIGHT WAY?" BREN PANTED.

Mal nodded. "According to Ronin, the elevator that leads to the lab is down this hallway."

The cheetah made a low roar and pushed by Bren. He raced down the hallway and turned the corner, and yowled as a man screamed hoarsely.

The two men and the bear quickened their pace, and Bren winced when he turned the corner and saw Fenton ripping out the throat of the human. He scooped up the man's gun as Mal ran to the elevator.

"Hurry!" he shouted. "We need to get down there before _"

Bren made a hoarse cry of surprise as a man appeared behind Mal. He locked his arm around Mal's throat and knocked the gun from his hand before pointing his own at Mal's temple. "Everyone, just stay cool."

Bishop roared angrily, and Clay shook his head. "Don't, bear shifter, or I'll kill him."

"Where the fuck did he come from?" Bren said as Clay turned his gaze to him.

"Drop your gun and kick it to me, please."

"I know you," Bren said. "You were at the park when we found the dead squirrel shifter."

"Gun, now," Clay said.

Bren hesitated, and Bishop shifted to his human form. "Do what he says."

Bren placed his gun on the ground and kicked it toward Clay. Without moving the gun from Mal's temple, Clay reached out with his foot and kicked the gun behind him.

"You were stupid to come here," Clay said.

"They're our friends," Bishop said.

"You'd risk your lives for them?"

"Yes," Mal said.

There were footsteps behind them, and Bren stiffened when a gun muzzle pressed against his temple. He stared at the dark-haired man holding the gun to his head. "Hey, how's it going?"

"You're dead, asshole," the man said.

His finger tightened on the trigger, and Bren flinched at the gunfire. The man holding the gun to his head dropped like a stone, a small smoking hole in the middle of his forehead. Bren stared at Clay as the man lowered his gun and stepped away from Mal.

"Wyatt has Kat and Ronin in the lab three levels below this one. There are two armed guards. Watch your backs."

He vanished, and Bren stared up at Bishop. "What the fuck just happened?"

———

CLAY APPEARED IN THE MIDDLE OF THE ROOM, WELL AWAY from the cages and any arms that might grab at him. Lora paced restlessly in her cage, roaring every few minutes, before staring at him. She roared again, baring her fangs and howling with rage when the other two creatures made their own screams of hunger. She threw her body against the cage, making it rattle, as she reached uselessly for Clay

He took a step toward the two smaller creatures, ignoring the alarm that immediately began to whoop and bray and aimed his gun at the porcupine shifter pacing restlessly in his cage. Clay fired once, the bullet finding its mark in the creature's brain, and the porcupine shifter fell to the floor of his cage.

Clay turned to the squirrel shifter. Her long bushy tail whipped out between the bars of her cage and narrowly missed his face.

"Goodbye, Sandra," Clay said before firing again. She made a loud chittering noise of surprise before sinking to the floor and falling on her face. Her body twitched once and then stilled as Clay turned to face Lora.

She made a low whine of hunger and tried to reach for him with her paw. He kept a safe distance from the creature, raised his gun, and waited patiently. The door to the room flew open, and the bear ran into the room. Wyatt roared, and Clay fired a shot. The bullet hit the wall behind Lora, and Wyatt snarled in fear and rage as he skidded to a stop in front of the cage.

Clay aimed the gun at Lora as she tried to reach the bear

through the bars. "Tell me where my brother is, or I'll kill your wife, Wyatt."

Wyatt shifted to his human form and held up his hands. "Clay, put the gun down."

"Tell me where he is!" Clay shouted.

"If you kill her," Wyatt said, "you'll never see your brother again."

———

RONIN SHOOK THE ASH FROM HIS FEATHERS BEFORE SHIFTING to his human form.

"Ronin!" Kat said. "Unlock the door!"

He bent and pulled the key card from the dead guard's belt and pressed it against the control panel. The door opened, and Kat stumbled out. She threw her arms around Ronin and kissed him repeatedly.

He returned her kisses, and she cupped his face and gave him a worried look. "Are you – are you okay?"

"Couldn't be better," he said.

"Oh my God," she whispered. "I was so afraid, Ronin. Every time he killed you, I didn't think you would come back."

"I'll always come back, sweetheart," he said. "Now, let's get the fuck out of here."

"I think Mal and Bishop are somewhere in the building," she said as he grabbed his pants from the floor and pulled them over his hips.

"They are. Fenton too. We find them and get out."

"What about Clay and Wyatt?" she asked. "We have to kill Lora, Ronin. If we don't, Wyatt will never stop hunting for you."

He closed his eyes, and she squeezed his hand. "I'm sorry, honey. We have to."

"I know," he said.

"Do you know where they're keeping her?"

"Yes."

They ran out of the lab, and Kat's jaguar purred happily when the bear shifter lumbered out of the elevator. He shifted to his human form, and Bishop ran forward. He picked her up and hugged her tightly, pressing a rough kiss against her cheek.

"Jesus, Kat! Are you okay?"

"I'm okay, big guy," she said before returning his hug.

He set her on her feet and stepped aside as first Mal, and then Fenton hugged her tightly.

"Hello, Ms. Frost."

She stared at Bren, who was splattered with blood. "Hello, detective."

"What are you doing here?" Ronin asked.

Bren shrugged. "I was in the area - thought I'd join in the fun."

"Come on. We need to get the hell out of here," Mal said.

"We can't leave yet," Kat said.

"Any particular reason?" Fenton said.

"We need to kill Lora."

"Question," Bren said. "Who's Lora, and why are we killing her?"

"She's Wyatt's wife, and she's infected. If we don't kill her, Wyatt will never stop hunting Ronin."

"Not to mention that sooner or later she'll infect someone else," Bishop said.

"Ronin knows where she is. We have to move quickly," Kat said.

"TELL ME, WYATT," CLAY SAID.

The bear shifter shook his head, and Clay fired his gun. The bullet hit Lora in the right thigh, and she squealed with pain.

"Lora!" Wyatt shouted before growling at Clay.

Clay smiled thinly and fired again. The bullet hit Lora's upper shoulder and drove her back against the bars.

She squealed again before roaring angrily and charging the bars. She slammed against them, the cage shuddered but held, and Wyatt shouted angrily. "Enough!"

"Tell me what you did with my brother." Clay said. "Tell me, or I'll kill her. I swear to God, I will."

The door opened, and Ronin, followed by Kat, ran into the room. They stared in surprise at Wyatt and Clay as the door slammed shut automatically behind them.

Bishop pounded on the door. "Kat! The door! Open the goddamn door!"

Kat snatched the card key from Ronin, but before she could swipe it, Wyatt rushed forward, snarling and shifting into his bear form. He grabbed Ronin, barely flinching when the bird shifter shot him in the stomach. He threw Ronin across the room before picking up Kat and throwing her into the wall. She dropped to the floor and, hissing and yowling, shifted to her jaguar. She crouched on the floor and growled at the bear as he lowered his head and charged toward her. She leaped on him, digging her sharp back claws into his abdomen before tearing at his thick neck with her fangs. Wyatt screamed and dug his claws into her ribs, raking through her fur and tearing her open to the bone.

Gunfire rang out, the creature bellowed in pain, and Wyatt dropped Kat indifferently to the floor before whipping around. He switched to his human form, blood pouring out of his abdomen from the gunshot wound and Kat's claws, and staggered forward as Lora, half of her face gone, fell to her knees.

"Ma chérie," Wyatt said as Lora slumped to the floor of her cage. He turned and stared at Ronin as the bird shifter lowered the gun. "You killed my love."

"Wyatt, that isn't Lora anymore," Ronin said. "Lora is gone."

His hands shaking, Wyatt punched a code into the glowing keypad outside the cage. The door opened with a quiet click, and Wyatt shambled into the cage before kneeling beside the fallen creature.

"No. Lora, no," he moaned and buried his face in the creature's shaggy shoulder. Clay moved toward the bear shifter, holding his gun at his side as Ronin knelt beside Kat. Panting heavily and whining softly under her breath, she shifted with a soft pop before making a harsh cry.

"Hold still, sweetheart," Ronin said. He kissed her lightly before leaning over her torn and bleeding side. She could see the bright white of her broken ribs, and she stared up at Ronin when he rested one hand on her shoulder and one on her thigh.

"I'm sorry, Kat," he said as tears dripped down his cheeks and landed on her side. She screamed as pain rocketed through her body and tried to squirm away. Ronin held her down as her broken ribs straightened with a loud crack, and her torn flesh healed. It took less than thirty seconds to heal her, and he straightened and helped her into a sitting position.

"Fuck, that hurts," she said.

"I know, I'm sorry," he said before pressing a kiss against her forehead and helping her to her feet.

"Wyatt, tell me where my brother is," Clay said.

"Go to hell." Wyatt stroked Lora's matted fur. "You might as well kill me, Clay. I'll never tell you where he is. I won't -"

He made a strangled little yelp when Lora's arm shot up, and her claws sunk deep into Wyatt's shoulder. She sat up with a roar, and Ronin, Kat and Clay watched in stunned silence as she bared her fangs at Wyatt.

"Ma chérie," Wyatt said. "I love you, Lora. I love -"

Lora buried her face in his throat and ripped it open. She lapped at the blood spraying from Wyatt's throat as Clay screamed in rage and shot her in the head. She growled and jumped to her feet as both Ronin and Clay fired at her repeatedly.

Clay threw down his empty gun and vanished. Lora lumbered out of her cage and stretched before lowering her head and staring at them with her remaining eye.

"Why the fuck isn't she dying?" Ronin said.

"We need to leave," Kat said breathlessly. "We need to leave right now."

"She's blocking the door," Ronin said as he bent and snagged the key card from the floor. "I'll distract her away from the door. As soon as there's a path, you run, Katarina."

"Ronin," Kat said. "She'll kill you, and what if – what if this time you don't come back?"

"I told you, sweetheart, I always come back," Ronin said as Lora cocked her head and sniffed the air before taking a step toward them. "Get ready to run."

"What? Are you just going to let her kill you repeatedly until she gets tired of her prey catching on fire?" Kat said.

"It's not a *bad* plan," Ronin said before pressing the key card into her hand.

"It's the worst fucking plan in the world, Ronin," Kat said as the creature took another step forward.

"Come back with a missile launcher and blow it to smithereens," Ronin suggested.

"Where am I going to find a missile launcher?" Kat said.

"You're resourceful. You'll find one," Ronin said as his body tensed. "Get ready to run, Kitten."

"Ronin, I -"

There was a puff of air behind them, and Clay grabbed Kat's wrist. Lora made a roar of surprise at his sudden appearance and ran forward with surprising speed.

"Grab him!" Clay snarled into Kat's ear. She hooked her arm around Ronin's neck and pulled him toward her as the creature leaped. There was darkness and a horrible feeling of spinning out of control, and then she was lying on the floor of the hallway, Ronin's warm body beneath hers and Clay standing over them.

"Kitten, move," Ronin groaned, "I'm gonna barf."

She rolled off of him, her stomach churning with nausea as Ronin climbed to his knees and vomited loudly. Warm hands gripped her arms, and she was hauled to her feet. She gagged and bent over, throwing up bile as Bishop held her hair back.

"Kat, you okay?"

"I'm good. Just a little motion sickness," she rasped before gagging again. She straightened and gave Bren a smile of thanks when the detective pulled off his shirt and held it out. Bishop helped her into it, steadying her when she nearly fell, and she patted his cheek with one trembling hand before hobbling to Ronin.

"Hey, Kitten," he said. He was horribly pale, and he leaned against the wall as she wrapped her arms around his waist. "Just so you know, I might throw up on you. I feel like I've been through the goddamn spin cycle on a washing

290

machine. I don't suppose you have any Pepto Bismol on you?"

She laughed, she couldn't help it, and kissed his warm chest. "You were just tortured and killed repeatedly for hours, but a little teleportation turns you into a wimp?"

"I've got a sensitive stomach, sweetheart," he said before squinting at Clay. "Thanks."

"You're welcome," Clay said.

"So, I hate to interrupt the moment," Bren said as there was another bellow of rage, and Lora rammed her fists against the door, "but we've still got a rather large problem."

Lora hit the door again, and it shuddered in the frame as the small group backed away.

"Anyone got a missile launcher?" Ronin asked.

"Leave the building," Clay said. "I'll take care of this."

"How?" Mal asked. "We heard you guys firing. If bullets won't take this thing out, how exactly are you planning on killing it?"

Clay reached into his jacket's inside pocket, and Kat stared at the object in his hand. "Is that a...grenade?"

"Who the fuck just carries a grenade around in their pocket?" Bren said.

"Go," Clay said.

"You heard the man, let's go," Ronin said. He pushed away from the wall, and Kat grabbed him around his waist as he staggered forward.

"Jesus, I am never fucking teleporting again," Ronin said. He glanced at Bishop, "I think you're gonna have to carry me, handsome."

Bishop rolled his eyes before striding forward.

"Just kidding," Ronin said. "I just need a minute to get my land legs back and – shit!"

Bishop had bent and heaved him over his shoulder, and

Ronin grinned at Kat as the bear shifter carried him down the hall. "When you think back on this night, promise me you'll remember the part where I tried to sacrifice myself to save you, rather than the part where I'm carried out of the building like a damsel in distress by a naked bear shifter."

She laughed and squeezed his hand. "No promises, little bird."

---

"Jesus, I will never get used to that," Fenton muttered when Clay appeared on the lawn beside them.

There was a low rumble, like the distant boom of thunder, and the entire building shuddered delicately.

"Huh," Ronin said. "I expected something bigger."

"The lab is underground, and that entire floor is reinforced with thick steel," Clay said. "In case something ever escaped its cage. I'll be right back."

He disappeared again before reappearing less than a minute later. "She's dead."

"You're sure?" Mal asked.

Clay grimaced before nodding. "I'm sure."

"I'm sorry about your friend," Kat said to Ronin.

He squeezed her waist and kissed her throat. "She died a long time ago, Kat."

He straightened and turned to Clay. "What are you going to do now?"

"Go back into the lab, see if I can find something in Wyatt's email that tells me where my brother is."

"I'm sorry about your brother," Kat said.

Clay just grimaced as Bren said, "I'm making an anonymous call in an hour to the police station. You shouldn't be here when the cops arrive."

Clay held his hand out to Ronin. "I'm sorry for my part in this, Ronin."

Ronin hesitated and then shook it briefly. "Goodbye, Clay."

"Goodbye."

He vanished, and Ronin threw his arm around Kat's shoulders. "What do you guys say we get out of here and go get tacos? I'm starving."

_TWO WEEKS LATER_

"I HOPE YOUR MOM ISN'T MAD THAT WE'RE LATE FOR dinner," Willow said as they pulled into the driveway of Mal's parents' house.

"She won't be. While you were talking to your ghost friend, I texted her and told her we'd be late," Mal said.

"Thanks, honey." Willow unbuckled her seat belt and climbed out of the car, grabbing Mal's hand as they walked toward the house.

"Ghosts have the worst timing," she said as Mal opened the door. "Still, I'm glad we could help Eddie with...."

She stared in surprise as Mal led her into the living room. Mal's entire family, as well as Ava and Bishop, Kat and Ronin, and Ginger and Fenton were gathered in the room, and she stared blankly at them for a moment before turning to Mal.

"Why are they all staring at us?" she asked.

Mal grinned at her, and Willow's eyes widened when he dropped to one knee and pulled out a small, velvet box. He opened it and held it up. The ring gleamed softly in the light, and Willow started to cry as Mal took her hand and squeezed it gently. "Willow Blossom Tanner, will you marry me?"

"Yes," she said. "Hell, yes."

He slipped the ring onto her finger and stood as Willow stared at the ring. "It's beautiful. I love it, Mal."

"I love you," he said as their friends and family cheered and applauded.

"I love you too," she said.

He picked her up and held her tightly before kissing her soft mouth. She returned his kiss and cupped his face. "Thank you, honey. Now put me down so I can show off my new ring."

---

WATCHING MAL PROPOSE TO WILLOW MADE KAT TEAR UP A little. She blinked back the tears as Ronin leaned closer to her.

"They look really happy," he said. They watched as Mal set Willow on her feet, and Ava hugged her tightly before Mal's family crowded around her. Ronin put his arms around Kat's waist and tugged her back against him. Kat leaned against his chest and smiled up at him as he placed a soft kiss on her mouth.

"I'm so happy for Mal. He and Willow are perfect for each other," she said. She studied Ronin's face for a moment. "Ronin, there's something I wanted to ask you."

"Whoa, Kitten. I get that all this marriage stuff has got your biological clock ticking, but this bird needs to fly free," Ronin teased gently. "I mean, I'm flattered and frankly, not that surprised that you want to put a ring on it, but…."

"Shut up, Ronin," she said before slapping him lightly on

the arm. "I'm not asking you to marry me. But I am asking you to move in with me."

He tugged on a lock of her dark hair before squeezing her hip. "I thought you'd never ask, Kitten."

She turned and pressed her body against his. "You belong to me, little bird. Always."

He smiled and kissed her again. "Yes. Always."

Keep reading for an excerpt from book four in the Shifters Series, "Porter's Mate".

# PORTER'S MATE EXCERPT

## (THE SHIFTERS SERIES BOOK FOUR)

Porter took another drink of beer and stared moodily at the smooth top of the wooden bar as Arlo stopped in front of him.

"Hey, Porter. What's up?"

"Not much."

Arlo swiped the cloth in his hand across the already-gleaming surface of the bar. "You working later?"

Porter shook his head. "No, it's my night off."

"And yet, here you are. You know there are other bars out there where a guy can get laid."

"Shut up, Arlo."

Arlo laughed. "I'm just saying."

"Ask Mike to make me a house burger and fries, would you?"

"Sure."

There was a sharp whistle, and Arlo frowned irritably at the shifter waving at him. "Yeah, yeah, I'm coming. Keep your fur on."

He wandered away as Porter took another drink of beer. Tonight was Mal's and Willow's engagement party, and after it was over, feeling bored and a little lonely, he had stopped in at the bar on his way home. He was thrilled that Mal had found his mate, but he was also jealous for the first time in his life.

He groaned inwardly. What was happening to him? Since when did he want to settle down with one woman? Sure, he was thirty, and his mother had been bugging him for years to find a good woman and give her grandpups, but that had stopped the moment Mal brought Willow home to meet them. He didn't think she had given up on her quest for him to find a mate, but the upcoming wedding had taken away some of the pressure.

He laughed a little bitterly. It was ironic that his mother had stopped voicing her desire for him to be mated, and now it was something never far from the back of his mind. He shook his head. He was being ridiculous. His brother's happiness with his mate was just making him a little jealous. Nothing more. He might enjoy taking as many different women to his bed as possible, but it didn't mean he didn't occasionally wish for something more. Who didn't come home from work and occasionally wish there was a warm and willing woman waiting in his bed? Someone to ask him how his day was, someone to listen when he'd had a bad day, someone to curl up against when the nights were cold and –

He snorted loudly. He was acting like a love-struck school girl. These ridiculous feelings of – he could think of no other word than nesting – would fade, and he would find himself perfectly content with bedding a different woman every night. His mother might act like he was on the verge of dying old and alone, but he was only thirty, for God's sake. He had plenty of time to find a mate.

There was a startled yell from behind him, and he turned to see a boar shifter glaring impudently at the bouncer. A tall and imposing bear shifter, Judd returned his look with an amused grin.

"I am not too drunk to enter your establishment!" The boar shifter raised himself to his full height, looking ridiculously puny next to Judd, and puffed out his chest. He snorted loudly, his round cheeks bright red, and Porter rolled his eyes when he poked Judd in the chest.

"Do you know who I am?" He poked Judd in the chest again.

"You're about to become a side of bacon," Porter muttered. His eyes widened when the man suddenly launched himself at Judd. Taken by surprise, Judd staggered backward into a table and roared in anger.

As the two of them began to scuffle - the boar was shockingly strong and giving Judd a run for his money – a flash of pink caught Porter's eye. He watched as a woman wearing a stained and dirty pink dress slipped into the bar past the angry Judd and the indignant boar.

Porter frowned. It was cold out, but the woman wasn't wearing a jacket, and her dress was thin and short sleeved. He studied her pale legs. They were bare and streaked with dirt, and the heels on her shoes had been broken off.

She hovered in the corner for a moment. She was too far away for him to see her face clearly, but she was obviously nervous. She was short like Willow and, although not as slender as Mal's mate, it still looked like a strong wind would blow her over. Her light brown hair was shoulder length, and it hadn't seen a brush in a few days.

He watched as she took a deep breath, straightened her spine, and looked around the bar. Her gaze landed on him, and she twitched all over as he stared silently at her before nodding slightly and turning back around. He studied the bottle of beer in front of him and wasn't at all surprised when he felt a light tap on his shoulder.

"Excuse me?"

The woman's voice was low and raspy, and a weird little shiver went down his spine at the sound of it. He turned his head and gave her a once over. She was even dirtier up close. He could smell her fear pulsing through her like a living, breathing thing and underneath that the sour odour of her sweat. Her pale face had streaks of dirt, and he frowned at the scratches that ran across her forehead and down her right cheek. Her eyes were a lovely shade of blue, and they were staring at him with a hint of desperation mixed with fear.

"This is a paranormal only bar, and you," he inhaled deeply, "are definitely not a paranormal."

She flushed and pulled nervously at a rip in her dress. "I'm sure there are other humans here."

He shook his head. "Nope. You're the only one."

She looked around the bar, noticing for the first time that all of the patrons close to them were staring at her with suspicion and hostility. Her eyes widened, and she stepped a little closer to Porter.

"The only human?" she whispered.

"Yes. You should leave," he advised before taking another drink of beer.

Arlo approached them and smiled easily at the woman. "Can I get you a drink?"

"She's human, Arlo."

"So? Humans aren't forbidden." Arlo shrugged. "What will you have, pretty lady?"

"Oh, um," she touched her rat nest of hair self-consciously before clearing her throat, "could I trouble you for a glass of water?"

"Sure."

She cleared her throat again and gave Porter a weak smile. "So, um, what's your name?"

"Porter."

"I'm Maggie. It's nice to meet you." She held her hand out, realized it was covered in dirt and dried blood, and snatched it back. She wiped it hurriedly on her equally dirty dress before giving him an apologetic look.

"Forgive me, Maggie, but you don't look like you're having a very good day." He studied her face and body again, and she flushed to the roots of her hair.

"It's been a rough few days," she mumbled.

"So, you decided to make it better by waltzing into a paranormals-only bar?"

"Humans aren't forbidden," she echoed Arlo's words desperately.

"True. But shifters in this place aren't always appreciative of humans who wander in off the street without an invitation."

"Are they dangerous?"

"Yes."

"Good."

He frowned at her. "Excuse me?"

Arlo set down the glass of water in front of her, and she smiled in thanks before snatching the glass and drinking all of it in four large gulps. She wiped her hand across her mouth as Arlo raised his eyebrow at her. "Do you want another water or something stronger?"

"Another water would be great."

She studied the paranormals in the bar as Arlo left. "Which one is the most dangerous?"

"What?" Porter said. What was going on with this human?

301

"Which one of these shifters would you say is the most dangerous?"

"Why?"

"Because I want to speak to them." There was a touch of impatience in her voice, but she cringed back when he touched her arm.

"You really should leave, Maggie."

"I – I can't." The desperation was back in her voice. "Please, can you just tell me which one of these shifters is the most dangerous?"

"Tell me why you want to know first," he said.

Frustration crossed her face, and she leaned against the bar. "I'm in trouble, and I need some protection. I want to hire a paranormal."

"Why not just go to the police?"

"They can't help me," she said with a new thread of fear in her voice.

"What kind of trouble?"

She picked at the rip in her dress again. "I don't want to talk about it when there are so many people around."

Oddly fascinated by the woman, Porter slid from the barstool and took her arm. "Come with me."

"Wh-where are we going?" she squeaked out.

"Just to one of the booths. It's more private, and you can tell me what's going on."

She followed him willingly enough to the booth and slid in across from him before giving him a careful look. "Are you dangerous, Porter?"

"As dangerous as they come, darlin'." He winked at her.

"What kind of shifter are you?" she asked.

"I'm a wolf shifter."

Her eyes widened, and she blew out her breath in a shuddering rush. "Wolf. Good, that's good. You're big and strong, right?"

He nodded. "I am."

"Okay, good."

One of the servers, Tori, stopped in front of them and set down the plate of burger and fries in front of Porter and the glass of water in front of Maggie. "You want something to eat, hon?"

"Oh, um, no, thank you. The water is enough." Maggie smiled faintly at her.

Tori nodded and grinned at Porter, running her fingers affectionately through his dark hair before sauntering away. Porter watched the sway of her hips for a moment. Two years ago, he had slept with the pretty brunette shifter, and she had made it clear she was willing to have another go at him. He hadn't taken her up on the offer.

She'd been a firecracker in bed, full of unlimited energy, but rabbit shifters were notorious for accidentally getting pregnant. They loved nothing more than having babies, and with three kits already, Tori was no exception.

He turned back to the human. She stared at his plate of food with a look of feral hunger, and he clearly heard her stomach when it growled.

"Would you like some?" He pushed the plate toward her, and she shook her head.

"Oh no, I don't want to eat your food. I'm fine."

"Take some, I insist." He was reasonably certain she was going to start drooling any moment.

"I'll just have one fry. Thank you." She reached out, her hand trembling badly, and plucked a French fry from his plate. She popped it into her mouth and chewed slowly, her eyes closed in utter bliss. He used his knife to cut the burger in half before pushing the plate a little closer.

"Take half the burger and the fries," he said.

Her eyes popped open, and she stared at the burger, swallowing thickly as she shook her head. "Oh no, I can't."

"Yes, you can. It's a lot of food. I'll never be able to eat it all."

There was a stack of four appetizer plates on the table, and he grabbed one and transferred half the burger and half the fries to the small plate. "Eat."

"Well, if you're sure?" she said tentatively. Porter could see the shame in her eyes, and his stomach twisted a little.

"I'm more than sure. Eat, Maggie."

"Thank you," she said.

He blinked in surprise, a small smile crossing his face when she nearly inhaled the burger. She ate quickly and enthusiastically, shoving the fries into her mouth and chewing loudly. When her plate was clean, she sat back and gave him an embarrassed look.

"I'm sorry."

"Don't be. I like a woman with an appetite." He grinned at her, and she blushed again.

"When was the last time you ate?" he asked.

She shrugged. "It's been a few days."

He cursed under his breath before leaning forward. "So, tell me about this problem."

She took a deep breath. "There's a man – a shifter – stalking me, and I need someone to make him stop."

"Why aren't you going to the police?"

"They can't help me," she repeated.

"Of course, they can. It's their job to -"

"They can't!" There was a slight note of hysteria in her voice, and he made a soft, soothing noise as she stared nervously around the bar.

"Please, just believe me when I say they can't help me,

okay? I'm not stupid! I would have gone to them if I thought it would help."

"Okay, okay. I know you're not stupid, Maggie," he said quietly. "What kind of shifter is after you?"

"A hyena shifter," she said.

He grimaced. He hated hyena shifters. They were sneaky and cruel bastards and often looked upon as the scum of the shifter world. They had earned their reputations honestly, and he wasn't surprised that one was harassing Maggie. When they wanted something, they stopped at nothing to get it.

"How did you meet him?"

"At a party," she said. "At first, he was nice and sweet, but then he started to act differently. He kept showing up at my apartment or job, then at random places when I was out. I told him I wasn't interested and broke it off with him, but he – he got a lot worse after that."

She grimaced and clutched at her stomach for a moment.

"Are you okay?"

She nodded. "Yes. I think I, uh, ate too fast."

"So, you broke it off with him, and things got worse?" he prompted.

"Yes. At first, it was just him showing up but then more and more of his friends started appearing too."

"Hyenas are most comfortable in packs."

"Right," she said before rubbing gingerly at her stomach. "Anyway, he showed up at my apartment a few nights ago, and he – he broke the door down when I wouldn't let him in. He was so mean and rough, and he said that I – I was his now and that there was no point in fighting it. I was going to be his mate, and that was that."

Her trembling grew worse, and tears slid down her face. He reached out and touched the top of her hand gingerly. "It's okay, Maggie."

"It isn't," she said. She swiped at the tears on her face before taking a deep breath. "I played along and offered to make us something to eat. He agreed, and I went into the kitchen and got the biggest butcher knife I could find and then I – I tried to stab him with it."

"Did you?"

She nodded. "I stabbed him in the thigh. It made him so angry, and he pulled the knife out, and there was blood everywhere, and then I just ran."

She suddenly latched onto his hand and held it tightly. "I waited a few hours, and then I went back to my apartment, but I was careful, you know? I hid in the park across the street, and I watched my apartment building. I was pretty sure he would still be there, but I was wrong. Vaughn had left, but his pack was there. All ten of them were just, like, prowling around my apartment building. They were trying to blend in, but I saw them. So, I ran again. I work at a coffee shop, and I went there the next morning. They were waiting there too. They – they went to my job and my apartment, and I didn't know what else to do."

"So, you've been running since then?"

She nodded and sniffed loudly before staring at their clasped hands. "Oh, I'm sorry." She yanked her hand free and slid it into her lap, where it twisted and turned against her other.

"Do you not have any family? Friends who can help?"

"I don't have any family. My parents died when I was young, and I went into foster care. I have a few friends, but I can't involve them in this. Vaughn is dangerous, very dangerous, and my friends are only humans. It's why I came here. I thought maybe what I needed was a shifter. A bigger, stronger shifter than Vaughn."

He studied the dark circles under her eyes. "When did you sleep last?"

"Wh-what?" she said.

"When did you sleep last?"

"I don't know. What does it matter?" she asked a bit impatiently. "I'm sorry, I don't mean to be rude, but can you help me? I can pay you for your protection."

He doubted that statement was true. The woman had no purse and was obviously starving. "What exactly do you think a shifter can do for you?"

"Well," she leaned forward eagerly, "I thought maybe they could talk to Vaughn and tell them that I was their mate, not his. I know a little about shifters, and I know most are very protective of their mates. If a bigger, stronger shifter – a wolf shifter like you – told Vaughn that I was dating them and that I was their mate, he would back off. Right?"

"Maybe," he said.

"Once Vaughn gave up, we could go our separate ways. And if pretending we were dating didn't work – I thought maybe the shifter could, I don't know, beat him up?"

He pressed his lips together. The woman was almost ridiculously naïve when it came to shifters, but then again, most humans were.

"Not that I condone violence," she said hastily, "and I would only ask for that if we had no other choice."

He didn't reply, and she rubbed at her stomach again before giving him a tentative smile. "Do you think you could help me, Porter?"

"You said you would pay for protection. Forgive me, Maggie, but you don't look like you have money."

She took a deep breath. "You're right – I don't. I didn't think to grab my purse when I ran, and honestly, I don't have much, uh, cash anyway. Working at a coffee shop doesn't pay very much."

She leaned forward and gave him a hesitant smile. "But I have something better than money. Something I know will appeal to you even more."

"What's that?" he asked.

"My virginity."

———

# ABOUT THE AUTHOR

Elizabeth Kelly was born and raised in Ontario, Canada. She moved west as a teenager and now lives in Alberta with her husband and a menagerie of pets. She firmly believes that a person can survive solely on sushi and coffee, and only her husband's mad cooking skills prevents her from proving that theory.

For more information about Elizabeth, check out her website at

www.elizabethkelly.ca

facebook.com/EKellyBooks

twitter.com/ElizabethKBooks

instagram.com/elizabethkelly_author

amazon.com/Elizabeth-Kelly/e/B00EOHZ0MS

bookbub.com/authors/elizabeth-kelly

Broken

An Unlikely Seduction

**Holiday Romance**

The Christmas Wife

The Christmas Rescue

The Christmas Nanny

The Christmas Boss

Sordid Games